THE HANGING TREE

Even the darkest of secrets deserve an audience

JOHN REGAN

ACKNOWLEDGMENTS

It goes without saying that no one finishes, or indeed begins a novel without influence from other people. Having always had a love of the English language in general, words and their meanings in particular and, fast approaching my fiftieth year, I decided to do something about it.

It wasn't until having enrolled in a creative writing class held in Middlesbrough on a Monday evening that my writing bug took hold. Encouraged not only by Liz Bielok, the teacher but enthused by the other members of the class, the genesis of this novel began.

After the classes finished and taking a brief interlude away from writing, I found myself drawn back towards it. Having sought out a few of my former classmates who still met regularly at one of their houses, I was invited to join them.

My grateful thanks go to Kate, Christine and Anne-Marie, for their enthusiasm along my journey. Extra thanks to Christine and Anne-Marie who read my book offering invaluable advice on plot changes, some of which I've implemented.

Special thanks to Anne-Marie for reading chapters and assisting with grammar and punctuation. A huge thank you to Deb, who diligently read the entire novel and highlighted solecisms, helping me greatly to achieve this finished book.

Finally, as I'm sure everyone's aware, we're the sum total of the experiences, good and bad, that we go through in life. So, to anybody who I've met, laughed with, cried with, travelled, further along, the road on life's journey with, whose influence, however small, manifests in some way in this book, many thanks.

John Regan, June 2015.

DISCLAIMER

Many of the places mentioned in this book exist. However, the author has used poetic license throughout, to maintain an engaging narrative. Therefore, no guarantee of accuracy in some respects should be expected. The characters depicted, however, are wholly fictional. Any similarity to persons living or dead is accidental.

PROLOGUE

JUNE 1992 - The man leant against the back of his van. In front of him a freshly dug grave containing the naked bodies of two young boys. He lights a cigarette, the flame from the match briefly illuminating the darkness of the small wood. The man inhales deeply, the smoke slowly drifting back out from his mouth and nostrils. He finally finishes and nonchalantly tosses the butt aside. Picking up his shovel, he begins the arduous task of filling in the hole, pausing briefly every now and then to gather his breath before resuming. An owl, high up in the trees, looks down indifferently at the man as he continues his grisly work. Slowly and relentlessly, shovel after shovel, burying his unfortunate companions.

SEPTEMBER 2006 - The man sat fastened to the chair, his face puffy and swollen from the beating he'd received. On the floor in front of him, his five severed toes lay close to the bloody stump of a foot that once housed them. A man, with a scar running from under one eye to his upper lip, casually plays with the secateurs in his hand. A second much bigger man holds a knife, the spider's web tattoo on his neck adding significantly to his menace. He stands and wanders across to the tethered man.

'Her name?' The tattooed man asks. 'We need her name. You've been brave, and I'm sure your friend would be proud of you.'

The tethered man lifts his head a little, blood running from his nose drips onto his chest. 'I can't tell you.'

The tattooed man allows the tip of the knife to rest on his victim's chin. 'If you're not going to tell me, I might as well cut out that tongue of yours.'

'Please, she had nothing to do with this. She's got a young daughter … I can't.'

The tattooed man pulls a mobile from his pocket and holds it up. 'Surely you want this torture to end? I can leave you with my friend if you like?'

'Please ... I ...'

'Her name. That's all I need for this to be over.'

The man in the chair begins to sob like a child. 'Sandra,' he says. 'Sandra Stewart.'

The man with the tattoo passes the knife to his colleague, who quickly dispatches their victim. Searching through the contacts on the phone, he finds her name and rings. 'Sandra Stewart?' he says.

AUGUST 2014 - Vale Farm had stood empty for the previous eight years, potential buyers put off by the horrific events in 2006.

The house that had once reverberated to the happy sound of voices lying dormant throughout this time.

If a house could talk, what would it say? Would it give up its secrets and tell us what happened?

Inside its walls, a sign, a hint from the past.

Enclosed between the darkness and the light sits a clue. Hiding deep in the shadows, lies the truth.

SEPTEMBER 2014 - The woman enters the front door of Sunny View Nursing Home carrying a small bag in her hand. The care assistant, on the phone, acknowledges her as she passes the reception desk and heads along a corridor towards the rooms. She reaches a door, pauses outside to glance left and right, satisfied, the woman taps lightly and enters. The man in the wheelchair slowly turns to face her, his shoulders and neck hunched.

She smiles at him. 'Hi, John. How are you?'

'Much the same,' he slowly enunciates. His illness hampering him significantly. 'Have you brought it?'

She opens her bag and pulls out a syringe. 'I've loaded it up for you already. Are you sure you can manage?'

He forces a smile. 'It would be better if you did it.'

'I can't do that. You know I can't.' She leans forward and touches his face with her hand.

'I'll manage. How hard can dying be? Hundreds do it every day.'

She stands and places her hand on his cheek again before turning towards the door.

'You will get them, won't you?' he asks.

She nods. 'Don't you worry about that.'

The man puts the syringe in the bedside drawer, covering it with some underwear. Sitting back in his chair, he closes his eyes again. A brief snooze he thinks, before his appointment with death.

SEPTEMBER 2014 - The man is running after them, his effort to close the gap in vain. The woman and the girl keep their distance, thwarting any attempt by him to get closer. He pauses to gather his breath as they stop ahead of him. The woman, whose features he cannot make out, taunts him. The girl struggles to break free from the woman's vice-like grip. The girl stares back, her eyes imploring him, but as he moves again, they set off once more.

Eventually, they reach the top of some stairs and begin their descent as the man desperately tries to catch them up. Only a few feet from them now, but as he turns the corner, he stops in his tracks. He's at the top of more stairs and below him, at the bottom, lies the prostrate body of a man. He grips the bannister with his child-like fingers and closes his eyes in horror.

The beep, beep, beep of his alarm jolts him rudely from his dream. Glancing at the clock on the bedside cabinet he sighs. The realisation of what today entails smashes headlong into him as he slowly brings his hands up to his face.

'Even the darkest of secrets deserve an audience.'

CHAPTER ONE

The car travelled along the quiet lane, passing hedgerows and fields as the late summer sun beat down on the already parched land. Turning a corner he saw the farmhouse ahead of him, the same as he remembered it years ago. The trees and shrubs had grown taller over the intervening years of course, but in every other sense it remained identical. *The photo in the estate agent's portfolio didn't do it justice,* he thought, as he pulled the car up opposite the driveway. Stephen Stewart reached across to the passenger seat and picked up the agent's house details. Getting out of his vehicle, he ambled towards a man waiting outside the front door of the property. The man, approximately 30, was tall with blonde hair cut short. He wore a grey suit, white shirt and blue tie, the sort that comes together in a pack from M&S. If there was a typical looking estate agent, he was it.

The man held out a hand. 'Mr Roberts?' Stewart nodded. 'Hi, I'm Steve Robinson from White Leas Estate Agents.' Trying to maintain his friendly attitude, he continued. 'Have you come far?'

'I'm staying at The Fat Ox, in Guisborough.'

'Ah! The Fat Ox. Has their food improved any?'

Stewart smiled. 'It won't be getting a Michelin star anytime soon.'

The estate agent chuckled as he turned and placed a key in the lock. The door opened with a loud groan as if the house itself resented the intrusion. 'Well, this is it ... Vale Farm.' Stepping into the hallway with Stewart following close behind, he paused. 'I'll tell you the history of Vale Farm, Mr Roberts ... It's just that ...'

'I know about its history. It isn't a problem.'

'That's fine then. Do you want to start upstairs or down?'

'Do you mind if I look around by myself? I'd like to get a feel for the place. If that's all right?'

'No, not at all,' the agent said. 'I've a couple of calls to make. Take your time. Give me a shout if you need anything.'

Stewart thanked him and began looking in the downstairs rooms one by one, feigning interest here and there, enough to convince the agent he actually wanted to buy the property. Desperately, Stewart tried to maintain his composure as he swam within the memories of his past. Finally, he felt safe enough to climb the stairs to the first floor. He glanced across at the bathroom, the door wide open, enabling him to see the familiar but now somewhat dated interior. He headed for the master bedroom at the rear of the property stopping to glance downstairs at the agent, still buried in conversation on his phone.

Stewart felt his heart rate quicken, momentarily unsure if he wanted to proceed any further but deep down knowing he had to. He reached the bedroom door and pushed it open before entering. Once inside the room, he gently closed the door behind him. He stopped to gather his thoughts, dizziness caused him to stagger as the smell of perfume - her perfume - filled his nostrils. Queasiness threatened to overcome him as he battled successfully to stop himself from vomiting. Distant memories pushed hard for his attention. He felt a presence in the room to the left of him but resisted the urge to look, knowing what he'd see. The hallucinations had increased over the past week. A sign his illness was progressing much more quickly now. Realising he couldn't allow himself to become distracted from his task, Stewart pressed on. He headed for the cupboard in the corner of the room but stopped a few feet from the door as he caught sight of the apple tree in the garden. Replete with red fruit, dozens of windfalls scattered around its trunk like cherries on a fruitcake.

'Of course,' he muttered to himself. 'The apple tree.' He'd almost forgotten. The traumatic memory buried deep for so long. His emotions very nearly overwhelmed him. He puffed out his cheeks, blowing out air, and succeeded in subduing them again. He turned his attention back to the cupboard, opened the door, and dropped onto his haunches, pulling back the carpet at the corner. The tacks holding it easily yielding, to reveal the floorboards below. He took a penknife from his pocket and gently prised a small piece of one of the boards up. Putting his hand inside he searched beneath the other boards, finally locating something metal. Pulling it out, he stared at the small rectangular tin in his hand. The board and carpet now replaced, he quietly closed the cupboard door. He had waited so long, and with a combination of dread and excitement, he brushed the years of dust from the tin before prising off the lid.

Inside were three items. A key, a small gold locket and a folded piece of paper. Secreting the key in his pocket he opened the piece of paper to reveal a list of names, numbered one to four. Next to number five, a question mark. Refolding it, Stewart popped it into the top pocket of his jacket before switching his attention to the locket. Closing his eyes, and blowing out air once more, he managed to again keep his emotions at bay. But as he opened the locket, his hand began to shake, and Stewart gazed at the face of a young girl within it. Unable to hold back the emotional floodgates any longer, he dropped to his knees and began to weep like he'd never wept before. Every memory a dagger, every teardrop a waterfall.

Stewart stopped the car within view of the church but far enough away so as not to cause any undue attention. Getting out, he removed a small rucksack from the boot and headed for the church as the rain fell slowly. He reached the entrance to the graveyard, scanned left and right, and pushed open the gate leading towards the graves. The cemetery, though not huge, had enough graves within it to make his task difficult. Opening his rucksack and removing a torch he began checking the names on the headstones one by one, ignoring any ancient-looking ones. Eventually, he shone his light on one of the graves, brushed the dust and dirt from it, and read the inscription.

* * * *

IN LOVING MEMORY OF
SANDRA STEWART
DIED OCTOBER 10TH, 2006, AGED 34 YEARS.
MOTHER OF JESSICA STEWART
DIED OCTOBER 8TH, 2006, AGED 10 YEARS.
* * * *

Falling to his knees next to the gravestone, he opened his rucksack and removed a trowel. With it, he pushed away the white stones covering the top of the grave to reveal the earth below. Digging with the tool until he'd created a small hole, he delved into his pocket and removed the gold locket. Opening it, he gazed at the face of the young girl as tears rolled down his face getting lost in the falling rain. He closed the necklace, kissed it, and placed it carefully inside the hole he'd dug. Pushing the soil back in, he replaced the stones over the top. Satisfied the grave appeared undisturbed, Stewart stood and headed back to his car. He still had a few hours to wait until the Reverend was due to arrive, so he decided to try to sleep until then.

Unsure how long he'd slept, Stewart rubbed his eyes to remove the tiredness from them but stopped midway sensing her presence. Briefly resisting the urge to look at the passenger seat, he slowly turned his head and stared at the face of Sandra seated next to him. Stewart knew it was only a hallucination - having experienced them many times before - but she seemed so real. Almost as Stewart remembered her alive, except for the red mark encircling her neck and the slight blue tinge on her lips. He could smell her favourite perfume too, as all his senses joined forces in the deception. She smiled at him. He, lost in the moment, smiled back, his reason and logic pushed aside.

He lowered his eyes. 'I'm so sorry.'

She smiled. 'What for?'

He brought a hand up to his mouth. She had never spoken before in his previous hallucinations, but now the smell of her perfume, the sound of her voice, seemed so real, so tangible. There had always previously been a slightly ethereal quality to her, but it appeared as if his long-dead wife was seated next to him. Skin and bone, flesh and blood. Not just a vision conjured up by his mind. He'd smelt her perfume back at Vale Farm, but now it was much stronger. Maybe the closeness to her grave was heightening the experience. Coupled with his illness and tiredness, his subconscious was running amok.

'I should have been there,' he said. Happy to play along with this mental illusion.

'You weren't to blame, Stephen. They were.'

He glanced up at the rearview mirror and seated on the back seat he could see Jessica. She smiled at him, her blonde hair tied back in a ponytail, the tell-tale blue tinge around her lips the only incongruous feature.

'Hello, kidda,' was all he could say to her.

'I love you, Daddy.'

Stewart put his hands up to his mouth to stifle his emotions, as tears queued patiently for their inevitable appearance. Distracted by a car pulling up outside the churchyard, he watched as a man wearing a large grey overcoat, carrying a bag, got out of the vehicle and headed towards the church. He waited until the man entered the building before looking back at the passenger seat. He was alone. Stewart's reason and logic returning him back to reality. Getting out of his car, he collected the rucksack and headed after the man.

Reverend James entered the cavernous interior of the building and made his way to the vestry at the back. After putting away his bag, and hanging up his overcoat, he headed inside the body of the church. He began laying out the hymn books along the pews. The Reverend reached the second row when footsteps sounded behind him. Turning, he saw the figure of a man approaching along the aisle.

'Can I help you?' he said. Stewart continued his progress, stopping 10 metres from him.

'Reverend James?'

The Reverend narrowed his eyes. 'Yes. Do I know you?'

'No, but you knew my wife and daughter.'

'Oh yes?' The Reverend moved closer to Stewart.

'They're buried in your graveyard.'

'I'm sorry for your loss.' He resumed placing the Hymn books on the pews. 'What were their names?'

'Sandra and Jessica Stewart.'

The Reverend stopped as their names penetrated his memory and flung open the doors to his past. He turned to face Stewart. 'Yes ... Sandra and Jessica ... From Vale Farm. Very sad.'

'The thing is Reverend.' Stewart edged closer. 'Sandra left a list of names for me. If I ever returned.'

'A list of names? How intriguing. I'm not altogether sure how this concerns me?' He resumed the laying out of the hymn books and moved further away from Stewart.

'I thought the names on the list would interest you?' Stewart raised his voice a little.

The reverend spun around and met Stewart's stare. 'Why would you think that?' He turned and continued his task.

'Because your name is on it.'

'My name is on it?' Stopping, he turned and looked directly at Stewart again.

Stewart sneered. 'We could play this game of yours all morning, Reverend, but I'm not in the mood. So, I'll cut to the chase. There are four names on the list, numbered one to four, and a question mark next to number five. What I need from you is the missing name.' Stewart edged closer to the Reverend, a scowl filling his face.

The Reverend half-laughed. 'I've no idea what you're talking about. I don't know anything about a list, or why my name is on one. So, if you don't mind, Mr Stewart, I'm rather busy.'

Stewart ambled towards the Reverend, stopped 3 metres from him, and pulled a large knife from his rucksack. The Reverend gasped. 'It's up to you,' Stewart said. 'We can do this the hard way if you wish? I'm not bothered.'

'Please, Mr Stewart. I think there's been a misunderstanding.'

'I know all about it,' Stewart snapped. 'I know all about your little secrets. How does it go?' He continued. '*Be sure your sins will find you out.* So please, don't insult me anymore.'

The Reverend sighed. 'I'm sorry. I knew you could return one day. I thought of moving away ... running away actually, but some things in life one cannot escape.' He brought his hands up to his face. 'I know what we did ... what I did, was dreadful. I'm sorry, you have to believe that.'

'Save me the sermon.' Stewart waved the knife at him. 'Tell me the fifth name.'

'I'm sorry. I can't help you, I don't know it.'

He pushed the knife closer. 'You're lying.'

'I'm truly sorry for your loss, but I never knew his name. I only knew he was in an influential position. Shelby knows his name. He's the only one who had any contact with him, I swear.'

Stewart scoffed. 'On the Holy Bible, no doubt?' Putting the knife back into the rucksack, he pulled out a gun. Raising the weapon, he pointed it at the head of the Reverend. 'The fifth name!'

'Please, Stephen. I'd tell you if I knew. I don't know.'

Stewart pondered for a moment before lowering the gun. 'I think I believe you, Reverend. I'm an atheist, so all of this nonsense means nothing to me.' He waved his hands around the church. 'But if I'm wrong, and there is a God, you'll have some explaining to do.'

'Yes. Yes, I will,' the Reverend said. 'And now?'

'There's no happy outcome for either of us, I'm afraid. Make peace with *your* God.' Allowing the gun to drop to his side.

The Reverend crossed himself and uttered a prayer under his breath. 'Forgive me,' he whispered at Stewart.

Stewart raised the gun again and fired. The bullet tearing through the Reverend's forehead and exiting the back of his skull. Fragments of bone and brain, along with blood, splattered across the altar. The Reverend momentarily stayed upright before slowly falling backwards, his body hitting the floor with a giant thud. The noise reverberating off the walls in hot pursuit of the sound of the gunshot. Stewart ambled towards the body. Lifeless eyes stared back as a large pool of blood billowed out from his head. Dropping the gun into his rucksack, he strolled outside, jumped in his car and drove away. Only after putting some distance between himself and the church did Stewart finally pull into a lay-by. He removed his mobile, opened his contacts at the name *Ang,* and called.

'Steve, how did it go?' said a woman's voice on the other end.

'Reverend James is dead. He told me Shelby's the only person who knows the fifth name.'

'Shelby's away, I've checked. On holiday. He's back on Tuesday.'

'I'll go after the Johnsons, then.'

'That will alert Shelby.'

'I know, but I haven't much time. Maybe I could make it look like a robbery?'

'Yes, not a bad idea. Although I'm not sure it'll convince the police.'

'The police don't concern me,' Stewart said.

'I've made an appointment for you at the solicitors on Tuesday under the name Roberts. Ten o'clock. I'll keep working at this end.'

'Thanks, Ang.'

'Good luck,' she said.

CHAPTER TWO

Detective Inspector Peter Graveney entered Ratano's coffee shop and headed for the counter. A curvaceous woman prepared coffee for a customer, and spotting Graveney, she smiled pleasantly. Graveney waited patiently for her to finish serving. Eventually, she turned her attention to him, leaning across the counter, displaying her ample cleavage as she did so.

'Morning, Peter. How are we?' A welcoming smile filled her attractive face.

'Very well, Becky.' He folded up his newspaper and gave the woman his full attention.

'Usual, honey?' she said

'Am I that transparent? I might go for something different. I've got a rare day off today, and I may do something *totally* out of character.'

She raised her eyebrows. 'Day off. What are we going to do together? I'm sure Andrea wouldn't mind looking after the shop for me.'

Graveney leant in closer, his face no more than a foot from her now. 'What would you like to do, Becks?' he whispered.

'What I'd like to do to you, *Mr Policeman,* would get most people arrested,' she whispered, even quieter.

Andrea entered from out of the storeroom, glanced across at Graveney and Becky, and gave them a look of someone who'd witnessed the same scene many times before.

Graveney winked. 'That's all right. I'll pull some strings at the station.'

Andrea tutted. 'Will you two give up. You're like a pair of teenagers.'

Becky stood up straight and blew him a kiss. 'Americano is it?'

'Americano.' Winking at them both.

Becky picked up a cup and began preparing the coffee. 'How come you're off anyway? Who's going to keep our streets safe?'

'Oh, you'd be surprised. There's plenty of others like me back at the station.'

'Surely not?' Becky said.

Graveney reached into his pocket and pulled out his wallet. 'None of them know about this shop, though.'

Becky picked up the cup and put it on the counter in front of him. Graveney handed her a £5 note. She gave him his change and looking Graveney in the eyes, popped a small cake next to the coffee. 'For energy.' She smiled. 'On the house.'

'Sorry, Becks. I'm off sweet stuff at the moment, but I'll save it for Louisa if you don't mind?'

'Is she coming in today? I may have a couple of shifts if she's interested?'

Graveney glanced at his watch. 'She's late actually.' Tucking his newspaper under his arm, he picked up the coffee and cake before winking at Becky again. He headed for his favourite seat, vacated by an elderly couple, and pushed their used cups aside. Graveney gathered up his paper and read while keeping one eye on Becky and Andrea. He knew he was the topic of conversation by their body alignment, and secretly found it most amusing.

Graveney read his paper for ten minutes or so when Louisa finally arrived. Spotting Graveney, she headed over to him and looking up he recognised instantly something was wrong. In the two years he had known her, he had learnt to read every nuance and emotion. Today he could see concern etched on her face.

He put aside his paper. 'What's up?'

She sat next to him. 'My cousin phoned. My mam's in the hospital and wants to see me.'

Graveney put a hand on hers. Louisa's head dropped a little. 'Would you like me to take you there?' he said.

'It's ok. My sister's picking me up from town. They'd only want to know who you are, and it's no one else's business but ours.' She squeezed his hand.

'Are you sure? I'm off today. I don't mind?'

'Thanks, but I'll be ok,' Louisa said. She stood and glanced at her watch. 'I'd better get going.'

'Aren't you having a coffee before you go?'

'No. My sister's waiting.'

Graveney forced a smile. 'You keep me informed, do you hear?'

'I will.' Bending, she kissed him on the cheek. Louisa left the coffee shop giving a half-hearted wave towards Becky and Andrea as she did.

Becky walked across to Graveney's table and began gathering up the dirty cups and plates. 'Is Louisa all right? She seemed a little off.'

'Her mam's ill in hospital. She's meeting up with her sister. Her mam wants to see her, and I've a feeling it's bad news.' Graveney rubbed his chin. 'Louisa didn't say, but I sensed it's something serious.'

Becky patted him on the shoulder. 'Give her my love.'

He nodded. 'I will.' Becky headed back towards the counter.

Graveney was concerned. His mind drifted back to when he'd first met Louisa. Almost two years ago, outside this very coffee shop, he remembered smiling to himself. A scruffy looking kid, who had apparently been sleeping rough, asked him for some change. He didn't know what it was that struck a chord with him. After all, it wasn't unusual in his job to meet kids like her, and on occasions when they'd come to some sad end. But he had to be dispassionate in his line of work, otherwise seeing life at the bottom end of the scale affected you, and stopped you doing your job efficiently. You had to become detached, somehow. It hardened you, police work. Deaths and murders, drug overdoses, rapes, and all manner of other crimes people inflict on each other, had to be met with a large measure of indifference.

Louisa was different though. There was something about her, something he couldn't put into words. When he looked at her, he saw the pain in those eyes. The sadness, the abuse he was sure she'd suffered, writ large. She was like an open book to him. A stray dog that, if you feed and give it a bed for the night, never leaves your side. They'd never talked about her past, or indeed her family. He thought that in time, she would maybe open up and tell him what had happened. She never had though. Secretly he hoped she never would. He would listen, of course, but he had the feeling this little girl, then only fifteen, and now just seventeen, would break his heart if she told him what she had gone through. Graveney rubbed his face, trying to push away the images his imagination conjured up.

He had taken her into the coffee shop on that day two years ago and bought her a meal. He gave her some money and even offered to get in touch with social services regarding finding her somewhere to live. But when he had gone to the toilet, she disappeared. Only to show up later at his flat. She must have followed him home he reasoned, and against all his better judgement he had taken her in.

There hadn't been a plan, initially, with what they would do. Or how they would explain to people what she was doing there. Eventually, they agreed to tell anyone who inquired she was his niece. Graveney confided in only a small number of people, including Becky, and life moved on. In the beginning, it had been hard. Louisa barricaded her bedroom door at night fearing, Graveney supposed, he would try something.

To begin with this upset him, but he understood Louisa was broken. Time and trust were needed to put her back together. Graveney wall behind her as she fell to the ground, dead. The man's flight or fight mode kicked in immediately, he turned and tried to make his way out of the rear of the shop. Stewart acted quickly, levelled his gun again and fired into his back. The man fell down, groaning. Attempting to escape his assailant, he crawled along the floor. Stewart casually lifted the hatch to gain access behind the counter, strolled towards him, and shot him through the back of the head. He put the gun away, replaced his gloves and raced for the front of the shop, bolted the door and entirely closed the blinds. The workmen outside, digging up the road, banged noisily with their digger. Stewart, hopeful the noise from them had masked the gunshots, walked calmly back to the till. He grabbed the banknotes, pushing them into his jacket pocket, and headed for the back of the shop. He opened the rear door of the property leading into a yard. Striding forward he unbolted a gate at the far end of it, and checked in both directions. Satisfied there was no one about, he stepped into the alleyway and headed for his car.

Graveney left Middlesbrough Police Station having decided to go for something to eat, and possibly a few pints at The Farmers Arms. Not wanting to go home to his empty flat, he put the key in the ignition. A couple of weeks had passed since he'd seen Liz, and he was in the mood for some pleasant female company. His mobile started to ring as he started the engine. Graveney put his head on the steering wheel and blew out hard. It had been a long, tiring day, and the last thing he needed was more police business. Tempted to ignore it he paused, but thinking it may be Louisa he pulled the phone from his pocket. His face dropped when he saw the name DCI Phillips. 'Yes, sir?'

'Peter, there's been another shooting. In Stokesley high street this time.'

'They've got to be linked, haven't they?' Graveney said, 'I mean, two shootings within days.'

'No idea. Forensics, Jones, and Hussain are already there. Get yourself over, and see what's happening. I don't need to remind you that the Chief Super only lives half a mile from there. Imagine what he's going to say when he hears about it.'

'I'm on my way, sir.'

'And Peter. I don't care what time it is, I need to know what's going on. Keep me informed.'

'I'll phone later, sir.' Ringing off he rubbed his eyes before putting on his seat belt and unenthusiastically headed off.

Stokesley high street was awash with flashing blue lights as he approached. Putting down his window, he showed his card at a diligent PC who had flagged him down. The officer, assisted by another PC, opened the roadblock allowing him through. Graveney pulled up at the first available space and got out of his car, as DS Jones headed towards him.

'Evening, sir,' Jones said.

'Well?' Graveney said. Jones, not his favourite police officer. Jones' attitude never failed to annoy him.

'There's been a shooting at Johnson's bookshop. There are two bodies believed to be Roger and Sheila Johnson, the shop owners.'

'Who found them?'

'A neighbour. He'd arranged to meet them here after closing, but there wasn't an answer when he knocked on the front door.' He followed after Graveney, who headed towards the bookshop.

Graveney stopped and glared at Jones. 'No one heard the gunshots?'

'No, sir. They're digging up the road outside the shop. The sound of the jackhammers masked them.'

Graveney strode on, Jones following in his wake. 'How convenient that is. If you're going to shoot someone in broad daylight, with a police station 50 metres away, wait until there's a water leak.'

'I think it was Transco, sir.'

Graveney stopped again. 'What?'

'Digging the road up, sir.'

'Jones, who cares?' he said. 'How did the neighbour get in?'

'He went around the back when he couldn't get an answer at the front. The gate at the rear of the property and the back door were unlocked. He went inside and found them.'

'Have we any witnesses?'

'There's a lady who remembers leaving the shop just before closing and seeing a man still in there. Her description isn't great,' he said, getting his notepad out. 'White male, tall, maybe six feet, dark brown hair. Possibly a beard.'

Graveney sneered and walked on again. 'Well, we've narrowed it down a bit.' Hussain joined the two of them as they finally reached the shop.

'What have you got, Raz?'

'The neighbour arrived just after five, sir. The shop witness said she left at about 16.50, so we've got a 15-20 minute gap.'

'I don't suppose we have any CCTV?'

'Not really, sir,' Hussain said. 'I mean, there's a police station on the high street. Who would be stupid enough?' Graveney rolled his eyes.

'It's Stokesley,' Jones said. 'There's not much call for security cameras, sir.'

Graveney looked at the pair. 'Ok, boys. The usual. Knock on doors and ask some questions. The Chief Super will be all over us on this.'

'Yes, sir,' they both said in unison and marched away.

Bev Wilson came out of the shop and Graveney followed her as she headed for her vehicle. 'We'll have to stop meeting like this, Bev.'

'Nothing would please me more, Graveney.'

'You're not still pissed off, are you? Christ. *Hell hath no fury like Beverley Wilson scorned!*'

She sighed loudly. 'Yeah well. It's been a long, hard week and it's not going to get any easier.'

'You think you've got problems? The Chief Super lives half a mile away, and that's his local.' Pointing at a pub across the road.

'You'd better dot all the i's and cross all the t's, then.'

'Can I have a look at the crime scene?'

'Not yet. We've got lots to do, and if you want a result on this, we'll have to be thorough.'

'What have you got so far, so I can keep the DCI up to speed?'

Bev turned to face him. 'Two bodies, one male, one female. They're probably the shop owners, although we'll need official ID. The guy who found them said it was the owners, but he's a little freaked out. The woman has a single gunshot wound to the forehead.'

Graveney raised his eyebrows. 'The same as the Reverend?'

'Very similar. The man has a gunshot to his back and another to the back of the head. It looks like the woman was shot first.'

'What makes you think that?'

'It appears the man was trying to flee. I'm suggesting the murderer shot the woman, and as the man tried to run shot him in the back before finishing him off. That's my first guess.'

'This guy, the murderer, seems cold and calculating.'

'How do you know it's a man?' she asked.

'A witness said there was a man still in the shop when she left, so he's probably the killer.'

Wilson laughed. 'Good description?'

'Usual. Narrowing it down to 10 per cent of the white male population. She may be able to identify him ... If we ever catch him, that is.'

'Your domain, Graveney.' She took a box from the boot of her car.

'Anything turned up inside?' he said.

'You mean like an eight by ten photo of the killer with his name and address on the back? Not yet, but its early days.' Faking a smile at him.

'Has anyone ever told you that you have a great sense of humour?'

'You! When you asked me out for a drink, and then, oh, let me see ... *stood me up.*'

'That was low, Bev.' He turned and walked away.

'There's something else.'

'Yes?' Graveney stopped and spun around. Half expecting to be greeted with Wilson's middle finger.

'We found a book on the floor. A John Keats poetry book. Are you familiar with Keats, Peter?'

'Isn't everyone?'

'We found it next to the counter. It didn't look like it'd been knocked off a shelf, so, we've bagged it just in case. Who knows, we may get lucky.'

'We may indeed. We'll have to have a drink sometime, Bev?' Turning away again before getting the inevitable finger from Wilson.

Graveney phoned DCI Phillips when he got back to his car informing him of what had happened. The DCI seemed unusually calm when he relayed the intricacies of the case. Probably due to the bottle of red wine he had almost certainly imbibed when he got home. Graveney told him of the possible clue of the poetry book. Experience had taught him not to over-egg the pudding where evidence was concerned though. After instructing Hussain and Jones on what he expected of them, he had another quick chat with Bev Wilson. Deciding there was nothing else he could do that day, and feeling exhausted, he resolved to start afresh in the morning.

He drove back towards Marton from Stokesley, dropped his car off at his flat, and walked the relatively short distance to the Farmers Arms. The pub was quiet, even for a Monday night, and Graveney positioned himself on a stool at the far end of the bar waiting to be served.

'Now then, Peter. What can I get you?' the barman said.

'All right, Nick,' Graveney said. 'Pint, please. Liz about?'

'Liz!' Nick shouted.

An attractive woman appeared in the doorway. In her late-forties with long brunette hair. She glanced about, trying to see what the barman wanted, as he nodded towards Graveney. 'Hi, stranger,' she said.

'Liz. How are you, darling?'

'Very well, thanks,' she said. 'Bit quiet in here tonight though. There's no live football on. Have you eaten?'

'I had a sausage roll earlier.'

'How does lasagne grab you?' she said.

'Sounds fantastic.'

Liz lifted the hatch that gave access to behind the bar, he picked up his drink and followed her into the back.

'Sit down.' She pointed at the table and chairs in the centre of the room. Graveney sauntered up to her and wrapped his hands around her waist, kissing her on the side of her face. 'They say the way to a man's heart is through his stomach.'

She smiled. 'Well, let's see if it's true.'

Graveney kissed her again and patted her backside before sitting. 'The food smells lovely.'

Liz dished up her homemade lasagne and wedges. They chatted like old friends about nothing in particular while sharing a bottle of Pinot Noir. Liz went back into the bar to check Nick was coping ok, satisfied, she returned to find Graveney finishing the washing up.

'You didn't have to do that, Peter. I've got a dishwasher, you know?'

'I know you have. What do you think of him?' He held out his arms.

'Well, you're no Zanussi, but you'll do.' She walked over to him. 'Nick's going to look after the bar tonight, and I've got one of the girls coming in later, so I'm free and easy.'

'Well, that's a coincidence because I'm at a loose end myself.'

'Follow me, young man,' she said. 'I promise I'll be gentle with you.' The two of them ascended the stairs to Liz's flat above.

Graveney got up early and made his way downstairs where Liz prepared breakfast for him. They chatted briefly before she had to start sorting out the pub for the day ahead. Graveney kissed her goodbye and walked back to his flat to get a shower and a change of clothing. He checked his answer phone, chiefly to see if Louisa had been in touch, but there weren't any messages. He set off for the police headquarters in Middlesbrough, and the inevitable pandemonium awaiting him.

CHAPTER FOUR

Graveney pulled up in the busy car park of Middlesbrough police headquarters as his mobile started to ring. Seeing the name of Louisa on the screen, he quickly answered it.

'Hi, Peter, how are you?'

'Never mind me. How are you?'

'I'm ok. I thought you'd be worried, so I rang.'

'Of course I'm worried. How's your mam?'

'She's ...' her voice faltered. 'She's dying.'

Graveney didn't know how to respond, her bluntness taking him by surprise. 'I'm so sorry. How long?'

'Mam's comfortable in the hospital. I got the chance to talk to her, but with the drugs they're giving her now she's drifting in and out of consciousness. My sister thinks it won't be long.'

Graveney clearly heard the emotion in her voice. He wished himself there. He wanted to hug her tightly and pull her close into his arms. He had never felt so useless in his life, but he knew he had to be strong. Strong for Louisa. 'I can come over there straight away.'

'I've seen the papers,' she said. 'I know your hands are full at the moment. My sister and cousin are here with me,'

'Are you safe, though?' Although he was unsure of what she would be safe from.

'I'm all right,' she half-laughed. 'My stepdad isn't here. He left when Mam got ill.'

Although Graveney didn't know what made Louisa leave home, he knew she must have suffered some sort of abuse. This, the first indication she'd given him regarding what had happened to her. He felt angry but fought to suppress it. This wasn't the time to open up old wounds. 'I see.'

'I'd better go. I want to be there when ...' her voice trailed off.

'Louisa, if you need anything, anything at all, ring me, do you hear?' his voice slightly shaking with emotion.

'I will, thanks. I love you,' she said.

Graveney put a hand to his mouth, as he desperately tried to keep his emotions in check and speak. 'I love you too, Lou.' Was all he could muster.

They both rang off. Graveney closed his eyes and tried to compose himself as he clicked into policeman mode and headed into the station.

Louisa thought for a moment. She had almost told Graveney. He deserved to know, and she hated keeping secrets from him. She just wasn't ready to tell him everything yet. Putting her phone away, she headed back to the ward and her dying mother.

Graveney entered the incident room. Uniformed and plain-clothed police officers milled around the crowded space. Spotting DS Hussain, he motioned to him. 'Raz, have you got a minute?' He entered his office closely followed by the officer. 'Shut the door. What have you got for me? I'll be getting a call from the DCI, shortly.'

'I'm waiting for a telephone call regarding the gun,' Hussain said.

'Nothing from Forensics about any other evidence yet?' Graveney said.

'Not yet, sir. I could telephone them if you like.'

Graveney sat back in his chair. 'No. I'll give Bev Wilson a call. Keep working on the gun.'

'Yes, sir.' He left as Graveney's phone rang.

Graveney sighed, and with a degree of trepidation, he answered it.

'Peter,' Phillips said. 'Can you come to my office ASAP, please. The Chief Super is on his way down. He's looking for an update.'

'I'm on my way, sir.' Graveney exited his office and wandered over to DC Sarah Cooke, busily sifting through paperwork on her desk.

'Sarah, I don't suppose there's any decent coffee going is there?'

'Yeah, in the kitchen. I'll get you one, sir.' She smiled up at him.

'No, it's fine. I'll get one myself.'

Graveney cradled his coffee as he looked over at the whiteboard against the far wall. The photos of the Reverend and the Johnsons on it, but little else. Armed with his coffee he headed upstairs to DCI Phillips' office, pausing to knock on the door before entering. Phillips sat behind his desk while Chief Superintendent Charles Oake stood next to him.

'Sit down, Peter,' Phillips said. 'I was getting the Chief Super up to speed.'

Oake nodded at Graveney and looked at Phillips. 'What can you tell me? I don't need to remind you two of the grief I'm getting over this. One shooting is bad enough, *but three.*'

Phillips nodded. 'We understand, sir. It's all happened a little quickly. We're still gathering information on the two shootings. We're not sure at this point if they're linked, isn't that right, Peter?'

'Yes, sir. We're waiting for Forensics to get back regarding any evidence from the murder scene, and I've got one of the boys chasing up the weapon. We're not sure if it's the same person or persons. My gut feeling is ...' He paused. 'They're linked.'

'What makes you say that?' Oake said.

'Just a feeling, sir. I could be wide of the mark. The way the Reverend and Mrs Johnson were killed struck me as similar. Two separate shootings close by? I can't believe they're random.'

There was a knock on the office door, and Hussain popped his head in. 'I'm sorry to interrupt, sir, but there's a call for DI Graveney from Dr Beverley Wilson.'

Phillips nodded towards the door. 'Go and see what she wants. She may have some news on the shootings.'

Graveney got up and made his way to his office, closing the door behind him and picking up his phone. 'DI Graveney.'

'Putting you through, sir,' said a female voice on the other end.

'Peter.' Wilson said.

'Yes, Bev. What have you got for me?'

'The guns match.'

'That doesn't surprise me.'

'Something that might though. Remember the book we picked up in the shop?'

'I'm not wanting to rush you or anything, but I'm in a meeting with Phillips and the Chief Super, so I'm going to have to hurry you.'

'There were two different prints on the book. One was the bookshop owner, Johnson. The other's a match for someone called Stephen Stewart.'

'Stephen Stewart?' Graveney said. 'Where do I know that name from?'

'The Vale Farm Murders.'

'Right,' he said, pausing as the information sank in. 'So why is someone, wanted in connection with the murder of his wife and daughter, shooting people eight years later?'

'Can't help you with that. I can only give you the facts. It's possible Stephen Stewart was just visiting the shop, and he didn't shoot them. Maybe he happened to be in the area.'

'I don't think I'm going to buy that.'

'Neither would I,' she said.

'Well, it looks to me as if Forensics didn't do their job properly.'

'Right. Any reason they wouldn't?'

'None I can think of. Sandra Stewart's body is fascinating as well. She was probably murdered in the front room of the house, but for some reason she was taken outside, and then brought back in.'

'How do you know that?'

'Her clothing was wet. It'd rained.'

'Maybe Stewart tried to move the body and changed his mind?'

'Possibly. But here's a strange thing. She had two types of fibres embedded in her neck. One from a tie they found in the front room and another from a kind of ordinary rope.'

'Did they find the rope?'

'There's no mention of it in the report. Again, a bit slapdash if you ask me.'

'Is it possible he began to strangle her with the tie, and then finished her off with the rope?'

'Maybe. But where was the rope? Why leave the tie and take the rope?'

'All this amounts to is the poor capture of evidence.'

'Then there's the knife found at the scene. It had Stephen Stewart's DNA on it, and Sandra Stewart had quite a lot of Stephen Stewart's blood on her clothing. She was definitely in close contact with her husband.'

'The knife had her fingerprints on it, didn't it?' Graveney said.

'It had Sandra's prints all right, but even they aren't convincing.'

'In what way?'

'When someone grips a knife handle or any other implement, it leaves a specific type of print displaying the grip the person uses. But, to me, the grip appears as if it's not complete. Almost as if someone put the knife in her hand and then squeezed her hand shut. Why would Stephen Stewart fake the fact his wife stabbed him?'

Graveney frowned. 'What you're saying is someone else pressed the knife into her hand, but why?'

'No idea. It looks to me as if someone tried to make it look as if she had stabbed him.'

'Who was the pathologist on the case?'

She laughed and shook her head. 'Ernie Simpson.'

'Didn't he get struck off, or something?'

'Ernie Simpson was an alcoholic. He'd been walking a tightrope for some years because of poor practices. The CPS even lost cases because of his evidence. He'd let anybody walk all over the crime scene and contaminate it. He was sacked not long after this investigation ended.'

'Poor evidence collecting, as I said?'

'All I know is, any barrister worth his salt would drive a bus through this evidence.'

'Is he still alive, do you know?'

'He died years ago. Washed down a handful of pills with a bottle of whisky.'

The waiter arrived with their food, placing it in front of them. Graveney thanked him, the waiter nodded and left them to it.

'One more thing, Peter. I'd check if she was right or left-handed. The print was from her right hand.'

'Most people are right-handed.' Graveney said. 'If she was left-handed, it adds more weight to your theory?'

'It's all circumstantial of course, but there's enough doubt.'

Graveney nodded. 'Yes, I believe there is.'

Bev picked up a forkful of food. 'Who found the body?'

'There was an emergency call from Stewart's mobile. I've heard the recording and it's a bit muffled.'

'What did he say?'

'He said he'd murdered them, and then gave his address before ringing off. His family couldn't say for certain if it was Stewart or not.'

Bev sipped her wine. 'Wasn't his mobile traced?'

'The signal was lost a couple of miles from the house. Presumably, he got rid of the phone.'

'Don't know about you, but it all looks fishy to me.' She put a forkful of food in her mouth.

'Maybe. We'll dig a little deeper and see what we find.'

CHAPTER FIVE

Graveney spent most of the afternoon bombarded with information from his team, most of it useless. The only link between the Johnsons and the Reverend was that they lived relatively close to each other, which didn't seem a good enough reason for anyone to murder them.

He couldn't help but think of Louisa and how she was getting on at the hospital. Sooner or later the inevitable would happen to her mother, and Graveney needed to be there for her. This case had all the hallmarks of dragging on for some time, and he didn't see it reaching a conclusion any time soon. His thoughts were interrupted by a knock on the door and Mac entered.

'What have you got?' Graveney said. 'I hope it's good news or something in a glass?'

'The former, unfortunately, Peter. Have you ever heard of *Winterton Boys' Home*?'

'Yeah. A home up near Sedgefield. Got closed down after it turned out some of the staff were abusing the boys. Why?'

'The Johnsons both worked there. They weren't married at the time, but that's how they met. In addition to them, guess who visited to counsel the boys?'

Graveney smiled. 'Our friend, the Reverend?'

'The same.'

'We've got a foothold in this case then. What about Stewart? Did he stay there?'

'No. But I've been doing some digging into Winterton. There were all sorts of rumours flying about at the time regarding what went on. Only one person ever got convicted of abuse. Arthur Stevens. He was found dead in his prison cell near to the end of his sentence.'

'Murdered?' Graveney said.

'Stabbed to death. They never found out who did it.'

'Dig some more, Mac. See if there's a link to Stephen Stewart. If he wasn't a resident there, he possibly knew someone who was. Find out the names of the staff when it closed down. Maybe Stewart was related to a member of staff who was afraid to speak out.'

Mac smiled. 'I've already got some of the gang onto it now.'

'Sorry. I wasn't trying to teach my granny to suck eggs.'

'Don't worry. I know the score. It's your case. You're the one who'll have to keep the Brass happy. Anyway, work wasn't the only thing I wanted to talk about. Fancy a drink tonight?'

'Like a date, Mac?'

'Not quite, mate. Maria and I've separated, but I'm not desperate.'

'Sorry, I didn't know about that. What happened?'

'Long story. Maybe I'll bore you with it over a drink tonight?'

'Yeah, no problem. My local do?'

'Has it got good beer and a comely barmaid?'

'Both. The landlady's a friend of mine.'

'I'll get the address from you later.' He headed out the door.

Graveney hadn't even thought about why Mac moved to Teesside. Apparently, his marriage to Maria had hit some problems and if he'd relocated here permanently, it must be bad. He'd find out tonight. Mac had on occasion, been a sort of confidante to Graveney. It looked as though he was about to return the favour.

Chief Superintendent Oake arrived at Wyndbourne Hall at around six in the evening. He'd been greeted by William Foxley, his friend and owner of the hall. Foxley ushered him into a sitting room, handing Oake a large brandy as he sat opposite him.

'What did you want to discuss?'

'As I told you on the phone. The murder of the Johnsons and the Reverend. It appears it was our friend Stephen Stewart. We've got a positive match on a fingerprint left at the scene of the second murder.'

'Should we be worried?'

'Of course, we should. The force is going to start digging deep into this. It'll only be a matter of time before they make a connection with Winterton.'

'But I thought we sorted Winterton out. I mean. We got rid of Arthur Stevens and nobody knows where the bodies are buried, literally and metaphorically. Can they link us to the Stewart murders after all these years?'

'Good coppers find links, and the DI I've had to assign is one. Luckily, I've been able to keep Phillips away from it with additional responsibilities. But it won't stop this investigation running its course.'

'What about Shelby. Should we warn him?'

'No. I think we should let Stewart do our dirty work for us. The problem is Shelby will almost certainly have some incriminating evidence on us all. We need to secure that. The fat devious bastard hinted as much in the past.'

'What sort of evidence?'

'No idea. But we don't particularly want it coming to light, do we? I should've had the odious bastard done in years ago. The thing is, this is going to cost. We need to speak to our friends in London.'

'Money isn't a problem, but isn't there any way you could scupper this investigation?'

'It's not easy, I'm too high up now. If I interfered, people, especially Phillips, would get suspicious. Unfortunately, we haven't got an easily-manipulated, piss-head pathologist in our pocket this time either.'

'You've still got Jones, haven't you? Surely he can help?'

'Jones is becoming a liability. He's run up a gambling debt and has a drug problem. He's already asked me for more money. The DI on the case, Graveney, doesn't like him either, so we'll have to keep our eye on Jones.'

'How can you do that?'

'I've got someone else coming in. A woman. Graveney is a ladies' man. I'm hoping she can get close enough to him to be of value. We'll keep Jones in the loop for the moment. When the time is right, we'll eliminate him.'

'Isn't that risky?'

'I think once they look into his bank account, see who he's been rubbing shoulders with, and find out he's been taking drugs, it won't be a problem.'

'Charlie, I'm grateful for this.'

'*Bill*, old school ties only go so far. I'm getting sick of clearing up yours and your friends' mess. This has to be brought to a conclusion because I'm not about to lose everything I've worked for.'

Foxley sneered. 'Not to mention the large Swiss bank account we've filled for you.'

Graveney sat on a stool at the end of the bar in the Farmers Arms talking to Liz. He'd arranged to meet Mac at around 07.30pm and glancing at his watch, his arrival was imminent.

'Who's this friend you're meeting?' Liz said.

'A colleague of mine who's transferred from Strathclyde. He's separated from his wife, and I think he's looking for a new start down here.'

'Is this him?' Nodding towards the door as Mac entered. He stopped to look around and then headed into a corner.

'Yeah, that's him.' He got up from his stool and smiled at her. 'See you later, darling.'

Liz smiled back. 'I hope so.'

Graveney headed over to a table in the corner with two pints, Mac smiled at him as he sat down. Graveney handed him one of the drinks.

Mac nodded towards Liz. 'Is that your friend, the landlady?'

'Liz,' Graveney said.

'Very attractive. How did you meet?'

'This has been my local for years. My flats only a ten-minute walk from here. She ran this pub with her husband when I first started coming in.'

'So, there's a husband then?'

Graveney sneered. 'Was. Not anymore.'

'I've a feeling there's a story there?'

Graveney laughed. 'What makes you say that?'

'Come on, Peter. You're an open book where women are concerned. Not to mention my copper's nose.' Tapping the side of it.

Graveney looked at Mac, who raised his eyebrows, suggesting he wanted him to tell him more.

'Liz and her old man ran this pub when I started coming in here, as I said. She was always friendly to me, but then I suppose running a bar, being friendly goes with the territory. Her husband didn't like me, especially when he found out I was a copper. Bit of a dodgy character. Knocked about with a few local villains. More uniform stuff, rather than anything of interest to me. Liz interested me though.'

'Oh yeah?'

'Not like that, Mac. A bit quick with his hands, her husband. I got sick of coming in here and finding Liz with another bruise or black eye. I lost count of the number of doors she'd supposedly walked into. Liz was scared of him, and I don't think she'd have ever left him. One day I heard from someone at the station that he was being investigated for passing on stolen gear. So, I had a quiet word in his ear about it. Told him the word on the street was he'd grassed up the rest of the villains, and if he valued his life, he'd leave town.'

'And he left town?'

'Three years ago. No one's seen hide nor hair of him since.'

Mac raised his eyebrows. 'And did they really think he grassed them up?'

'No. But he wasn't to know I lied.'

'Naughty boy. You'll give us coppers a bad name.' Mac laughed. 'You and Liz took it from there?'

'Not really, it was a while after. Liz and I have this understanding. After her old man, she didn't want another relationship. That suited me. So, we sort of spend time in each other's company when we feel like it.

I like Liz a lot. She's funny and intelligent, and the situation suits us both.'

'Knight in shining armour.' Mac laughed again. 'I'm with you where wife-beaters are concerned, though.'

'It took me back to my childhood, as well,' Graveney said. Surprised by his own candidness, he continued. 'My dad was a violent alcoholic.'

'I think you mentioned it to me on one of the courses we were on. You tried to explain to me how you got so good at reading body language if I remember. We were so hammered I've forgotten most of what you told me.'

'You don't want to hear that stuff, do you?'

'Of course, I do. It's interesting.'

'Well, go and get another round in then. If we're going to have a soul-searching session, I want to be pissed.'

Mac got up and headed to the bar. Graveney smiled as Mac talked to Liz, and wondered what they were saying about him. He knew he was the topic of conversation by their body alignments, and small gestures the two of them displayed. He smiled to himself. He liked Mac. He had this way about him. No subterfuge, no artifice or veil. A genuineness Mac had that put Graveney at ease. He wouldn't usually open up to anyone about any of his past, let alone his childhood. Occasionally though, normally drink-fuelled admittedly, he felt a need to unburden himself. And if he was going to bare his soul to anyone, he couldn't think of anyone better. Mac headed back from the bar carrying two pints and two shorts in his massive hands.

'We're not on the shorts already, are we?' Graveney said.

'Just the one. We've got work in the morning.' Mac raised his glass. 'To the investigation.'

Graveney lifted his Jack Daniels up, clinking glasses. The pair downing their shorts in one.

'What were you and Liz talking about?'

'Nothing in particular,' Mac said. 'You were telling me about your dad.'

Graveney's smile vanished. He closed his eyes and exhaled. 'He was an alcoholic, as I said earlier. My mother, younger brother and me, lived in fear of him and his drunken, violent moods. Sometimes he'd come back from the pub, collapse into bed and not bother us. Other times, maybe when he'd argued with someone or lost money at the Bookies, he would change. I learned to become hyper-vigilant. I got excellent at sensing the cues. A rise in his tone of voice, the lowering of his eyebrows into a scowl, that sort of thing. I found as I got older, the better I got at it.' Graveney took a swig of his pint and continued.

'At college, I could for example, tell when one of my female classmates was having an affair with the tutor. I noticed how their bodies became synchronised in a sort of subtle dance. They'd shift together and move in unison. When she moved, he moved too. When I saw them so intimately attuned, at a body level like lovers, I knew he was shagging her. Couples don't know they're doing it. They become responsive to each other on a subconscious level. Over the years I got better and better at it. It's like anything else in life. If you practice long and hard enough, you become an expert.'

'What do you see when you look at people?' Mac said.

'Whenever I'm with someone, I'm aware of loads of information other people don't sense. Like the lift of an eyebrow or the movement of a hand. Small gestures like that. I find it disruptive, being overly aware, so sometimes I tune it down a little. I used to tell people what I was doing, a sort of party trick, but I quickly found out how much people dislike the fact you're reading them. They become self-conscious, so I've learned to keep it to myself wherever possible.'

'When you say you find it disruptive, sometimes,' Mac asked. 'What do you mean?'

'I remember once when I'd started on the force, and I had this meeting I was late for. When I arrived, people were outwardly perfectly friendly to me, smiling, saying hello, etc. But their bodies were telling me a different story. Their postures, and the fact no one made proper eye contact, showed me how angry they all were. You can imagine how off-putting that was.'

'What about the thin thingy you mentioned before?'

'Thin-slicing. I went to a few lectures held by this American professor. He taught this technique of how to read people's faces. Building on stuff I'd already learned. I thought it'd help in my line of work. When you talk to people or ask them questions, especially under duress, their faces often betray their real emotions.'

'You can tell if they're lying, for example?' Mac asked.

'It's not as simple as that. I can believe people are not being entirely honest, or if they're trying to cover something up. You ask one question, and because you're the Police, and they feel guilty about something else - entirely unrelated - this can lead me to believe they're hiding something. I can't mind-read or anything.'

'But how can you see it, if it happens so fast?'

'For example. When Roger Federer plays tennis at Wimbledon, there's no way he'd ever return a 125 mph serve if he reacted once the ball had been hit. It'd be past him. So, over years of training, his brain learns to look for subtle signs in his opponent's game. Clues, etc. How he throws the ball, how he swings his racket, and so on. Scientists call this chunking. The information is quickly processed by the brain as if time has slowed down. The same thing occurs with thin-slicing. After hundreds of hours of watching videos of faces, you can almost slow time. When someone is asked a question and they don't want to give a truthful answer, or if they're trying to mask how they're really feeling, there's a split second where the genuine emotion shows itself. Before the person's conscious self, covers it up. Most people wouldn't see it, or recognise it for what it was. They may get a vague feeling that something's not right. What we call intuition. When you get the feeling that someone, or something, doesn't ring true.'

Mac took a drink. 'But you can see the emotion?'

'Often, I can,' Graveney said. 'This is getting serious, Mac. I think I need another pint.' He drained his glass.

'What happened to your dad?' Mac asked. Graveney thought carefully for a moment. He wasn't sure he wanted to allow the conversation to head in this direction, his childhood littered with bad memories which Graveney kept buried. He knew Mac wasn't likely to give up, so reluctantly continued.

'When I was twelve, he came home drunk one night in a terrible mood. Mam and my brother, Andrew, barricaded themselves in one bedroom. I hid in another. He flew up the stairs threatening to kill us all but slipped at the top and fell. He suffered a hyperacute subdural haematoma and died in hospital three weeks later.'

Mac shook his head. 'Sad end.'

'Yeah, it was.' Picking up the empty glasses, he headed for the bar. Graveney almost told the truth. Thankful Mac couldn't thin-slice, as he'd kept his own counsel on what happened all those years ago. He couldn't tell anyone his dad came rushing up the stairs with a hammer, ready to smash down the bedroom doors. Or how he'd tripped his dad at the top of the stairs and watched him as he tumbled down them. How could he tell anyone, no matter how special to him they were? He had murdered his own father. Graveney pushed the memory back into the far corner of his mind to gather some more dust and headed back to Mac with two more pints.

Liz brought some sandwiches over and popped them on their table. 'I thought you boys might be hungry?'

'Thanks,' Graveney said. Liz winked at him and headed off.

'She's a lovely lady, Liz,' Mac said.

'Anyway, I thought you were supposed to be bearing your soul tonight regarding you and Maria separating?'

Mac blew out. 'Soon to be divorced.'

'Is it that bad?'

'Afraid so. That's what this job does to marriages, wrecks them. I don't hold it against her. She was right what she said to me.'

'What did she say?'

'There were three people in our bed. Her, me and the force. She told me she'd brought the kids up as I was hardly ever there. It came as no surprise when she told me she'd met someone and was leaving me.'

'What's he like, this new fella?'

'Fine. The kids like him. It would have been easier if he'd been a dick-head, but he's not. He runs his own business, lots of cash, a beautiful house, and to be perfectly honest what Maria deserves.'

'What about the kids? Do you still see them?'

'Yeah, you know. The usual. Weekends and birthdays, job permitting. Anyway, enough of this depressing talk. Let's cheer ourselves up and talk about the case for the length of time it'll take me to finish this pint. I'm knackered, and I don't know about you, but I've a feeling this one's going to run and run.'

Graveney raised his eyebrows and nodded. 'Me too.'

Liz locked up for the night. Graveney helped her to tidy up before they headed upstairs to her flat.

'You ok. You look a little down?' she asked.

He sighed. 'Mac was asking me about my childhood, and it brought back memories I'd prefer to stay in the past. I'm worried about Louisa, too.'

'Look at you getting all emotional. You big softy.' Hugging him tightly, maternally. 'Come on let's get you to bed.'

CHAPTER SIX

David Shelby parked his Mercedes outside the offices of *Shelby & Mathews solicitors,* Yarm Village. In his mid-fifties, with thinning grey hair, his rotund figure a result of too many brandies and long business lunches. His small stature, at only five-feet-two, further exaggerating the size of his waistline. Wearing an expensive, bespoke, navy blue suit, white shirt, and a cream coloured tie, he entered the building and slowly climbed the stairs to the first floor, panting with the effort involved. His tanned complexion taking on a somewhat rubicund appearance as he finally reached his secretary's office. Mary Jacobs, his secretary for the last ten years, smiled at him. A spinster in her late-forties with the sort of dress sense that would make even the primmest of women look fashionable.

'Morning, Mr Shelby.'

'Morning, Mary,' he said, through panting breaths. 'Those stairs will be the death of me.'

'Did you enjoy your holiday? You look tanned.' In all honesty, he always looked tanned. Six or seven trips a year to sunnier climes only added to his colour.

'Marvellous. Fantastic weather,' Shelby said. 'Can you get me some tea, Mary, and let me know what appointments I have today, please? Back to the grindstone.'

'I'll bring one through, sir.'

Shelby plodded through to his office and sat at his desk. He picked up the local newspaper - diligently placed by his secretary for him to read – and stared in disbelief at the headline:

**HUSBAND AND WIFE BOOKSHOP OWNERS KILLED IN
BUNGLED ROBBERY.**

He recognised the shop instantly as Johnson's Bookshop, owned by Roger and Sheila Johnson. Mary entered the room carrying a tray with a pot of tea, hot water, and a small plate of biscuits. 'Terrible business, Mr Shelby.' She put the tray on his desk.

Shelby's mouth momentarily fell open. 'Yes, it is.'

'Didn't you know them?' she asked.

'I've met them once or twice.' Reading the story as he spoke. 'But I can't say I really knew them.'

'It's getting terrible around here, what with that and someone murdering poor Reverend James.'

Shelby gaped at his secretary. 'Reverend James?'

'Yes. In church, on Sunday.'

'Do they know who did it?'

'No. Apparently someone saw some youths hanging around there, and the police are looking for witnesses. If you ask me, it's probably someone high on drugs or something.' She left the office and closed the door behind her.

Shelby removed his mobile phone and called a number. From her desk Mary heard Shelby's raised voice, and listened intently to his one-sided conversation.

'It's Shelby, have you seen the news? The Johnsons and the Reverend … come off it, bungled robbery. He's come back … Listen to me. I know everything. Every name involved. And I've got documents too … I'm not waiting for Stewart to turn up and put a bullet in me. He has to be got rid of, quickly, or I'm spilling the beans. You got it!' Shelby rang off, put his phone back into his jacket pocket, and pressed the intercom.

'Mary, cancel my appointments for today.'

'Is everything ok, Mr Shelby?'

'Yes, yes. Something's come up, that's all,' he said.

He walked over to the other side of the room, took a key from his trouser pocket, and opened the top drawer of a filing cabinet. Inside lay an old World-War-two service revolver and a box of bullets. He loaded the gun and returned to his desk. With shaking hands, he placed the weapon in the top right-hand drawer.

Mary began ringing around the list of appointments to cancel them when Stewart walked up the stairs.

'Can I help you?' she asked.

He stopped in front of her desk. 'Mr Roberts. I've an appointment with Mr Shelby, but I'm a little early. Could he fit me in now?' He glanced at the clock on the wall.

'I'm sorry, Mr Roberts. I'm afraid Mr Shelby will have to cancel his appointment with you today. Something important has come up.' She looked towards Shelby's office.

Stewart followed her gaze and raced towards the door. 'He'll see me.' He burst into the office, his right-hand tucked inside his coat. Shelby turned and glanced at his hand, spotting the outline of something he presumed a gun.

'I'm sorry, Mr Shelby. I told him you weren't seeing anybody today, but he barged in.'

'That's ok, Mary. I know this gentleman. It's fine. You can leave us now.'

The secretary nodded at Shelby and threw an anxious glance towards Stewart as she left the room. She intuited all was not well. Unsure of what to do she sat back at her desk, picked up the phone, and dialled.

Shelby sat back in his chair, trying to appear calm, knowing he was in grave danger. Realising, however, he had something to bargain with. Trying not to glance at the drawer, he allowed his right hand to slightly open it before the nerves got the better of him, and he put them back on top of the desk.

'Stephen Stewart, I presume?' Hardly recognising Stewart from the pictures posted in the papers years earlier. Stewart's hair much longer, his face much thinner, and sporting a full beard.

Stewart pulled the gun from his pocket and sitting opposite Shelby let it rest on his thigh. 'Shelby, I'm going to get straight to the point. Who's the missing name?' He pushed a piece of paper across the desk. Shelby viewed it, four names numbered one to four, his name number three. The others had a line crossed through them, the significance of which wasn't lost on him. Number five was blank.

Shelby rubbed his chin. 'If I tell you the name, how do I know you won't shoot me anyway?'

'I don't think you're in a position to bargain.'

'You don't know what you've got yourself into here, Stewart. There are a lot more people involved than these. The fifth name is just the tip of the iceberg. I've information which would astound you. I've papers to help you to get the real culprits. The people responsible for your wife and daughter's murder.'

Stewart followed Shelby's momentary glance towards a filing cabinet on the other side of the room. 'Where are these papers?'

'Not here. My safety deposit box.'

'What's in the filing cabinet, Shelby?'

'What filing cabinet?'

Stewart walked over to it and pulled at the top drawer. It was locked. He turned back towards Shelby, holding out his left hand. 'Give me the key, Shelby.'

'It's in my car.'

'And I suppose I should let you go and get it?'

'I could send Mary if you like, while I stay here ... Just to show I'm not trying any funny business.'

Stewart thought for a moment. Shelby could be telling the truth he reasoned. And in any case, the secretary wouldn't know what was going on. 'Ok. Ask her to come in here. If you try anything, you're dead. You understand me?' He thrust the gun in his pocket.

'Yes, Mr Stewart. I understand perfectly.'

Shelby pressed the button on the intercom. 'Mary, can you come in here please?'

There was a light tap on the door to the office and Shelby's secretary walked in. 'Ah, Mary. Nip downstairs and get my filing cabinet keys from my car? I think I left them in the glove-box.'

'Of course, Mr Shelby,' said his secretary, holding out her hand.

As she leant forward to collect the car keys from him, Shelby pulled open his top drawer and snatched the gun aiming it towards Stewart. Stewart reacted quickly to Shelby's sudden movement and drew his own gun from his pocket. Shelby fired past his secretary and hit Stewart as Stewart shot at Shelby. A sharp pain exploded in Stewart's side momentarily causing him to stagger back. The noise terrific as Shelby, hit full in the chest, slammed against the office wall and slowly slipped towards the floor. Stewart moved swiftly still pointing his gun. He manoeuvred around the secretary, who was crouched on the floor with her hands covering her ears, and peered over the top of the desk where Shelby had sat. He lay slumped against the wall. Blood smeared down it from where his body had slid. Stewart crept closer and stood no more than a foot away from the stricken Shelby, half expecting him to spring to life at any moment. But when he prodded him with his foot, the solicitor rolled onto his side, dead. He sighed loudly, allowing the breath he'd been holding to escape. Dropping to the floor, he rifled through Shelby's trouser pockets. After discarding several items, Stewart picked up what looked like the filing cabinet key. His attention drawn back to the secretary, who was now sobbing.

'Are you injured?' Leaning over her, he helped her to her feet.

'No ... I ... don't think so,' she stammered.

Stewart led her over to a chair on the other side of the room and helped her into it. He studied the terrified-looking secretary, who was clearly, to his mind anyway, in shock. She stared at the inert body of her employer lying on the floor. Stewart, shaken from his thoughts wondered what to do. He glanced out of the window and into the street. A large crowd gathered below, looking up at the building. He hurried to the filing cabinet on the other side of the room and searched the top drawer. He paused, about to move onto the second drawer but something gleamed in one corner. Picking it up, he held it in his hand. He hadn't seen anything like it before, and he hoped it was the safety deposit box key Shelby had spoken about. Stewart slid it into his pocket and pondered, trying desperately to keep his mounting panic in check. He couldn't go out through the front door, not with all the people outside, he reasoned. Heading out of Shelby's office and into the secretary's, he closed and locked the entrance to the staircase. Pulling the desk across from the other side of the room, he jammed it up against the handle. Hoping this would give him more time, he raced back to Shelby's office.

'Where's the door to the fire escape?' he said to the secretary. She sat quietly, still staring vacantly at the body of the solicitor, appearing not to hear Stewart. He decided to look for another means of escape but halted in his tracks, as Police sirens sounded outside. He rushed to the window and peeked out. Two police squad cars, lights flashing, were parked opposite. Stewart slumped onto a chair. Realising all his exits were now probably covered, his mind raced, as he pondered what to do. Taking his mobile from his pocket, he texted. *It's all gone wrong. Shelby's dead. I'm injured. What should I do? Steve x.*

Within seconds he received a message back: *Sit tight, I'll get back to you, Ang x.*

Stewart looked over at the secretary, who appeared still in shock, as she lifted a shaky hand to her face. He stood, and walking across to her, gently put his hand on her shoulder. 'Are you ok?'

She looked at him and nodded.

What's your name?'

'Mary,' she said.

'Listen, Mary. I won't harm you. You've nothing to worry about. If you do what I say, there won't be a problem. Do you understand?'

'Mr Shelby is dead,' she said. Tears rolled freely down her cheeks.

'I know he's dead. There's a lot about him you don't know. He deserved to die for what he did. But I'm sorry you had to witness it.'

She stared at Stewart, her face a deathly white. 'I'll do what you say, Mr Roberts.'

'Stephen,' he said. 'Call me Stephen.'

She nodded. 'Ok, Stephen.'

Graveney sat at a table in the coffee shop, a black Americano in front of him, he looked up as Becky made her way over. She'd been busy in the stockroom when he'd arrived, so they hadn't enjoyed their usual banter.

'Hi, Honey.' She stopped close by, smiling broadly at him.

'Well, hello there,' he said in a fake American drawl.

'I meant to ask.' Glancing back towards Andrea, who was oblivious to them both. 'Have you heard from Louisa?'

He sighed. 'She phoned this morning. She couldn't speak though. She said she'd ring later on, so I'll know more then.'

Becky placed a hand on Graveney's shoulder. 'I hope everything's ok. Louisa's been through a lot already.'

Graveney liked Becky, her warmness and concern genuine. That was one of the reasons he'd confided in her about Louisa. Knowing he could trust her implicitly. To Graveney, there were few things more important.

'What you up to today, fella?'

'Work. I'm on my way in now.'

'Another coffee?' she asked.

Graveney consulted his watch. 'To go. I'm going to be late.'

'I sometimes think my coffee's the only reason you come in here,' she said. Graveney smiled. She was obviously fishing for a compliment.

He leaned in closer to Becky as she bent to pick up his cup and saucer. 'The coffee's an excuse to see you, Becks. You know that,' he whispered.

Becky stood straight and beamed at him. 'You know, Peter,' lowering her voice. 'One of these days you're going to wake up in bed with me beside you, and think, wow! How did that happen?'

'I'll look forward to that,' he said, and leant back in his chair.

Becky walked back to the counter, but couldn't resist looking back at Graveney over her shoulder with her best sexy-vamp look.

Andrea rolled her eyes. 'You can't help yourselves,' she said.

Becky joined her. 'You've got to admit it, he's gorgeous.'

'In an obvious sort of way.'

'He reminds me of a young David Essex.' Ignoring Andrea's remark.

Andrea studied Graveney, who'd picked up his paper again. 'I see what you mean. It's the dark wavy hair. Definitely a bit of gipsy in him.'

Becky leant across the counter. 'Mmm.'

Andrea nudged her. 'I thought you were seeing Tim?'

Becky sighed. 'Tim's - how can I put it - a little backwards coming forward. If you know what I mean?'

'What are you talking about?' Andrea said.

'Two dates and all he's managed is a little peck on the cheek.'

'Maybe he's a gentleman?'

'Come off it, Andrea. This is the twenty-first century, not Victorian England. We're both in our early forties, not teenagers.'

'My sister in law, Anne-Marie, swears by the three-date rule,' Andrea said.

'The three-date rule?'

'You know. She won't have sex until at least the third time.'

Becky laughed. 'How quaint. Well, my best friend Kate says life's too short, and you should jump in with both feet. If he's sticking to this three-date rule, thingy, Saturday could be interesting.'

'Why?'

'He's taking me to the pictures. Our third date.'

'You'd better put your best undies on, Becks.'

'Definitely. If nothing happens, I'm sending you to the corner shop for some more batteries. Sanjay will be wondering what I'm doing with them all.'

They both broke out into laughter. Graveney glanced up over the top of his paper and smiled to himself, assuming it was probably something to do with sex.

He glanced around at the other occupants. The shop half-full of coffee-sipping, button-pushing people. He returned to his morning paper, flicking through the pages, barely pausing to digest any of the headlines. Quickly becoming bored with this, he once more continued to survey the other customers in the shop. A young couple caught his eye, the two of them staring across the table at each other. Apparently in love, subconsciously mimicking each other's movements. Something people in love do. Young love. What an illusion it was, he thought, but then admonished himself for his cynicism. A black man on the table next to him spoke on his mobile phone. Immaculately dressed in a bespoke suit. The usual accoutrements surrounded him. Briefcase, laptop and The Financial Times. A businessman, Graveney thought, something in the financial sector no doubt. A young woman with a toddler in her arms, an older lady opposite her - her mother perhaps - she talked incessantly to the older woman, fed the baby with some food from a bowl, while simultaneously tapping on her phone. He moved his gaze to a female sitting in the corner, surreptitiously watching him. Graveney tried not to let her know this by keeping his glances in her direction to a minimum. Tall, perhaps five feet ten, especially with the killer heels she was wearing. Her long brunette hair somewhat sternly tied back in a ponytail, so tight it stretched the skin on her face. Smartly dressed in a skirt, jacket, and finished off with a crisp white blouse. Attractive, her bright-red lipstick looking somewhat out of place though. Nearly, but not wholly meretricious. She was somehow managing to pull the look off though. Whoever she was, she was used to having her own way and not afraid of using her looks to achieve it. A woman in a predominately male environment, he guessed. Graveney summed this up in a matter of seconds, his thin-slicing and reading of body language quickly stripping away any subterfuge, intentional or otherwise.

His phone sounded in his pocket. Moving his attention away from the brunette, he retrieved it and answered the call. 'Graveney.'

'Guv, it's Jones.'

Graveney rolled his eyes. 'Yes, Jones, what is it?'

'We've got an incident on Yarm high street.'

He stood and took hold of the coffee Becky held out to him, handing her some money, he winked and marched towards the door. He glanced across at the brunette who was gathering her things and leaving too. 'What sort of incident?' Graveney said.

'Gunshots in a firm of solicitors. The firearms boys are here, but we're not sure how to proceed. I tried ringing DCI Phillips, but he's not answering.'

'I'm on my way. I'll have to phone for a car. Don't do anything rash for the moment.' Graveney hung up and searched through his contacts on his phone.

'DI Graveney?' the brunette said.

'Yes, and you are?'

'DS Marne, sir. Chief Inspector Phillips sent me. I'm your new DS.' She flashed her ID.

'Have you got a car, Marne?'

'Yes, sir.'

'Get it then,' he said. Marne hurried over the road to a parked car, Graveney closely following her as they both jumped in and headed off.

'Do you know where Yarm is?' Graveney asked.

'Yes, sir.'

'Head for the high street. Some sort of incident. Gunshots from a firm of solicitors. Have you a first name, Marne?'

'Stephanie, sir. Steph.'

'Well, Stephanie. Steph. Put your foot down.'

Marne accelerated, weaving in and out of traffic as she went. He glanced across at her. She was beautiful. A strong smell of perfume, one he recognised instantly, briefly distracted him. He picked up his mobile and dialled Phillips.

A voice answered on the other end. 'Yes, Peter?'

'I'm on my way to an incident in Yarm, sir. Possible shooting. The firearms are there. What do you want me to do?'

'I'll let you handle it. I'm on my way up to see the Chief Super. Keep me informed on this one. Some bigwigs live in Yarm, so we don't want a bloodbath or anything.'

Graveney smiled. 'I'll see what I can do, sir.'

They careered along at an alarming rate, Graveney impressed by Marne's level of driving skill. Every now and then she'd glance in his direction, not even attempting to hide it, and Graveney, no stranger to the fairer sex, grew increasingly interested. They pulled up at the top of the high-street, two rows of quaint looking shops spread out along its length. Some of the buildings dating back to the eighteenth century providing an archetypal-looking, traditional English village. Both ends of the high-street had been cordoned off by uniformed police, and a line of police tape spread across the length of the road at one end. Two police vehicles blocked the way at the other. Further away, a paramedic van parked with its lights flashing furiously. Graveney got out of the passenger seat and turned towards a group of uniformed and plain-clothed officers fifty metres away.

'Your phone, sir,' she shouted.

He turned and reached out to take the phone from her. Marne placed it gently on the palm of his hand, allowing her hand to fleetingly touch his. She looked at him. Their eyes met, and for what seemed like minutes to Graveney, they stared at each other.

Marne leant forward towards him, her face only inches from him now. 'I think you'd better go, sir,' she whispered.

Graveney smiled as he pushed the phone into his pocket. He marched away but couldn't resist one final glance back at Marne, still seated in the car. Never had a woman delivered a sentence to him so loaded with sexual tension. If Marne intended to grab his attention, she had indeed succeeded.

CHAPTER SEVEN

Stewart sat quietly in the solicitor's office, the pain in his side increasing. A small pool of blood had formed on the floor beneath his seat. 'Mary, are there any towels?'

The secretary awoke from her daze and looked across at Stewart. Her eyes darting between the blood on the floor and the large, red stain on his clothing. 'Yes,' she said. 'In the bathroom.'

'Can you bring me some, please?'

The secretary nodded, stood and raced from the office, returning moments later with two hand towels. Stewart thanked her and pressed one of them against his wound. His phone beeped. He fished it from his pocket and opened the text from Ang, reading it under his breath. 'Ask for Graveney, no one else.'

He typed: 'Probably won't get out of this alive, thanks. Steve x.'

Ang replied: 'For S and J, Ang. x.'

Graveney was met by Hussain as he approached the group of officers. 'What have you got for me, Raz?' He looked over at DS Jones, deep in conversation on his phone. Jones waved an acknowledgement at him.

Hussain nodded across at the building. 'From what we've gathered, sir, there's been a shooting at the solicitors. Witnesses reported hearing one, maybe two shots. There are usually only two people in the office.' Taking out his notebook. 'David Shelby, solicitor, and his secretary, Mary Jacobs. Tony's on the phone with some guy in there now.'

Jones placed his hand over the mouthpiece of the phone and ambled towards Graveney. 'Guv,' he said. 'He wants to speak to you. He asked for you by name.'

'He asked for me?'

'Yeah. He said he'll only speak to you.'

Graveney snatched the phone from Jones and put it to his ear. 'Detective Inspector Graveney speaking. Who am I talking to?'

'My name doesn't matter. Just listen to what I'm saying. I've got Mr Shelby's secretary here with me. She's uninjured but obviously shaken. I'll let her come down in return for you coming up.'

'What about Mr Shelby?'

'Mr Shelby's not in a position to do anything.'

'I see,' Graveney said. 'Can you give me a moment?'

'Five minutes, Graveney. The clock's ticking.'

Stewart slumped back in the chair and dropped his head a little. He felt light-headed. Shaking his head, he tried to clear the fog now masking his thoughts.

Mary peered over at him and frowned. 'Can I get you a drink, Stephen?'

He forced a smile at her. 'Yes, please.'

Graveney turned to the officers now present. Marne wandered up to the assembled group, causing some to look in her direction.

'This is DS Stephanie Marne.' Indicating in her direction before continuing. 'He's holding the secretary hostage. I think Shelby's dead, so we'll tread carefully. This is probably the man who carried out the other three shootings, so we know what he's capable of. Our first concern is the secretary. It's vital we get her out unharmed.' He paused a moment before adding. 'He's prepared to swap her for me.'

'Surely you're not considering that?' Jones said.

'It's not procedure,' Hussain added.

Graveney held up his hand to stifle the protests as he phoned DCI Phillips. The phone went straight to answerphone and Graveney hung up. 'Ok, Jones. Get him back on the line.'

Stewart's phone rang. He put down the glass and answered. 'Yes?'

'It's Graveney. I'm on my way up, but I need assurances the secretary won't be hurt.'

'It's not about her, Inspector. She'll be ok. I'm warning you, Graveney. If you try anything, anything at all, this will end up as a bloodbath.'

'You have my word,' he said.

Graveney turned to the assembled officers. 'Can someone bring me a jacket? Jones, try and get hold of the DCI and keep him informed of what's happening. I want everyone to know this is my decision. Have we got that?' The group nodded in agreement as a firearms officer handed Graveney a bulletproof jacket.

Marne moved towards Graveney, slightly closer than necessary. 'Guv,' she said. 'You should take a radio with you and insist on calling in at pre-agreed intervals.'

'Raz. Sort me one out, will you?'

The senior firearms officer pulled Graveney to one side. 'We've got men out the back, and I've got someone covering the front. Do you want me to take a shot if the opportunity arises?'

'No. Let's hold our nerve for the moment and see what his game is.'

'Ok, sir.'

Graveney slid on his bullet-proof vest and then his brown tweed jacket over the top. He picked up the radio, put this into his pocket and headed towards the building. Entering, Graveney climbed the stairs to the office above and reached a closed door with the name of the Solicitors on the front. Graveney knocked and listened as he heard movement inside, as if something substantial was being pulled away from the door. Someone unlocked it. The door opened just wide enough for someone to enter or exit, and Graveney stepped through. Stewart, holding a gun, nodded for the secretary to leave. She quickly headed for the door, as Stewart closed and locked it behind her. He pointed the gun in the direction of the solicitor's office, and Graveney walked towards it. Once inside, Stewart motioned for Graveney to raise his hands in the air and performed a body search.

'What's in your pocket?' Stewart said.

Graveney slowly removed the radio from his jacket pocket and placed it on the desk nearby. He looked at Stewart, and the large red patch on his clothing. 'It's a police radio. I have to call in every fifteen minutes.'

'Take your jacket off.'

Graveney did as he was told and handed it to Stewart. Stewart searched through it and seemingly satisfied, gave it back to Graveney who placed it on the back of a chair.

Stewart nodded. 'That's fine. Take a seat.' Pointing to a chair positioned opposite the one Stewart slumped into.

'You are?' Already knowing the answer to his question.

'Stephen Stewart, Inspector.'

'The Vale Farm Murders. Why did you ask for me?' Graveney studied Stewart, as an immense look of sadness crossed the injured man's face. He sat back in the chair and grimaced from the pain Graveney was sure he must be suffering. He stared directly across at Graveney and for the briefest of moments, Graveney recognised an emotion that flickered, and then was gone. A look of absolute desperation. The kind of look someone displays when hope has all but faded.

'Why I asked for you by name is unimportant, Inspector. I want you to find the people who killed my wife and daughter.'

'Isn't that what you've been doing already? The Reverend, the Johnsons, Shelby. Clearly, they had something to do with it or am I wide of the mark?' Graveney turned and pointed at the dead body of the solicitor lying against the wall.

'I thought I was nearing the end with Shelby. My wife left a list of names.' Indicating for Graveney to look at the paper still on Shelby's desk.

Graveney picked it up and read the names. 'The people you've killed? Who's number five?'

'That's just it. I thought I was looking for only one name. The Reverend told me Shelby knew the person. He also said that the fifth person was in a powerful position.'

'I'm confused here. You say your wife left these names for you?'

'Inspector.' Stewart grimaced again. 'I haven't time to go into the finer details now. All you need to know is the four of them, and the missing fifth person were involved.'

'I see,' Graveney said.

Stewart shook his head slowly. 'Shelby knew.' Glaring across at the dead man. 'Unfortunately, he decided to get into a gunfight with me. You can see the outcome.' Stewart smiled ruefully. 'The thing is, he indicated those four names and the missing fifth, are just the tip of the iceberg. There are more people involved.' Stewart reached into his jacket pocket and pulled out a key. 'This is a key to my room where I'm staying. The Whitestone in Great Broughton. In my room, you'll find a rucksack with everything I've got on the murders. Please find them and bring them to justice.'

Stewart slumped back against his seat.

'Stephen,' Graveney said. 'Do you want me to call for a paramedic?'

'No. I just need a drink of water.'

The police radio sprang into life. 'Guv, you ok?'

Stewart motioned for Graveney to answer the radio. As Graveney strode across to it, Stewart hauled himself up and moved closer to the chair where Graveney had sat. 'Jones, I'm fine. I'll speak shortly.'

'Ok, Guv.'

Stewart now stood next to Graveney's vacated chair, as he used his left arm to steady himself. 'Would you mind getting me that drink from the kitchen? I'm rather thirsty.'

Graveney, now growing concerned about the state of Stewart, raced next door to get some water. Stewart plucked the safety deposit key from his trouser pocket and slipped it into the top pocket of Graveney's jacket. He turned unsteadily and made his way back towards his own chair but stumbled and fell before reaching it. Graveney came rushing back into the room and grabbed the radio. 'Jones. Get the paramedics up here, straight away.'

Graveney stood on Yarm high street surrounded by police officers as the ambulance carrying Stephen Stewart set off, its siren sounding and lights flashing furiously.

He called over to DC Sarah Cooke. 'Sarah, I need you to go to the hospital. Keep me informed of his condition.'

'Yes, Guv.' She headed towards one of the cars. The other officers surrounded Graveney, listening intently as he gave out instructions. 'Jones and Marne. You two with me,' he said. 'Stewart gave me a key to his room at The Whitestone Hotel in Great Broughton, so we need to get across there and secure any evidence.'

'What room?' Jones said.

Graveney fished in his pocket and pulled out a key, holding it aloft for everybody to see the number 10 on the key ring. 'Raz. I've phoned through to the station to arrange for the necessary paperwork. I need you to go there and bring it to the hotel, ASAP.'

'Yes, Guv.' Heading for his car along with Jones, racing ahead for his.

'Steph, go and get the vehicle. I'll be two minutes.'

Marne headed for her car as Graveney made his way over to Bev Wilson who was entering the solicitor's office. 'Bev!' he shouted, making his way towards her. 'Just a quickie. The other day when you rang me about the fingerprint on the book.' Bev nodded. 'Did you speak to anyone else before me?'

'No,' Bev said. 'You were the first to get the news.'

'Thanks,' Graveney said. He turned and marched away from her.

'I hope all your quickies aren't as quick,' she muttered under her breath.

Graveney walked towards Marne's car when his mobile rang. 'Mac.'

'Peter. The paperwork should be ready when Raz gets here. Where are you off to next?'

'Great Broughton. Stewart gave me the key to his room and said he had information on the Vale Farm Murders there. So, I'm hoping to secure that. I'll ring and let you know what we find.'

'I've spoken to Phillips and he's up to date with events,' Mac said.

'Good.'

Jones made excellent time getting to Great Broughton. He pulled into the car park at the front of the hotel and opening the boot to his car, slipped a small crow-bar and a pair of latex gloves into his jacket pocket. Although hazardous, Oake had promised him £20,000 if he managed to recover any evidence Stewart had left behind. Jones crept into the hotel and glanced towards the reception area. Luckily no one was about, so he quickly raced past the desk towards the bedrooms. He turned a corner leading down another corridor and paused. The cleaner, in front of him, slipped out of sight. He knew the hotel well, having stayed there on a couple of occasions, and quickly located room 10. Taking the gloves from his pocket, he put them on, removed the crow-bar and gently forced it between the door frame and the door. The door quickly gave way, and Jones stepped through into the room, quietly closing it behind him. He began systematically searching through the drawers and wardrobes. Finding nothing he moved towards the bathroom, and then stopped, spotting a holdall on the floor in the corner partially covered by a curtain. Throwing the contents of the bag on the bed and picking up a folder, he flicked through the pieces of paper inside. Smiling to himself, Jones put it into his jacket and headed towards the window. He moved the curtains to one side checking the yard was clear and opening one of the sash windows, stepped outside. He kept a watchful eye as he strode back around to the front of the hotel and his car. He opened the boot, deposited the folder, gloves and crowbar inside. He gave one last glance about the car park, smiled to himself again as he headed back to the reception desk and pressed the bell for attention.

Graveney and Marne screeched into the car park of The Whitestone Hotel, Marne sliding to a halt on the loose gravel next to Jones' car. They jumped out and marched towards the entrance, just as Jones and a middle-aged, grey-haired man came outside.

Jones pointed at the other man. 'Guv. This is the hotel manager. I've informed him of the search we're hoping to carry out and that the paperwork's on its way, but he's happy for us to have a look inside the room now.'

Graveney introduced himself and Marne. The four of them turned towards the hotel as Hussain pulled into the car park.

Graveney waved a hand towards the manager as Raz reached the entrance. 'Give this gentleman the paperwork, Raz,' he said.

The manager accepted the envelope from Hussain and led the officers along a corridor towards the room. Stopping outside a door with the number 10 on it.

Graveney paused, noticing the damage to the door frame he gently pushed it open. 'Looks like someone's beaten us to it,' he said, as the four officers entered the brightly lit room.

Graveney rang Mac on his mobile. 'We've hit a blank at the hotel. Someone beat us to it. Do you remember the phone I recovered from Stewart? The contact on it?'

'Ang?' Mac said.

'It could be her. I don't know why she'd take Stewart's things unless something was implicating her. Whatever the reason is, we need to find her. I've a feeling she's the key to all this.'

'There may be prints in the room?'

Graveney sighed. 'We'll check, but I wouldn't hold your breath.'

'I'll see you when you get back.' Mac hung up.

Graveney's mobile rang again. 'It's Cooke, Guv. I'm at the hospital. Stephen Stewart died on his way here.'

'Christ,' Graveney said. 'Get back to the station, Sarah. I'm sure Mac could do with an extra pair of hands.'

Graveney glanced at Marne. 'Stewart's dead.' He got into the car next to her and threw his mobile on the dashboard.

'Sorry to hear that, sir.' She turned away from Graveney and looked out of the side window.

'Back to Middlesbrough, Steph.' Graveney rubbed his face and slowly pulled his hands down. He sighed loudly. 'Phillips and Oake will be over the moon.'

CHAPTER EIGHT

Marne pulled the car up outside a block of flats as Graveney peered out of the window at the large, recently constructed building.

She glanced at him. 'Would you like to come up, sir? I've got the documents you gave me earlier in my flat, and it's quite a walk back. Especially with the lift broken.'

Graveney thought for a moment. That feeling again. The uneasy something which didn't ring true. A something he couldn't put his finger on. Attractive, confident, and apparently intelligent, but what was her motive for asking him up?

She stared at him. 'I've got a bottle of Jack Daniels ... If you're interested? It's been a long day.'

There it was again. How did she know his favourite drink was Jack Daniels? Coincidence? Possibly, but years of experience had taught him that where people were concerned, there was no such thing as coincidence. 'Maybe a quick one.' Putting aside any doubts, he got out of the car.

It was unprofessional of him. He was Marne's superior and shouldn't even contemplate going up, but she had her reasons for inviting him in. His weakness for women and alcohol trumped anything else, and if he was honest he was eager to see how this would pan out.

Graveney followed Marne up the stairs of the building. He trod slightly behind her, viewing her sinuous figure as she snaked in front of him. The tight pencil skirt she wore clung to the contours of her body, the faint outline of her briefs visible below. She stopped at the door on the third floor and opened it, indicating for him to enter. Graveney eased into a darkened room, immediately illuminated as she turned on the light. He found himself in a sitting room, sparsely decorated and furnished. Boxes still stacked in one corner. It appeared to him she had only recently moved in. Marne continued through into the kitchen, Graveney following closely behind. She opened a cupboard on the wall and taking out a bottle and two glasses, placed them on the table in front of her.

'Have you just moved in?' he asked.

'Yeah. How much?' Tilting the bottle over the glass, she waited.

'Not much.' He indicated around an inch with his index finger and thumb.

Marne handed him the glass, allowing their eyes to meet as she did so, holding onto the glass slightly longer than necessary. 'I'll get the folder.' She smiled and headed for what Graveney supposed was the bedroom.

He wandered around the kitchen opening cupboards, looking for any sort of clue as to who she was. What lay behind her facade. He prided himself on his ability to pick up little nuances and hints about people from where they lived. An acumen of sorts. One honed over years of practice. He was getting nothing here. The flat appeared staged. Nothing he could swear to, but as if put together by an interior designer who had not quite finished their work. The furniture, what there was of it, was what you would expect to see in a show home. It didn't ring true. He rubbed his chin and took a sip of his drink as Marne re-entered the room carrying a folder, and placed it on the table. He studied her. Marne's hair now untied, hung loosely around her shoulders. The second button on her blouse open, giving Graveney a tantalising glimpse of the bra below. She picked up her glass and took a large swig, leaning back against the dining room table as she did so. Graveney viewed her suspiciously. He'd been seduced often enough in his life to recognise it. But doubts nudged him, something at the back of his mind rang loud. Being here in her flat was wholly inappropriate. He knew what could happen, what would happen if he allowed it to. But where women were concerned willpower had never been his strong suit, so once again he pushed the feeling aside.

'What's your take on the Vale Farm Murders?' he asked.

She turned away and reached for the bottle. Graveney caught the glance as she did so, almost imperceptible. Most people would have missed it entirely, but Graveney didn't. A look, an expression which spread briefly across her face. Gone as quickly as it appeared.

She picked up the bottle and turned back towards him. 'It seems clear cut to me. Stewart killed his daughter, Jessica, and got into a fight with his wife. Killed her, while getting stabbed in the process.'

He inwardly smiled. There it was again, that look. The thin-slicing going on in Graveney's mind latching onto the merest of nuances. Something lurked behind her calm exterior, but he couldn't put into words the emotion she expressed. A mixture of horror and sadness, maybe? The sort of sorrow brought about by loss, but more, much more. Perhaps she had suffered some trauma in her own life, and this case was unlocking painful memories. Maybe that was it.

'I don't believe he did it,' he said. Graveney held out his glass, looking to elicit some flicker of emotion from her. If Marne was shocked, she didn't show it.

She poured more of the drink into his glass, half filling it. 'What makes you think that?' she said, so casually it took him by surprise. 'What did Stephen Stewart say to you at the solicitors?'

Graveney turned away and stared out of the kitchen window, allowing himself time to answer. He thought for a moment. There had been the briefest of gaps between the names Stephen and Stewart, as if she intended to use his Christian name all along, but instantly recognised her error before adding his surname. Again, hardly perceptible. It was as if she knew Stephen Stewart.

'He told me so. But then, it's not unusual for people to profess innocence. Is it?' He turned to face her. 'But this was different you see,' he continued. 'Stewart was,' and Graveney emphasised it. '*Telling the truth.*'

She sneered. 'How can you know that?'

'Let's just say, I know. Oh, I couldn't prove it. And I'd get laughed out of a courtroom, but Stewart was telling the truth.'

'If Stewart didn't kill them, who did?' Slowly running her free hand through her hair as she gazed at him.

Another emotion flashed across Marne's face, long enough for Graveney to recognise it. Hatred. Pure hatred. What was her connection to this case? In Graveney's conspiracy world, nothing was straightforward. He loved to get behind the veil people displayed in public, and apparently there was much more of Miss Marne than met the eye.

'I don't know the answer to that, but obviously the Reverend, the Johnsons and Shelby were in some way involved. Unfortunately, none of them are in any position to help us with our enquiries. It'll be interesting finding out, though. Don't you think?'

Graveney and Marne locked eyes. He stared at her, keen to gauge her reaction. There was none. If she felt any emotion at all, she masked it well. He was surprised by this, sometimes her innermost feelings were there for him to see and yet, it appeared she could cover them if she so wished. An unusual thought entered Graveney's head. Perhaps she was playing with him. He sipped at his drink, his eyes never leaving hers. He'd have to be careful with this one, he thought.

'Yes, it will be.' The merest of grins shot across her face.

Graveney drained his glass and put it on the table, suddenly he felt uneasy and not in full control. Experiencing what people commonly call *cold feet.* A first for Graveney, at least where women were concerned. 'I'll leave the car with you,' he said. 'My place isn't far from here. I'll see you in the morning, Steph.'

She smiled and licked her lips. 'Stay the night if you want.' It took Graveney by surprise.

'No ... I don't think that's a good idea.'

'Why not, Peter? I know you're attracted to me. I saw the way you looked at me in the car. You might be good at reading emotions, but it's a different ball-game hiding them.'

'I don't attempt to hide my feelings, *Stephanie*. My emotions are there for all to see. I live in a world where lying and deception are commonplace. I choose to be as open as possible with people. You're attractive, but so are hundreds of other women and I don't jump into bed with them. Besides, it would be somewhat unprofessional of us both. Don't you think?'

Marne edged closer to him. Her perfume, stronger than before. She must have re-applied it when she went into the bedroom, he reasoned. Graveney knew what was about to occur, his aloofness, a front. In truth, he loved being seduced. Yes, it was both unprofessional and wrong, but there was something about Marne that captivated him. Some hidden depth within her. His weakness for women, like his weakness for drink, evident to anyone who knew him. Usually, he did nothing to fight either, but now, his conflicting emotions battled with each other for supremacy, desperately trying to reach an accord.

She leant towards him, her eyes never leaving his, as he at first passively stared back. She pushed her face closer, warm breath on his cheeks, and pulled him nearer. Motioning to kiss him she stopped short of his lips before slowly allowing them to meet. She smiled as she backed away towards the table, mischievously grinning at him. Graveney closed the gap between them and pressed his lips to hers. Marne slid a hand down towards his groin. She kissed him passionately, unfastening his belt and trousers, before slipping her hand inside his boxers.

'This unprofessional enough for you, Peter?' she said.

Graveney didn't respond as Marne pushed his boxers onto the floor, along with his trousers. She kissed him again, but then bit down sharply on his lip, causing Graveney to recoil his head. He put his hand to his mouth and dabbed at his lip. A small dot of red covered his finger-tip. Graveney licked his lip and tasted blood. He stared at Marne, shocked by what she'd done, and spotted an emotion that flashed across her face. Pleasure. She pulled at his jacket with her free hand and allowed it to fall to the floor. Graveney pressed his right hand against the front of her skirt while his left followed the contours of the back of her thighs, and then slowly underneath the material. Marne pulled at his shirt, exposing his muscular chest beneath. She traced the space from his neck to where the shoulder meets the arm with her lips, kissing and occasionally biting him playfully, along the way. Graveney brought his hands either side of Marne's thighs and slowly hoisted her skirt up, revealing her lack of briefs beneath. He pushed a hand between her legs as Marne opened them, allowing Graveney to easily slip his hand between. He felt a sharp pain in his right shoulder as she bit down hard. He glared at her, but Marne looked back at him, a defiant stare, taunting and goading him.

'Show me what you're made of Inspector,' she whispered. 'Show me where your boundaries lie.'

She smiled lasciviously at Graveney and opened her legs wider. Marne's breathing quickening in anticipation of what was to come, as she pulled at him. She leant back against the table and yanked Graveney nearer. Graveney's mind flooded with thoughts, a torrent of words that screamed at him. This was wrong, so wrong. Part of him wanted to stop and leave, another part pushed him on. The dichotomy disquieting. He heard Marne gasp, and then whisper obscenities at him. Pushing her mouth against his, she wrapped her legs around him and pulled them up to waist height. Graveney lifted her up onto the edge of the table. She mouthed more things at him. Graphic, explicit, uninhibited words. Graveney's breathing quickened further. The more she spoke, the more he edged towards total abandon. His crumbling resolve now a ruin. He felt pain again, this time on his back as she dragged her nails across it. Her eyes imploring him on, daring him, wanting him to push his limits further still. Graveney, shocked by her and reacting to the pain she was inflicting, grabbed her by the throat and squeezed. His huge hand half spanning it, an automatic reaction as any reason and any sense of sobriety vanished like snowflakes on the sea. Graveney squeezed, and Marne allowed her head to drop back, as ecstasy filled her features. He lessened his grip, and she half-laughed, mocking his hesitation, but also daring him on. Her eyes danced with delight as she whispered more words, enticing him still further, willing him to squeeze harder as unfettered rapture covered her face. Graveney, now completely caught up in the moment, grabbed hold of Marne and turned her around, bending her across the table. Her hand knocked over his glass, and as they watched, it slowly rolled off and smashed on the floor. Graveney lifted her left leg up onto the corner of the table and grabbed hold of her hair, pulling it back aggressively. Marne glanced back over her right shoulder, smirking at him, still egging him on. She seemed to sense she could push him even further, to somewhere he'd never been, a place he'd never wanted to go. His breaths stalled in his throat, he clumsily uttered obscenities - shocked by his own language - but his words appeared to elicit an even greater excitement in Marne.

Graveney tumbled, his boundaries crossed, his self-restraint and self-control swallowed up in one giant uninhibited moment. She let out a groan of pleasure as her excitement and passion heightened. Marne stared back, shouting expletives at him. Graveney, un-phased by her language now, continued. Any doubts and misgivings pushed aside, and unimportant. They kept on, the pair conjoined as time itself appeared to stall. It reached an apogee for Graveney, an apotheosis he had never before experienced, and then embarked on a slow descent. Marne's eyes momentarily rolled back in her head revealing only white, her body quivering, her legs shaking. She grabbed hold of the table with a free hand to steady herself, gasping she held her breath. Graveney watched as Intense pleasure engulfed her, coursing throughout her body. Parts of her brain switching off momentarily and others, the pleasure centres, exploded into life.

He slowed as she slumped against the table. Graveney stood and pulled away from her, as a tornado of shame smashed into him, laying waste to his recklessness. He backed away from her and gasped. After a few moments, he spoke. His voice tremulous, little more than a whisper. 'Can I use your bathroom?'

Marne pointed to the landing but said nothing. Graveney awkwardly pulled his underwear and trousers up and headed towards the door she had indicated.

He entered the bathroom and closed the door, staring at his reflection in the mirror, hardly recognising the face looking back. He looked dishevelled, his face flushed, his hair a sweaty, tangled mess. Graveney washed his hands thoroughly, rinsed them and soaped his hands again, rubbing his face. Rinsing his face with warm water, he caught his reflection in the mirror. The devil glared back at him. His mind raced with thoughts, both shocked and disappointed at himself. He slumped against the wall. He felt weak for allowing it to happen. Disturbed by how far Marne was prepared to let it go. Knowing the level she had wanted it to travel had nowhere near been reached. There was something dark within Marne, something he found slightly disconcerting. Both appalled and excited by what had happened he dropped his head against the mirror, blew out hard, and punched the wall. The pain in his hand, metaphorically shaking him from his thoughts. He stared at his reflection again, embarrassment washed over him in a tidal wave of guilt and disgust for allowing it to happen. He pushed a damp hand through his hair, fashioning it into something resembling order. He dried his face and hands with a towel. Reasonably satisfied with his appearance, he turned to face the door, sucked in a deep breath, and unenthusiastically trudged back to the kitchen. He paused at the threshold. Marne sat at the far end of the table, her face flushed red. Fully clothed and tidy, a drink resting in her hands. The end nearest his had a half-full glass in front of the seat. His jacket now on the back of the chair with the folder tucked into the side pocket.

He looked down, his cheeks burned with embarrassment, unwilling to meet Marne's stare. 'I should get going. I've got something to do first thing in the morning.' The words stumbling clumsily from his lips.

'Do you want me to pick you up?' Her demeanour in total contrast to minutes earlier. As if a different person had entered the room.

'No.' He briefly looked up at her. Disappointment fizzed across her face as she took a large gulp of her drink.

'It's personal,' he said. 'I'll see you at the station.'

Marne nodded. Graveney glanced at the drink on the table but resisted it, put on his jacket, and raced towards the door. Marne sat impassively as she heard it close behind him. She opened her hand and looked at the key within it, as a huge smile spread across her face.

CHAPTER NINE

Graveney headed along the street away from Marne's apartment. Stopping midway, he glanced back, trying to understand what had happened. Graveney shrugged, and not feeling much like going home, headed towards his sister-in-law, Heather's, in emotional turmoil over what occurred. Both apprehensive and excited about what could happen.

He approached Heather's house in Church Road unsure if Heather was in, or still awake. Glancing at his watch - almost midnight - he paused outside the door before knocking. Three months had passed since his last visit to Heather's and unsure as to what reception he would receive, he trudged up the path, stopping outside the door. A small slit of light glowed where the curtains hadn't been drawn fully, so she was probably up, he thought. He tapped gently on the window of the front room and waited. The curtain was momentarily pulled away from the corner as he saw the face of Heather looking out. He gave a half-hearted wave as the curtain closed and the hall light came on.

The door opened, and Heather stood there. Attractive, in her late-thirties and petite. She appeared smaller than he remembered. Her blonde hair cut into a bob, considerably shorter than their last meeting, and this somehow made her look much younger too. She smiled at Graveney and beckoned him in.

'Long time no see, Peter,' she said.

Graveney kissed her on both her cheeks as he stood and viewed her. 'Like the hair. Suits you.' He forced a smile. 'I've been busy … You know how it is.'

'Drink?' she asked.

'Love one. What have you got?'

'Only wine, I'm afraid.'

'Wine's great. I need a shower? Long day and I … well, you know.'

'Of course. If you look in the back bedroom, you'll find some of your clothes. I think you left them last time you were here.'

Graveney climbed the stairs towards the bathroom.

'There's a towel in the airing cupboard,' she shouted after him.

He quickly showered, washing away the sweat and grime of the day and any lingering trace of Marne. The hot water stung his back and shoulder from the marks inflicted by her, but he quickly pushed any thoughts of their encounter aside. Having changed into some jeans and a sweatshirt, and feeling suitably refreshed, he strode downstairs where Heather sat in an armchair waiting. Graveney sat opposite, picked up a glass of wine she'd poured for him and took a large swig.

'How are you?' she asked.

'Fine.'

'Luke misses you.'

'I know,' he said. 'There's a cup match coming up. I thought I'd take him.'

'He'd like that, but that's not the reason you came. Is it?'

Graveney dropped his head. 'Not really, I needed some company, that's all.'

'It's fine.' She topped up his glass. 'We're always glad to see you. You're welcome anytime you know that.'

They finished the bottle while reminiscing about old times, Graveney almost forgetting about earlier at Marne's flat. They talked until after one. Finally, Heather clasped his hand and led him upstairs. The pair climbed into bed together, and Heather hugged him close. His body, his warmth, almost enough for her, but months had passed since she'd last had sex. Sensing his lack of enthusiasm, she slid underneath the bedclothes. He hardened, and Heather climbed on top gently moving above while Graveney drifted.

He woke at six. Heather's arms gently enveloping him. He turned and kissed her on the forehead.

She opened a bleary eye and stared back. 'You've come back to life then?'

'Sorry about that, I was tired. Hope I wasn't too much of a disappointment?'

'Oh, you weren't that bad. I managed.'

'I'll have to go to the spare room,' he said. 'Luke will be waking soon.'

'Luke's at his mates. He won't be back until 10, feel free to have another go if you like … See if you can come up to scratch this time.' Heather smiled at him and kissed him on the lips.

'Well, let's see what I can do.' He rolled across on top of her.

She had noticed the bite mark on his shoulder the previous night, and now she could feel the deep scratch marks on his back, but pushed any thoughts aside, and happily succumbed.

Heather stood in the kitchen cooking a late breakfast as Graveney and his nephew, Luke, played football in the garden. She smiled at them. How happy they seemed. Her thoughts, interrupted by the doorbell ringing.

She opened the door to her best friend, Maddie, who pushed past her into the hall. 'Aren't you ready yet?' Maddie said. 'You do know we're supposed to be going shopping?'

'Sorry. I'm running a bit late.' A huge smile filled her face.

'You look in a good mood. Won the lottery or something?'

Maddie followed Heather into the kitchen. 'No, nothing like that. It's just ...' She hesitated and glanced out of the window.

Maddie followed her gaze and spied Graveney in the garden, wandering across to the window, she peered outside. 'I see someone's had their rocks off.'

'He's only visiting.'

Maddie leant against the table, folding her arms tightly.

Heather held up her hands. 'I know what you're going to say.'

Maddie frowned and shrugged. 'I don't suppose anything I say makes the slightest difference?'

'Maddie. What can I do?' she said.

'I'll tell you what you can do. Find yourself a nice man. Someone who'll look after you and Luke. Someone who won't just turn up after months for a quick shag. No offence, but where's the future in this. I know Peter's good looking and charming, but he's clearly not looking for a relationship. He's going to break your heart.'

Heather's shoulders drooped. 'You're right, but you don't really understand.'

'Try me.'

'Even when I don't see him for months, when he hardly ever rings, I miss him. I still want him. It's just ...' Heather paused, 'I love him.'

'But Heather, be realistic. He's probably got a string of women on the go. Is that what you want to be, another woman he pops around to when he's in the area?'

'Of course not. It's not that simple. You wouldn't understand, nobody would.'

'How can I, if you don't tell me what it is between you two?'

'It's a long story,' she said.

'Heather you'll be old and grey, and life will have passed you by.'

'I don't care. Even if it's only occasionally I see Peter, it's enough. It has to be enough.' The last words whispered.

'Have you told him how you feel?'

'He knows. We've never discussed it properly, but he knows.'

'So why doesn't he want to be with you and Luke then?'

Heather looked downwards and shuffled her feet. 'Guilt.' Regretting saying it instantly.

Maddie raised her eyebrows. 'Guilt for what?'

Heather paused, the words catching in her throat, and tearing off a few pieces of kitchen towel she blew her nose. Luke and Graveney came in from the garden by which time Heather had composed herself.

Maddie was her closest friend, but she found it hard to talk about Peter with anyone else. It was complicated, and she doubted anybody would understand.

Graveney smiled at Maddie. 'Hi, Maddie, lovely as ever. How are you?' Kissing her warmly on the cheeks.

'Fine, thanks. You?'

'Good,' he said. He looked across at Heather. 'I've told Luke we're going to the cup match, I'll ring in the week.'

Heather frowned. 'You're not going now, are you? I've cooked you some breakfast.'

'Can you do it to go? I'm going to get a quick shower. I've got an important errand to do.'

Heather put the sausages, bacon, and egg into a large bun and wrapping it up in foil, gave it to Graveney. He kissed her on the cheeks, gave Maddie a peck, and ruffled Luke's hair. 'See you next week, Luke,' he shouted as he left the house.

Maddie glanced across at Heather, a deep frown on her friend's face. She walked over to Heather and hugged her tightly, placing a hand up to her cheek.

Luke pulled a face. 'Err, get a room you two.' And he headed upstairs.

'Heather, we've been friends for three years now. What is it between you and Peter. You've never actually spoken about it.'

'What's there to talk about? It is, what it is.' Checking Luke was still upstairs, she closed the kitchen door.

'You're having sex with your dead sister's husband.' Maddie threw her hands in the air. 'There's obviously lots to talk about. I've told you everything about my past. All my secrets, everything. You're my best friend, but how can I help you if you won't tell me what's wrong. Isn't that what best friends do? Confide in each other?' Maddie said, in a hushed voice.

Heather sighed. Maddie was right. It was something she'd kept to herself all these years, but bringing it out into the cold light of day wouldn't be easy. She half-heartedly gathered the breakfast things together before putting them in the dishwasher and turned to face her friend. Maddie waited patiently with her arms folded for Heather to start. Heather, sensing Maddie wouldn't be put off this time, reluctantly began.

'What I'm about to tell you stays between us, you understand?' her voice barely a whisper.

Maddie moved closer to Heather and taking her friend's hand, gently squeezed it. She said nothing, Heather knowing instantly she could trust her friend. A tacit understanding passed between them.

'Peter was mine. I found him. I fell in love with him first. Gillian, my sister.' She blew out hard, 'Well ...'

Maddie squeezed her hand again.

Heather paused, remembering her painful past. 'Gillian and I never had a close relationship. We were alike, people often asked if we were twins, but there was an eighteen-month gap between us. That's where our similarities ended. Gillian was entirely different to me, much more outgoing and sexy. Everything I wasn't. Gillian dressed better than me, looked better than me, and possessed this air of confidence about her which men loved. When we were teenagers, she'd delight in pulling any boys I showed the slightest interest in and then dump them when she grew bored. Anytime I had a boyfriend, Gillian would be all over them until they succumbed to her charms. As we grew up, she never changed. If I had it, she wanted it. That was Gillian in a nutshell.' Heather sighed loudly. Composed herself again and continued. 'We fought loads over the years about it, but she wouldn't accept what she was doing was wrong. She had this massive chip on her shoulder and convinced herself I was dad's favourite. Funny that. He was the only man I've ever met she couldn't wrap around her finger.'

'And Peter?' Maddie said.

'I met Peter at University, and we hit it off instantly. Everything I ever wanted in a man.' She smiled as she remembered. 'We'd go out with a group of friends together, not as boyfriend and girlfriend just superb friends. We loved the same things. Theatre, movies, good books, that kind of stuff.'

Maddie squeezed her hand again. 'You ok?' Looking deeply into her friend's tearful eyes.

Heather nodded. 'Peter lost his dad when he was young, and his mother died when he was in the sixth form. His dad was a violent alcoholic and Peter, his brother, Andrew, and his mother endured a rough time from what I gathered. He was a bit cagey about his past. It was only by picking up little snippets from him over the years, usually when he was drunk, I learned about it.'

'What happened to his mother?'

'She died from breast cancer when he was eighteen. Peter and Andrew - who was a little younger than him - lived with their aunt for a while.

Heather smiled as she remembered. 'He came home with me one Christmas. I'd asked Mum and Dad if I could invite him. I'd planned this fantastic time.' She frowned and lowered her eyes. 'Gillian was supposed to be spending Christmas skiing with one of her admirers, but at the last moment she cancelled and came home.'

'Don't tell me. Gillian met Peter, right?'

'Yeah.' She sighed heavily. 'I knew I couldn't keep Peter away from her forever, of course, but I hoped if I did it for long enough, Peter would fall for me.'

'Let me guess. Peter fell for Gillian?'

Heather plucked a piece of kitchen towel from the roll and blew her nose. 'I was devastated but somehow hid my feelings. I hoped she'd become bored of him, as she had with so many others. Unfortunately, that never happened. It turned out Peter was, *The One*. Her words, not mine. They ended up getting engaged and then marrying shortly after Peter graduated.'

Maddie gently stroked her arm. 'Oh, Heather. How did you bear that?'

Heather forced a smile. 'What could I do? Peter was hers, and that was that.'

'How did she die?' Maddie asked rather abruptly.

Heather, slightly shocked at the bluntness of her question, took a deep breath. 'She was pregnant, and her and Peter were going through a rough patch. Gillian could be a real bitch when she wanted to be. Peter confided in me, you see, and well, you know … one thing led to another.'

'You mean you slept with him while Gillian was alive?'

Heather's features hardened. 'I won't lie to you. I took great pleasure in that. Peter was mine. She had stolen him from me, and I sort of hoped I'd win him back. I don't know if Peter felt the same way.' She laughed half-heartedly. 'We did discuss living together once or twice, usually after a bottle or two of wine. I was never convinced he was serious, though.'

'And then she died?' Maddie said, equally as bluntly.

'She went into early labour. Peter and I were at my flat. Peter's brother, Andrew, offered to drive her to the hospital and it turned out he'd been drinking. Not a massive amount, but enough to make a difference. They crashed on the way. Gillian was killed outright along with the baby.'

'God! What did you do?'

'Peter was devastated. He'd lost his wife and his baby. Andrew got a two-year prison sentence for causing death by drink driving. As far as I know, they have never spoken since. Shame that. They were so close.'

'How did you feel about Gillian's death?'

'Numb, actually. If I'm honest - and I know this sounds awful - I didn't grieve for her until years later. It hit me one day, how self-absorbed I'd been. I didn't want her to die, but I wanted Peter so much.' Reaching for another piece of kitchen towel she wiped her face.

'What about Peter. Did he blame you?'

'No, that's just it. Peter blamed himself. He said it was like fate punishing him for, as he called it, *The Ultimate Betrayal*. Any hope of us living happily together, gone. How could I hope to compete with a memory? Her death put paid to that.'

'What happened after, you know. The funeral?'

'Peter turned up occasionally. Usually the worse for drink. He'd cry in my arms and well, we'd usually end up in bed. Peter would leave feeling guilty and remorseful, and I wouldn't see him for weeks or months. It's as if he comes to see me because I remind him of her. Then it brings home to him what he's lost. He's put Gillian up on this pedestal and has this idealistic view of what their marriage was like.' Heather sneered. 'I knew Gillian, though. She never changed, even after marrying Peter, she was still flighty. It wouldn't have surprised me if she had a string of lovers.'

'Heather, I'm sorry. I didn't know.'

'Maddie, I love him so much it hurts.' She began to sob. 'I wish Gillian hadn't died. Maybe over time, we'd have grown close. Maybe Peter would have left her for me, and we'd have lived happily ever after.'

Maddie hugged Heather tightly. It was complicated, even for Maddie, who prided herself on her pragmatism. 'We can't change what's in the past,' she said.

'The moments I spend with him are my happiest,' Heather said. 'When he appears, the dark clouds disappear, and the sun shines again. I know I'm hanging on to the crumbs of a relationship, but I can't lose him entirely. Anything's better than nothing. It has to be.'

'Oh, Heather.' Maddie hugged her sobbing friend tightly.

CHAPTER TEN

OCTOBER 2006 - Sandra Stewart gathered together the breakfast things while Stephen, her husband of twelve years, sat at the table deep in conversation on his mobile. She glanced out across the garden, bright morning sunshine gently creeping its way over the grass.

Stephen ended his call, stood, and meandered over to Sandra wrapping his arms around her, he kissed her on her cheek. 'That was Graham. Apparently, the job is not as involved as they thought. I should be home next week.'

'Great,' she said. 'Maybe we can get away for a break somewhere?'

'I'll ask mum and dad for a loan of the villa for a couple of weeks.'

'Oh, yes please.' She kissed him warmly.

'What are you up to today?' he asked.

'I'm meeting Angela for lunch at one in town, and then I'm meeting Jimmy later today. He phoned me last night. Sounded excited, actually. Something about a lead on a big story.'

'How's it going with you and Angela, then?'

'Great. I mean you can't be separated for as long as we were and expect things to be ... well, as if we'd known each other all our lives. I like her though. She's intelligent and funny. I think we're going to hit it off together.'

'Good. When will I meet this sister of yours?'

'Soon. Dinner, here tomorrow night. She's excited about meeting Jessica and you.'

'Tomorrow, eh? I'll have to be on my best behaviour.' He kissed her again. 'What's this story Jimmy was talking about?'

'I don't know. We had this thing - a sort of pact when we did our degrees together - if either of us ever got a story, one to interest the tabloids, we'd work together on it. Jimmy's struggling as a freelance, and he's got this vision, one day, we'll be writing for The Times or something.'

'I'm not moving down south if you do make it big,' Stephen said. 'I'm northern through and through.'

'Me neither. I wouldn't hold your breath. Jimmy tends to exaggerate a bit. It's probably a lost dog story.'

'So, what else can we do before you rush off and leave me?' Pulling her closer towards him, he kissed her neck.

'Jessica needs dropping off for her riding lesson, and the garage needs cleaning out.'

'*Really*! Surely you can think of something better than that?'

'If you drop Jessica off at Susan's and get back here pronto, you may catch me in the shower.' She smiled at him and licked her lips.

Stephen kissed her again and turned away. 'Hold that thought. Jessica! Are you ready?'

Jessica stomped down the stairs. 'I've been ready for ages.' And headed outside towards the car.

'See you soon, sexy.' He blew his wife a kiss as she turned around and wiggled her pert bum in his direction, reminding him of what was waiting when he returned. Stephen grabbed his car keys and raced after Jessica.

As Sandra entered the little bistro, her thoughts returned back to earlier in the day. She had met her sister, Angela, in town and after having a pleasant lunch with her, the two of them had done a little shopping. Although having only recently reunited, both of them adopted and separated when young, Sandra already felt love and affection for her sister. The family resemblance was obvious too. She felt pleased, after avoiding searching for years, she had finally plucked up the courage to seek her out. Sandra, three at the time of the adoptions remembered having a sister, although only vaguely. Her adoptive parents never knew much about her past and couldn't offer her a lot of help. Angela, on the other hand, a baby at the time, had no such memories.

A couple who couldn't have children of their own adopted Angela. Her adoptive parents never mentioned the fact she was adopted. It wasn't until after the death of her mother, and her father lay dying in the hospital, she finally learned the truth. She told Sandra she was shocked at first, but she had enjoyed a happy childhood with two loving parents and decided whoever her birth mother was, had apparently not wanted her. In any case, parents are the people who love and bring you up not necessarily the ones who create you she said.

Sandra understood this as she too had enjoyed a happy upbringing. However, when Jessica's age, her parents sat her down and told her the truth. She vaguely remembered asking them something when younger, and they thought it best Sandra should know when a little older. Her dad died a couple of years previously and unbeknown to her mum, Sandra began searching for her sister. She did think about telling her mother but thought it better to see how the relationship progressed first. Now reunited with her sibling, Sandra was overjoyed. She had always wanted a sister and now felt her family complete.

As she walked through the door, she spotted Jimmy sitting in the corner with Colin, his boyfriend. She waved to them, and they waved back as she made her way over. Jimmy and Colin both stood, and Sandra hugged and kissed them warmly.

'How are you?' Jimmy said, 'I've got you one in.' Handing her a gin and tonic.

'Very well,' she said. 'Oh, you're a lifesaver.' Taking a large swig of the drink.

'You well, Colin?' she asked.

He smiled. 'Great thanks. Jimmy and I've moved in together.'

'Really. This is getting serious, boys. What next? Marriage?'

Jimmy gazed across at Colin. 'We'll see how living with this one works out first before we do anything rash shall we?' Nodding at Colin playfully.

Colin stood. 'Well, I'll leave you two journos to it. I've got some shopping to do.' He kissed Jimmy and Sandra and headed off.

'I like Colin. He's right for you, Jimmy, especially after you-know-who.'

'Let's not talk about the past,' he said. 'Anyway, we've more pressing matters.'

'What's this scoop then?'

Jimmy moved closer to Sandra, lowering his voice as he did. 'Do you remember Winterton Boys' Home?'

'Vaguely.'

Jimmy leant in close. 'A home for boys who'd been in a bit of trouble. Not major things which would get you sent to young offenders, just kids that got a little out of hand. Well, in the nineties, a scandal hit. It came to light some of the boys suffered severe physical abuse. A guy called Arthur Stevens was arrested, and he ended up getting sent down for ten years. The police weren't able to implicate anyone else over it. Insufficient evidence. Stevens wouldn't incriminate any other person who worked there, either.'

'If this is old news, where do we come in?'

'Well, I was put in touch with someone who lived at the home when the abuse happened. He has a rather interesting story to tell. He's coming here to meet us.'

'What sort of story?'

'I'll let him explain, but there's more. I managed to do some digging and a mate of mine, who works at Durham nick, where Stevens served his sentence, gave me the name of someone who shared a cell with him for two years. Towards the end of his sentence, Stevens told him some of what happened there.'

'Why tell this guy?'

'Apparently, it's not unusual for prisoners to confide in their cellmate. Maybe his conscience got the better of him. We'll meet him tomorrow when we go to his flat.'

Sandra frowned. 'I can't see a big story in this. We'd be raking over old coals.'

'Listen to Terry's story – that's his name – when he gets here, and then decide.'

'Ok. I'll see what this Terry has to say.'

They chatted some more about unrelated things for another fifteen minutes until a scruffy-looking individual made his way over to them. Jimmy warmly shook him by the hand, before introducing him to Sandra as Terry. Terry appeared in his late 20's, although probably much younger. He smelt of stale sweat and booze. Not what Sandra called a reliable witness, but she had learnt not to judge.

'Ok, Terry,' Jimmy said. 'In your own time. Tell Sandra what you told me.'

'Jimmy's probably told you.' Terry said. 'I stayed at Winterton back in the nineties. There was a group of about thirty boys at the time, and we'd all been in some bother. None of us was an angel, of course, but the regime inside Winterton was severe.'

'When you say severe, what do you mean?' Sandra said.

'They'd beat us. Lock us up in the hole, a small, dark, cold room where the staff put you if you misbehaved.'

Sandra made notes. 'What sort of misbehaving?'

'Stealing food, not doing our chores properly ... that kind of thing. In all honesty, though, Stevens didn't need any excuse. He was a sadistic bastard. He loved to beat us and carry out all manner of punishments.' Terry swallowed hard, the memories apparently causing great distress.

Sandra put a hand on his. 'Take your time, Terry. I know talking about this is difficult.'

He continued, telling Sandra and Jimmy about the abuse he and some of the other boys had endured while in Winterton. They listened to him dispassionately until he paused for breath, the ordeal of recounting it affecting him greatly. Jimmy pushed a drink in front of Terry, who gratefully swallowed it.

'Didn't the other staff know about this abuse?' Sandra said.

'They were all in on it. One teacher, although teacher is probably not the right name to use, knew what went on and loved to watch Stevens carry out his punishments. It gave her a buzz.'

'How come only Stevens went to jail?' Sandra said.

Terry sighed. 'Insufficient evidence to prosecute the police said. When interviewed, none of us spoke out. We were all petrified, so we ended up saying nothing. The thing was, a couple of kids disappeared. Stevens told me they'd absconded, but when the case came to light one of the staff members – Johnson they called him – said we'd end up like them if we spoke out. Six feet under.'

Sandra looked up from her notebook. 'Were those his exact words?'

'Exact.'

Jimmy rubbed his chin. 'So, Stevens took the rap?'

Terry nodded.

'Weren't these boys missed by their families?' Sandra asked.

'What you've got to understand, Miss, some of the boys in Winterton didn't have the sort of parents who bothered about their welfare. Their families were probably happy to see the back of them. Other boys, whose parents cared about them, didn't usually get punished as much. Maybe Stevens was afraid these kids would tell their relations, so they got away with more. The boys that disappeared?' He paused and emptied his glass. 'I don't think I ever remember them having visitors.'

'Can you remember their names?' Jimmy asked.

'George Appleby and Gregory Watts,' he said.

Sandra jotted the names in her notebook along with Stevens and Johnson.

'What were the names of the other staff members?' she asked.

Terry listed all the names he remembered. It was evident to Sandra that he had a drink and probably a drug problem. Brought on by what happened to him at Winterton, she presumed. They listened again as he recounted more of the horrors he and some of the others endured throughout their time there. Finally, after Terry finished, Jimmy gave him some money. He thanked them both, before disappearing.

'What do you think?' Jimmy said.

'Well, it has some promise, but it's far from a scoop. I mean, a lot of this will have been investigated after Stevens arrest.'

'I agree, but I want you to meet this other guy, Ray Hetherington. His story's a little more exciting.'

'Come on then, give me a taster.'

'Stevens had a pang of conscience or something because he told Ray, his cellmate, about sexual abuse that also went on. He hinted the missing boys were picked and handed over to a bunch of paedophiles, for … Well, you get the picture.'

'You're kidding?'

'No. Here's the clincher. Apparently, Stevens kept proof of who was involved in this paedophile ring. Some of them were, and are, quite prominent.'

'Who?'

'He wouldn't say. There's a little snag … He wants £10,000.'

'You're joking, aren't you? Where the hell are we going to get £10,000?'

'Colin's going to loan me my half, and I thought you'd be able to raise the other.'

'I see. So, this is not down to our university pact then. You need my financial muscle too?'

'Come on, Sandra. If the names he gives us check out, and we make a good job of this story, £10,000 will be chicken feed. Besides, a mate of mine from London knows the deputy editor of The Daily Mail. I've already sounded him out.'

Sandra thought hard for a moment, and getting £10 out of her handbag, handed it to Jimmy. 'Well, we'd better celebrate our deal then.' Jimmy smiled, plucked the note from Sandra, and headed for the bar.

SEPTEMBER 2014 - Graveney left Marne's flat at eight o'clock at night, both mentally and physically battered and bruised from his latest encounter with her. Flagging down a passing taxi, he headed home. Dropping his jacket onto the kitchen table, he made straight for the shower, setting it hotter than usual to wash away any lingering trace of her, along with the guilt and shame he felt. He got dressed, pulling on a pair of jogging bottoms and a t-shirt, then put the kettle on to boil while checking his messages on his mobile. Mac had phoned asking him if he'd be in his local tonight but Graveney, not feeling sociable, ignored it. Bev Wilson had messaged too, informing him she hoped to complete the post-mortem on Stephen Stewart the next day.

Graveney, disappointed there wasn't a message from Louisa paused, about to ring her when he heard a key in the front door. He waited in the kitchen as Louisa entered. They stood momentarily looking at each other before Louisa ran towards him and buried her head in his chest, sobbing uncontrollably. Graveney cried too, tears dropping from his eyes, and as Louisa clung tightly to him, he clung just as tightly to her.

Graveney eventually persuaded Louisa to go to bed. She looked physically and emotionally drained from her ordeal, and he stayed with her until she fell asleep. Happy she was settled he stood, picked up the overnight bag she'd brought home with her and emptied the dirty clothes out, to put into the washing machine later. He unzipped the side pocket of the bag and pulled out a small photo album full of pictures, he presumed of Louisa's sister, mother, and other members of the family. The likeness between Louisa and her mother obvious, Louisa a younger version of her. One of the spaces in the album was blank as if a photo had been removed or dropped out, and when Graveney put his hand back into the bag, he found it. He glanced at the picture of Louisa's mam and his younger self, at first not believing what he was looking at. He stared at the picture again and recognised her face from his past. Her name was Carol, he remembered. He'd met her while on a course in York, years ago. He turned the photo over, written on the back, *Me and Peter 1996*. Graveney glanced across at Louisa's still-sleeping form. Placing the picture in the album, and then replacing the album in the bag, he headed to his own room.

CHAPTER ELEVEN

Graveney arrived at work at 08.00, wanting to get started early. He had reluctantly left Louisa with her friend, after she had reassured him she was fine. He had plenty to fit in today. He intended to travel to Sleights and talk with retired DI John Watney at the nursing home. Ruth, the incident room manager, had organised the meeting for him. He hoped to carry on to Whitby after this to meet Sandra Stewart's mother. He wanted to give her the news regarding her son-in-law's death but needed to hold off on that bit of information, until Stephen Stewart's parents had been located. Apparently, they were out of the country but due back home today. He wasn't looking forward to breaking the news to either of them. Graveney was deep in thought when Marne tapped on his office door and entered.

'You wanted to see me, sir?' Closing the door behind her.

'Yes, Steph. I'm hoping to visit the original DI on the Vale Farm Murders today, and probably carry on to Whitby to see Sandra Stewart's mother. I'm looking to leave with you in half an hour.'

He glanced at Marne's scarf around her neck, presumably to cover up any marks, and for a moment Graveney felt guilt and shame course through him.

'Half an hour, sir.' She turned and left his office abruptly.

Graveney thought that strange. No flirting, no suggestive dialogue with her. Marne seemed somewhat distracted. Graveney mulled it over briefly but then let it pass. Maybe, like him, she felt a degree of embarrassment over the previous night.

Marne left the incident room and making sure no one saw her, entered the disabled toilet. She pulled out her mobile and rang DCI Phillips.

'Yes, Steph?'

'I need a favour,' she said. 'Graveney wants me to go with him to see Watney, at Sleights.'

'That's not a problem, is it?'

'It could be if I've got to go back there later. Graveney also wants to visit Sandra's mother in Whitby.'

'And you think she'd recognise you?'

'Maybe.'

'Ok, leave it with me,' he said. 'I'll sort something out.'

'Thanks.' She hung up and headed back to the incident room.

Graveney's phone rang seconds after he'd finished speaking with Bev Wilson, picking it back up he answered. 'Graveney,' he said.

'Peter, it's Trevor, I need a favour. I'm looking to borrow your new DS.'

'I've got lots on, Guv. I could do with her today. I'm visiting Stephen Stewart's parents, and it always helps to have a woman there, sir.'

'I know Peter, but it would help me greatly. Take one of the young DC's. It's a good experience for them seeing how a real Detective works.'

'I suppose so. If it helps you out.' Graveney viewed Phillips' flattery as slightly odd, but let it pass.

'Thanks. There's a pint in it for you.' Phillips said, and hung up.

Graveney marched into the incident room and shouted over at Marne. 'Steph. Change of plan. The DCI needs you today. Someone tell Sarah she's riding shotgun with me, and I want her ready in 15 minutes.' He left and headed back to his office. Marne exhaled audibly.

Graveney made a few more phone calls and checked his messages in case Louisa had phoned. Satisfied she hadn't, he gathered together his things and headed for Sleights and the beauty of the North Yorkshire Moors.

OCTOBER 2006 - Sandra picked Jimmy up from his apartment the next day and they drove to Ray's. She wasn't sure of what to expect, but when she heard he lived in the seedier part of Middlesbrough, she knew he wasn't exactly living *la dolce vita*. When they arrived at his dingy flat, it still shocked her. They knocked on the door, which opened slightly for whoever was inside to view Sandra and Jimmy before it opened fully. Ray beckoned them in without saying a word, the two of them following him into a small ground floor flat. The smell of the building hit them as soon as they entered. A combination of sweat, vomit, decomposing food and possibly human excrement. It took Sandra all her effort not to gag, but Jimmy appeared not to notice it as much.

'Needs a good clean,' Jimmy whispered to Sandra.

'Needs a bomb,' she replied.

Ray slumped onto a seat, appearing not to notice the half-eaten pizza he sat on. Jimmy cleared two chairs and placed one near to Sandra, who was now wishing she had bought one of the white suits people wear on those cleaning programs, rather than the £80 jeans she wore.

'Have you brought the money?' Ray asked.

Jimmy shifted in his seat. 'We've got the money, Ray, don't you worry. We need to be happy with what you've got before we go and get it though,' he said. 'First, tell us what you know. If we are satisfied, you'll get your money.'

Ray lit a cigarette, gulped from his can of lager, and began. He had been sent to Durham in 2000 where he met Arthur Stevens. At first, Ray hadn't liked Stevens, especially when Ray found out what he was in for. Eventually though, Ray warmed to him. Stevens gradually came to trust Ray, and they'd got on as best they could. When Stevens neared the end of his sentence, someone visited. A tall thick-set man with short-cropped hair and a spider's web tattooed on his neck. The man looked the sort of person not to cross, and when Stevens came back to his cell, Ray remembered, he was scared shitless.

Stevens told Ray what happened at Winterton and how he often had nightmares over what he had done. He also told Ray he had, on occasion, provided boys to these wealthy men for money. The two boys, presumably the ones Terry mentioned, were taken to a party at a smart house. Stevens claimed he had no idea what happened to them there, but a man he knew called Shelby called him and asked him to get rid of their bodies. Stevens hadn't wanted to get involved in that but Shelby warned him if he didn't help, he'd tell *The Man*. Ray said Stevens never told him the name of this man, but he did say he was powerful, and he got incredibly agitated just talking about him.

Ray went on to say, as an insurance policy, Shelby secretly videoed some of the people at the house on the night the boys died. He gave Stevens a copy, telling him to keep it safe. Stevens took the rap for the abuse that went on at Winterton after they promised him a significant amount of money. As he came to the end of his sentence, he contacted Shelby to ask for what they owed him. The tattooed guy who visited, a heavy for *The Man*, had put the frighteners on Stevens. Ray didn't know the name of this man either.

Stevens was terrified they'd come looking for him when he got out and told Ray that if anything happened, he would leave everything to him. Ray thought this just the ramblings of an old man. After leaving prison, Ray, through a mutual acquaintance, had heard that Stevens had been murdered in his cell. Much to Ray's surprise, Stevens *had* left him everything he owned.

Sandra and Jimmy listened intently to Ray's story, and Sandra gave Jimmy the sort of look which told him she was interested.

'Have you got the video here?' Jimmy asked.

Ray trudged into the bedroom and returned with a video case which he opened, showing them its contents. He tramped over to the video machine and pushed it in. The video began and Sandra and Jimmy watched as it showed a large country house where several men, at different intervals, entered followed by a man bringing two boys about eleven or twelve into the house. They only recognised one of the men, a member of Parliament. The video switched to inside the house, showing the occupants in a relaxed mood, and the two boys being plied with what looked like drink and drugs. Sandra and Jimmy, although both shocked, remained outwardly blasé.

'What happened to the boys, Ray?'

'Do you want a fucking diagram, Luv? They raped and killed them of course.'

'Do you know where Stevens buried them?' she asked.

'Arthur told me he wrote down the exact location. It's at his lock-up.'

Jimmy's eyes widened. 'His lock-up?'

'I told you. He left his belongings to me. His stuff, what's left of it, is stored in a lock-up. Lots of furniture and clothes, which I sold, but there's still some odds and sods in there. I'll throw in the key and address with the price if you like?'

'Can we have a minute to discuss this?'

'Christ, Jimmy. You're not pissing me about, are you? You see I owe some people money. Not the sort of people you want to be in debt to. You understand?'

Jimmy glanced at Sandra. 'We understand.'

Sandra nodded, and Jimmy put his hand into his inside pocket and pulled out an envelope stuffed with notes. Ray retrieved the video from the recorder and pulled a key from his pocket. He searched for a piece of paper and scribbling an address for the lock-up, gave it to Jimmy. Sandra and Jimmy left. Once outside, Sandra gulped in fresh air, glad to be away from the foul stench.

Jimmy held out the tape. 'You keep the video, key, and address, and we'll meet up tomorrow. Have a look around the lock-up. See if there are any more clues.'

'Ok,' Sandra said. 'I'll ring you first thing to arrange a time.'

Sandra drove home, both excited and apprehensive. Dangerous people may be involved, and if she and Jimmy blew the lid on this, it could be massive. But her main thought was of the two boys and how they must have suffered. More than getting a scoop, she wanted these evil bastards brought to justice.

Two men sat in front of the black Audi. One small and thin, a large scar – inflicted years earlier – ran from under his left eye to his lip, the result of an altercation with a knife. The other man much more substantial, his close-cropped hair and the spider's web tattoo on his neck providing him with a sinister look. The mobile in the pocket of the tattooed man sounded.

'Yes, Shelby?'

'The Man wants you to clear up some loose ends, Flint,' Shelby said.

'Ok. I'm listening.'

'Arthur Stevens' cellmate's blabbing. Stevens must have told him what happened at Winterton. The man wants him dealt with. Anything incriminating, he wants it getting. You understand?'

'Perfectly. Have you his address?'

As Shelby gave the address to Flint, he repeated it aloud as the smaller man sitting next to him jotted it down. He ended the call with Shelby, turned on the engine, and drove off.

They pulled up at the top of the road, 200 metres from Ray's flat, minutes after Jimmy and Sandra left. Getting out of the car they approached Ray's, the smaller of the two men carrying a little holdall. Flint knocked on the door while his mate kept a look-out, making sure they weren't watched. Ray opened the door to his flat, half expecting to see Jimmy and Sandra there. Shocked to see two scary looking men outside he desperately tried to close the door but Flint, not a stranger to this type of event, placed his boot inside preventing Ray from doing so. The two men easily pushed the door open. Ray backed away, stumbling backwards from the men, as the smaller man closed the door behind them.

'I've got Ricky's money,' he said.

'Money? What money?' Flint said.

'I thought Ricky sent you to collect the money I owe him?' Ray started to babble uncontrollably as fear grabbed him, and Flint, not the most patient of men nodded at his partner.

'Shut him up, Dec,' Flint said.

Ray, who hadn't stopped for breath, looked on bemused as the smaller man strode across to him and punched him full in the face. Ray tumbled over backwards from the force of the blow and lay, momentarily stunned. The two men lifted him to his feet, dragged him into the lounge and sat him on a chair, the smaller man securing him to it with gaffer tape around his legs, arms and waist. Ray looked on, his eyes darting between the pair as blood trickled slowly from his nostrils.

Flint sat opposite him. 'Now, Ray, in a moment I'm going to ask you some questions which I would like you to answer. I don't want you to speak until I ask you these questions. If you understand me, I'd like you to nod your head.'

Ray nodded he understood what Flint told him, his eyes flicking from left to right as the smaller man placed his holdall on the table.

'Ray,' Flint said. 'What did Stevens tell you?'

'Nothing. Honest,' Ray said.

Flint smiled. 'Ray. I thought we had an understanding here. I figured we had some rapport going and yet, at the first opportunity, you fucking lie to me.'

'Please. Stevens told me what he was in for, but never mentioned anybody. Honest,' he said, his voice trembling.

Flint nodded at the smaller man who opened the zip on the holdall and put his hand inside, pulling out a large pair of garden secateurs. Ray, on seeing them, could hold on to the contents of his bladder no longer and wet himself.

'Ray,' Flint said. 'Look at the mess you're making of your lovely flat.'

The two men smiled at each other as they surveyed the squalor Ray lived in. The small man bent down and removed the shoe and sock from Ray's left foot, wrinkling his nose at the smell emanating from it.

Ray trembled. 'Please, I'll tell you everything.'

Flint laughed. 'I'm sorry, Ray. You're already in debt to us now. I make that two lies.' He pushed a piece of cloth into Ray's mouth and wrapped some gaffer tape around it.

Ray stared in terror as the small man bent once more and casually cut off the two smallest toes on Ray's left foot. Ray screamed, but a combination of the cloth and tape prevented him from emitting much noise. Blood seeped from his foot into the filthy carpet, as tears streamed down his face.

'Now Ray, you're not going to lie to us again, are you? Because my friend here.' Nodding at the other man. 'Doesn't want to have to remove your other shoe given the stench coming from your left foot.'

Ray shook his head in answer. Flint removed the tape and cloth from his mouth.

'He told me what went on at Winterton,' Ray said. 'About the boys and what happened to them.'

'Did he give you anything?'

'A video.'

'Where's the video, Ray?'

'I sold it to some journalists.'

Flint looked up, shaking his head. 'Ray. Now that was a stupid thing to do, wasn't it?' Moving closer to him. 'What are their names?'

'I'm not sure … Jimmy … I think. I don't know the woman's name.'

'You're not lying to us again, are you?' Flint picked up the cloth and tape.

'Please. I ... think ... I've got a card he gave to me.' Nodding his head towards the mantelpiece.

The small man picked up a business card and handed it to Flint.

'Have you anything else to tell us. We need to be sure you've told us everything, you see.'

'Please. That's all I know.'

The smaller man searched around the flat. Opening a cupboard, he pulled out the envelope containing the money which he handed to Flint.

'You can have the money,' Ray said. 'I don't want it.'

Flint ambled over and squatted down, his face only inches from Ray's. 'Let's make sure you've told us everything, Ray.' Pushing the cloth back into his mouth.

The two men opened Ray's front door and glanced outside. Satisfied the street was empty, they left the flat. Ray's lifeless body, minus a lot of toes slumped in the chair. Flames gently making their way across the floor towards him.

They drove off in the Audi before Flint made a call, putting it on speaker phone as Shelby answered.

'Yes, Flint?'

'Ray Hetherington's no longer a problem. We have a bigger one.'

'What did he tell you?'

'Everything. We were quite persuasive.' He smiled at Dec. 'Stevens told him everything about Winterton, and he also gave Ray a video.'

'A video? Have you got it?'

'That's the problem. He sold it to a couple of journalists.'

'Do you know their names?'

'One of them is a freelance called Jimmy Hind. The other, a woman. I don't know her name.'

'Did Hetherington say how Stevens got the video?'

'No. That question didn't come up. You should've left a list you wanted answering, Shelby. He still had plenty of fingers left.' The two men smirked at each other.

'Ok. Sit tight for the moment.'

'Are you sure? This needs containing.'

'I know, but I don't want you to do anything until I've spoken to *The Man*.'

'Ok,' Flint said, and rang off.

After dropping Jessica at school and then taking Stephen to the airport, Sandra headed for Jimmy's. She couldn't help but think back to the previous night when her sister, Angela, had come around for dinner.

It was Stephen and Jessica's first meeting with her, and Sandra thought it went very well. She had discovered Angela was a police officer with the Durham Constabulary. Opting for this line of work because her adopted dad had been a police officer as well. She had an ambition to become a plain-clothes officer one day like him, and was studying hard to do that. They arranged another dinner when Stephen returned from working away, and even invited Angela to come to Stephen's parents' villa with them, which she enthusiastically agreed to. She wasn't married and only recently split up with her long-term boyfriend, which she didn't seem bothered about. She was beautiful, and Sandra doubted she would have trouble finding another.

Sandra finally pulled up outside Jimmy's flat, watching as he came bounding out of his apartment block with a spring in his step. He jumped into the passenger seat, giving Sandra a peck on the cheek. 'Did Stephen get away all right?' he asked.

'Yeah, I've dropped him off. The job he's on is only going to take a couple of days. Hopefully, he'll be home before the weekend. We're going away for a week or two when he gets back so, it'll be good if we can get a head start on this story before then.'

'Hopefully, there are more clues at the lockup. Did you remember to bring the key?'

She held it up. 'Yes. Won't they ask for proof of who we are?'

'I don't know. It depends on how security conscious the place is. I'll try dropping one of them a few quid if I have to.'

They reached the address Ray gave them, deep inside an industrial estate. Jimmy checked the name on the piece of paper. 'This is it, *Jameson Storage*. It doesn't look like a high-security place, does it? It looks like the sort of place people store furniture while moving house, rather than anything really valuable.'

Sandra nodded. 'Well, let's go and see.' They both got out of the car and strolled towards a white portacabin with *OFFICE* painted in black paint on the front. They went through a door and found themselves in a small room, another door on one side, and a little window with two closed wooden doors within it on the other. To the right of the window, a bell with a sign below which read: *PLEASE RING AND WAIT*. Jimmy pressed the bell, which they heard chime in the room behind the window. Footsteps sounded inside the room as the two doors opened, and a scrawny-looking middle-aged man popped his head through it. 'Can I help you?' he asked.

'Yes,' Jimmy said, glancing at Sandra. 'We've come to get some stuff from our lock-up.'

'What's the number?'

'Hold on.' Jimmy looked across at Sandra, who fished the key from her handbag.

'24,' Sandra said.

The man turned away and walked across to a cupboard on the wall with row upon row of keys hanging from hooks. He searched through them and selected a key numbered 24, before picking up a large ledger and returning to the window. 'Have you got your receipt ... Mr Stevens?' Finding the relevant entry in the book, he looked up.

'That's the thing. We've misplaced the receipt,' Jimmy said.

'Have you any proof of identity then?'

Jimmy leaned close to the man. 'We're sort of doing this as a favour for Mr Stevens. He's unwell at the moment. He didn't mention we would need a receipt. We've come a long way. He wants us to collect some old family photos, you see.'

'I'm sorry, sir, but my boss would go spare if I let you in without a receipt or ID.'

Jimmy put his hand into his pocket and pulled out his wallet. 'What if we were to give you something for your trouble?' He took out a £20. 'We only want ten minutes.'

The man looked first at Jimmy, and then Sandra, before glancing at the note. 'You two look like honest people,' he said. 'If you're quick because I'm expecting him back at any moment.' Pocketing the cash, he smiled at them.

The man closed the doors, emerging from the office. 'Follow me,' he said.

He led them to a piece of open ground towards the containers. The man edged along them until he reached one with number 24 painted on the front. Taking his key from his pocket, he opened one of the two locks on the container. 'There are two locks on each container,' he explained. 'Your key fits the other lock. When you've finished just close yours again, and I'll lock ours when you've gone. Keep your eyes open for a blue Mercedes, it's the boss and I don't want to lose my job.'

'One of us will keep watch, and if he turns up we'll make ourselves scarce,' Jimmy said.

'Good.' He nodded at the pair and headed back towards the office.

Jimmy opened the second lock on the container, and the two of them entered. It didn't contain much. A wardrobe, a chest of drawers and an ottoman.

'It looks like Ray didn't leave an awful lot,' Sandra said. 'Probably sold it for drink and drugs.'

'I'll keep watch,' Jimmy said. 'See if you can find anything,'

He stood near to the door with his head poking outside while Sandra searched through the furniture. There was nothing of note in the ottoman, just some old blankets. The wardrobe, virtually empty as well.

She moved onto the chest of drawers, which again disappointedly didn't seem to contain a lot. The final drawer, however, had a small black book inside.

She opened it, pausing when Jimmy spoke. 'I think the manager's back. You'll have to hurry.'

Sandra pushed the book into the pocket of her jacket, joining Jimmy at the door. A man, getting out of a blue Mercedes, headed inside the office.

'Did you find anything?' Jimmy said.

'A black book. We'll have a look at it when we get back to the car.'

Jimmy locked up the container, and he and Sandra gingerly made their way out of the compound, careful not to pass in full view of the window of the office. Once back to the car they sat and stared at each other, both of them blowing out their cheeks.

Sandra shook her head. 'You love this sort of thing, don't you?'

'Yeah, it's exciting. Like proper detective work. Let's see the book, then.'

Sandra held the book out towards Jimmy, as his mobile rang. 'Hi. Colin,' he said into it. 'You've done what? I'm on my way.'

'What's up?' Sandra said.

'Colin's flooded the kitchen. I'll have to go home.'

She drove Jimmy back to his apartment as he read the contents of the book on the way, none of it making much sense. There were numbers, dates and initials. Possibly people or places. He read the contents to the equally bemused Sandra.

He looked at Sandra. 'You keep the book with the other stuff, and we'll pay Ray another visit soon. See if he can shed light on any of it. I'm trying to check up on the two boys who went missing, so I'll continue with that. You see if you can identify anyone else in the video. I'll ring you in the morning.'

'No probs.' She kissed him on the cheek. Jimmy disappeared into his flat, while Sandra headed home to Vale Farm.

CHAPTER TWELVE

SEPTEMBER 2014 - Graveney and DC Sarah Cooke travelled along the moor road towards Sleights. They had already visited Stephen Stewart's parents and as expected, it turned into an incredibly sad and sombre affair. The part of the job Graveney detested most, but a necessary task. Once the news of their son's death sank in, Graveney questioned them regarding Stephen's relationship with Sandra. They described an idyllic marriage. Two people genuinely in love and could offer no explanation as to why Stephen would murder Sandra and Jessica. They'd had no contact with Stephen in the previous eight years, didn't know of anyone called Ang or Angela. Graveney, after gauging their reactions to his questioning, had no reason to doubt they were telling the truth. He, of course, never informed the Stewarts of his and Bev Wilson's suspicion that the murder had been staged, and left them having not learned a great deal more than he already knew.

They finally reached a large roundabout on the moor road and headed to the small village of Sleights, eventually pulling into the car park outside Sunny View Nursing Home. They announced themselves at reception and were escorted along a corridor, stopping at a door. The care assistant tapped lightly on it and showed them into the room. A man in his early sixties sat in a wheelchair watching the television, his body twisted at an awkward angle, with one side of his face slightly drooping.

The care assistant turned off the television. 'You've got some visitors, John.'

Graveney and Cooke positioned themselves on chairs opposite Watney.

'Hello, John. I'm DI Peter Graveney and this is DC Sarah Cooke. Did you get Ruth's message?'

'Yes. She phoned the other day,' he said audibly but slowly, his illness clearly making talking difficult.

'I'll leave you to it,' said the care assistant as she left the room.

'What can I do for you?' Watney said.

Graveney smiled. Typical copper, he thought, getting straight to the point. 'Do you remember the Vale Farm Murders?' Talking slowly to him.

'There's nothing wrong with my hearing, Graveney. Or my brain. It's my body that's buggered,' he slowly drawled.

'Sorry, John. Tell us what you remember?'

'A cock-up from start to finish. Missing evidence. Poor forensics.'

'Missing evidence?' Graveney said.

'The rope, Graveney. The fibres on the woman's neck. The bloody pathologist was useless.' He motioned for Graveney to pass him a plastic beaker from the table nearby, and Graveney complied.

'Did you think Stephen Stewart killed his wife and daughter?'

'No. Something was not quite right. I couldn't put my finger on it, but no, I didn't think Stewart killed his wife and daughter. With no one else in the frame, and Stewart missing, what could we do? Eventually, we were told to wind down the investigation by Superintendent Oake.'

'Chief Superintendent now,' Graveney said.

'Yeah, I heard. Doesn't surprise me. Oake always was an ambitious bugger. I wanted to follow a lead concerning a friend of Sandra's – I don't remember his name, a journalist like her – he'd gone missing just before the murders. I thought the two were possibly linked.' Watney thought for a moment. 'Hind. Jimmy Hind. That's his name.'

'So why didn't you follow that line of enquiry?' Graveney said.

'Oake told me not to. Said budget constraints wouldn't allow it. But I persisted anyway. Oake somehow found out and gave me a right dressing down. Said he'd discipline me for disobeying a direct order if I did it again.'

'Who knew about this line of enquiry?'

'Only DC Jones. He either told Oake, or he told someone else who did.'

Graveney finished speaking about the case with Watney and passed away half an hour talking about Ruth, and the other people still at the station from Watney's time there. Graveney and Cooke eventually got up to leave.

'Can your young DC go and fetch one of the carers for me, Graveney?' Watney asked.

'Of course.' And Graveney motioned for Cooke to do that.

As Cooke left the room, Watney beckoned him closer. 'Graveney, a piece of advice. Trust no one at the station except, Phillips.'

'Why Phillips?'

'He's a decent copper.'

Cooke returned with the care assistant, and Graveney shook Watney's hand and headed for the door.

'Remember what I told you, Graveney,' Watney said, as they left.

'What did he mean by that, sir?' Cooke asked.

'No idea, Sarah.'

Watney sat in his wheelchair and picked up his mobile from the table next to him. Although the buttons were overlarge to assist with using it, he still struggled to locate and phone the correct number.

'Hi, John,' said a woman's voice on the other end.

'Graveney's been,' he said. 'I told him what you told me to say. Do we still have a deal?'

'Of course. I told you I'd keep our bargain. When do you want me to come?'

'As soon as possible, Ang. I'm sick of living like this.'

'I'll see you tomorrow.'

Graveney and Cooke headed away from Sleights and up to Whitby. Turning left at Pannett Park, and travelling up Chubb Hill Road, they turned left onto Upgang Lane. Graveney checked the number of the house before they got out of the car, and knocked. The door opened and an elderly, grey-haired lady stood there. Graveney and Cooke both held out their badges.

'Hello, Mrs Francis?' he said.

'Yes. You're the policeman I spoke to?'

'I'm Detective Inspector Graveney, and this is Detective Constable Cooke. Can we come in?'

'Yes, of course.' She ushered them inside and led them to the living room. Mrs Francis sat in an armchair and indicated for the officers to sit on a settee opposite, which they did.

'How can I help you, Inspector?'

'Would you mind answering some questions about your daughter, Sandra, and your son-in-law, Stephen?'

'What sort?'

'Background stuff. Your view of Stephen and Sandra's marriage.'

'I know what you're going to ask, Inspector. If I think Stephen killed my daughter and Granddaughter. *Stephen Stewart did not murder them*. They both loved each other and adored Jessica.'

'Sometimes, Mrs Francis, we don't always know what goes on in marriages. Sometimes things are hidden, even from people we love.'

She shook her head. 'Inspector, I had a close relationship with my daughter and son-in-law, and I can state categorically, they were happy,' she said.

'I'm sorry. I have to ask these types of questions. I know it's difficult for you to talk about this. Can I ask you about the last time you spoke to Sandra?'

'Two or three days before she died. We met up in Guisborough for coffee.'

'What did you talk about?'

'Stephen, Jessica, that sort of thing. She told me they were hoping to go away for a little break to Stephen's parents' villa in Portugal. She appeared happy. I mean, does that seem like someone in an unhappy marriage?'

'No, Mrs Francis. Anything else you discussed?'

'She told me she was working on a story with Jimmy.'

'Jimmy?' Graveney feigned not knowing him.

'An old university friend of hers. They were writing about some boys' home or something. She was excited about it.'

'Winterton Boys' Home?' Graveney said.

'Possibly, I don't really remember.'

'This Jimmy …'

'Hind,' she interrupted Graveney. 'Jimmy Hind.'

'Is it possible Sandra and Jimmy were,' Graveney hesitated and looked across at Cooke. 'More than friends?'

'Inspector, my daughter and Jimmy were just good friends. Jimmy was gay.'

'Ah, I see,' Graveney said. 'This Jimmy. Do you have an address for him?'

'Jimmy went missing, just before Sandra and Jessica died.'

'Missing?' Graveney again feigned surprise.

'He wasn't at the funerals. I spoke to his partner, and he told me Jimmy had gone missing. Beside himself with worry as I remember. But of course, I had my own concerns.'

'Didn't anyone think it unusual, Jimmy going missing at the same time as Sandra and Jessica's murders?'

'The police told me they weren't looking for anybody else but Stephen in connection with their deaths. Jimmy's disappearance was just a coincidence. That's what they said.'

'Do you know if Jimmy ever turned up?'

'No idea. Speak to Jimmy's partner, Colin, he'll know,' she said.

'Do you know his surname?'

Mrs Francis got up from her seat and opening a drawer in a side cabinet, she fished about until she finally found an old diary. She leafed through the pages before she stopped at one. 'Colin Jenkins, Brenda Road, Hartlepool,' she said.

Cooke, making notes throughout the conversation, jotted down this information too.

Graveney held out his hand. 'Thanks for your help, Mrs Francis.'

'Can I ask?' she said. 'Why now after eight years? Do you know something?'

'I can't go into details, but I can say there are new leads we're working on.'

'Do you think you'll find their killers?'

'I hope so.'

'And Stephen. What happened to him?'

Graveney almost told her about Stephen Stewart but decided against it. 'As I say, Mrs Francis, I'll keep you informed of any developments. Thank you again. One more thing. Did Sandra know anyone called Angela or Ang?'

She thought for a moment. 'No. I don't think I've ever heard of anyone Sandra knew named Ang or Angela. She never mentioned anyone with that name.'

'And ...' Graveney paused. 'Was Sandra right or left-handed?'

'Left,' said a puzzled-looking Mrs Francis.

'Thanks again. I'll keep in touch.'

The two police officers left the house and headed back to the car.

'Can you write up that stuff as soon as possible, and get it to Ruth in the incident room?'

'Yes, Guv. Where to next?' she asked.

'Back to Middlesbrough.'

OCTOBER 2006 - Jimmy phoned Sandra. Telling her of his intention of going around and seeing Ray Hetherington again, in the hope he could shed some light on the book they'd found at the lock-up. Jimmy turned the corner and pulled up at the top of Ray's road. Even from quite a distance away, the fire damage to Ray's flat was evident. Police vehicles parked outside, and several houses to the sides of the property cordoned off. Jimmy got out of his car and stopped a passer-by.

'What's happening there?' he asked a man walking a dog.

'They've found a body in a flat,' the man said. 'Someone murdered, I've heard. There was a fire yesterday.'

'Do they know who the victim is?'

'A bloke called Ray, I think.' The man continued on his walk.

Jimmy got back in his car and drove off, stopping some distance away, he telephoned Sandra.

'Hi, Sand.' he said. 'Forget about talking to Ray, he's dead.'

'Dead?' Sandra said. 'How?'

'Apparently, murdered. Probably by the blokes he owed money to. Do you fancy having a spot of lunch?'

'Yeah, about twelve at Salvadori's near the marina. I'll pick you up.'

'Twelve sounds great,' he said. 'See you then.'

SEPTEMBER 2014 - Graveney and Marne headed for Hartlepool and the address for Colin Jenkins. He was the manager of a bistro in the town centre, and he had agreed to speak to the officers at his place of work. They travelled the short distance from Middlesbrough to Hartlepool, and found themselves in the centre of the town and parked their car. They walked to the bistro – situated in the Castle Gate shopping centre – just around the corner from where they had left the vehicle. On entering the bistro, and introducing themselves, they were ushered into an office upstairs by a woman. Colin was on his way back from the wholesalers, they were informed, and the officers sat drinking tea while they waited.

'This Colin Jenkins was the partner of Jimmy Hind?' Marne said.

'Yeah. Apparently, Hind went missing before the murders.'

'And you think they're linked?'

'It seems a little odd, don't you think,' Graveney said. 'Working on a story together. One went missing, and the other is murdered.'

'They were working on a story about Winterton Boys' Home, weren't they?'

'Yeah,' Graveney said. 'Maybe Sandra and Jimmy uncovered something serious, and someone wanted it kept quiet.'

'What do you think Colin Jenkins will say?' Marne said.

'No idea, but I'm interested if he's heard from Jimmy Hind since.'

The door to the office opened, and Colin Jenkins strode in. He marched towards the two officers and shook their hands as he introduced himself. Graveney and Marne doing likewise.

Jenkins eased onto a seat next to them. 'What can I do for you two?'

'We'd like to ask you some questions about Jimmy Hind.'

Colin blanched. 'Why?'

'We're re-examining the murders of Sandra and Jessica Stewart.'

'I knew it,' Colin said. 'I knew Jimmy's disappearance was linked.'

'What makes you say that?'

'We'd been together for about six months. He got a lead on a story about Winterton Boys' Home from a guy who used to be in there. He also spoke to someone who spent time in prison with Stevens, the guy jailed for the cruelty that went on in Winterton.'

'Arthur Stevens?' Graveney said.

'That's him, Arthur Stevens. Well, apparently, his cell-mate had some information to sell regarding what went on there. Jimmy and Sandra stumped up £10,000 to pay him. I loaned Jimmy his half, and Sandra put up the other.'

'Do you know the name of this cell-mate or the guy from Winterton?'

'No idea, but a couple of days later Jimmy disappeared. I reported it to the police, but they said he was an adult and it wasn't unusual for people to go missing.'

'And you didn't buy that?' Graveney said.

'No. Neither did Sandra. She dropped him off at the top of Brenda Road, and we never saw him again.'

'Haven't you heard from him since?'

'No. I thought that's the reason you're here. I thought maybe Jimmy had turned up.'

'I'm sorry, Colin. We haven't any information on that. Anything else you remember?'

Jenkins slumped in his chair. 'Not really, Inspector. I never got involved. It's always bugged me as to what happened to Jimmy. We were close, you see.'

Graveney nodded. 'Can you remember anything at all. A name Jimmy may have given you?'

Jenkins shook his head. 'No. That's all I know. What do you think happened to Jimmy?'

Graveney rubbed his chin. 'No idea. He's disappeared off the map. I'll leave you my card. If you remember anything else give me a ring, will you? If we come up with anything about what happened to Jimmy, I'll let you know.'

Colin thanked them and showed them out before heading back to his office.

Graveney looked at Marne. 'What do you think, Steph?'

'I think the two are linked, sir.'

'Me too.'

'Jenkins? Could he have been involved?'

Graveney stopped and looked back at the building. 'I don't think so. In fact, I'm pretty certain of it.'

Marne and Graveney drove back towards Middlesbrough. Graveney took out his mobile and phoned Mac. 'I need you to find a name for me. Arthur Stephens' cellmate in prison.'

'Another lead, Peter?'

'Possibly. We'll be back over there in thirty minutes. Do you think you'll have something by then? There's a pint in it for you.'

'Pint, eh? Leave it to me.'

Graveney hung up and put his mobile away. 'You ok, Steph?' Looking at the scarf around Marne's neck.

Marne smiled. 'Never better.'

Graveney and Marne reached Middlesbrough police station late afternoon. Graveney made his way to his office and motioned for Mac to join him as he sat at his desk. 'What have you got for me?' he asked.

'The name of Stevens' cell-mate in Durham was Ray Hetherington.'

Graveney leant forward in his chair and waited for Mac to continue.

Mac glanced at his pad. 'He was serving three years for burglary. Apparently, they became very close. When Stevens died, he left everything to Hetherington.'

'Do we know where he is now?'

'Ah, that's the problem. Hetherington's dead.'

'Dead?'

'Found murdered in his flat in 2006. Tortured before being stabbed to death. His property set on fire. Fortunately, a neighbour noticed the fire before it took hold and called the fire brigade.'

'When you say tortured, what do you mean?'

'Taped to a chair in his living room, and someone cut some of his toes off.' Mac blew out. 'Put it this way, there weren't many places for the people in the morgue to fasten his name tag too.'

'Do we know who did it?'

'The smart money was on a villain from Newcastle called Ricky Taylor. Apparently, Hetherington owed him money and the thinking was Ricky Taylor had Hetherington killed. Unfortunately, Taylor had a cast-iron alibi, and they couldn't prove any involvement. Hetherington's death remains open.'

'Call me paranoid here, but isn't it a bit of a coincidence he's connected to Sandra Stewart and Jimmy Hind. One of which we know is dead and the other missing, possibly dead?'

'Well, I'm with you. Taylor could be the killer, but apparently, £10,000 was recovered from his flat,' Mac said.

'The same £10,000 Jimmy and Sandra gave him?' Sitting back in his chair, he rubbed his chin. He looked at Mac who shrugged and Graveney continued. 'Jimmy Hind's partner said he loaned Hind £5,000, and Sandra Stewart added another £5,000. They gave it to Hetherington for information he got from Arthur Stevens.

'I see,' Mac said. 'Do we know what information?'

Graveney shook his head.

'If Taylor did catch up with him,' Mac said. 'Why didn't he take the money?'

Graveney nodded. 'Exactly. Whoever killed Ray Hetherington wasn't interested in the money.'

'Looks that way.

'So where do we go from here?' Graveney said.

'I've got some of the guys checking on inmates of Winterton. As you can imagine, quite a few passed through those doors before it closed.'

'Let's hope something turns up there then,' Graveney said.

'We've done some background checks on Shelby, but nothing as yet. If he had any information like Stewart told you, he kept it well hidden.'

Graveney raised his eyebrows. 'He could've just been saying that to Stewart, of course. I mean, someone pointing a gun has that effect.'

'Maybe. It's early days, so let's hope for a bit of luck,' Mac said. 'I don't suppose you fancy a pint tonight, do you?'

'Maybe a quick one after work. I need to get home to Louisa. Make sure she's ok.'

'Of course, I forgot about her. How's she coping?'

Graveney sighed. 'Her friend's staying for a few days. Louisa tends to bottle things up a bit, so it's hard to tell.'

'We'll have a swift one. Just to discuss what we know so far. See if we can crack this case.'

Graveney laughed. 'Something tells me we'll be sinking a few more before we crack this one.'

Mac stood and made towards the door, pausing with his hand on the handle. 'It's not all bad news then.'

Marne, after dropping Graveney in Middlesbrough, headed away from the station. Stopping briefly at her apartment to collect a small bag before heading up to Sleights, and her appointment with John Watney at Sunny View Nursing Home.

CHAPTER THIRTEEN

OCTOBER 2006 - Sandra picked Jimmy up from Brenda Road around noon, before heading over to the marina and Salvadori's restaurant. The waiter ushered them towards a table in the corner, taking their order for drinks.

'What do you think happened to Ray, then?' Sandra asked.

'Like I said on the phone, it looks as though the people he owed money to caught up with him.'

'That's terrible, Jimmy. Are you sure it wasn't someone else?'

'Who?'

'Do you remember Ray telling us something about a heavy who visited Stevens in Durham prison. How frightened he was? The man with a tattoo of a spider's web on his neck.'

'You don't think it was him, do you?' Jimmy said.

'The thing is, I've viewed the video again and identified some of the other people there. Four of them are members of Parliament, Conservative backbenchers.' Opening her notebook, she continued. 'I've a feeling some of the others are civil servants. This paedophile ring may be London-based. It could be much bigger than we think.'

'All the more reason to write this story,' he whispered. 'We don't know how long it's been going on and how many kids have been murdered. We've got to expose them. This is why we became journalists, *isn't it?*'

'I know, but I'm scared. This may be too big for us.'

'Are you saying we should go to the police?' Jimmy said.

'Maybe. I just don't know.'

'What about if we dig some more and hand over what we have to the police, then?'

Sarah blew out. 'Ok. But if I feel like this is going to blow up in our face, I'm out. I've got to consider Jessica and Stephen.'

'Fine.' Putting his hand on hers, he patted it.

The waiter came over to them and jotted down their food order, both opting for the pasta carbonara followed by tiramisu. After eating their meal and discussing the plan of action, Sandra opened her notepad. A list of names on one of the pages numbered one to four. Number five, a question mark next to it. 'We need to find out who number five is. The person who Ray called, 'The Man,' she said. 'One of the faces on the video is someone called William Foxley. The house in the video is his place, Wyndbourne Hall.'

'Right, now we're getting somewhere. This man, number five on your list. Could it be him?'

'Maybe. Seems plausible,' Sandra said.

'Well. I've been having some thoughts of my own. The numbers in the book we retrieved from the lockup? Possibly grid references?'

Sandra frowned. 'Grid references?'

'Yeah. I did some digging on Stevens, and he was in the army, so he'd know all about them.'

Sandra gave Jimmy the book they'd taken from the lockup, and Jimmy showed her the twelve-figure number. Sandra jotted the number in her notebook on a fresh page, below the heading POSSIBLE BURIAL SITE, adding the names of the two murdered boys.

She tapped her book with her pen. 'Stephen has some ordnance survey maps at home. I'll check them when I get back.'

'I'll do likewise and see if we come up with the same location. You keep the video safe, and we'll meet up tomorrow.'

They headed back towards Jimmy's flat, Sandra stopping at the top of his road.

'I'm going to nip into the newsagent for a map,' He said. Kissing Sandra on the cheek and waving goodbye.

She drove home to Vale Farm, and on her arrival located the map under the stairs. She briefly checked on the internet as to how to plot the grid reference numbers before she tried it out on the map. If her calculations were accurate, and sure they were, the location was within the grounds of Wyndbourne Hall. The estate was extensive, and the site near a small wood on the outskirts of the land. She excitedly called Jimmy, disappointed when it went straight to voicemail.

SEPTEMBER 2014 - Graveney agreed to meet Mac at the coffee shop on Monday morning. Mac had travelled back up to Scotland to sort out some details regarding his divorce from Maria, and Graveney used the opportunity to spend some time with Louisa. They headed up to Whitby on Saturday, eating fish and chips on the quayside while watching the boats come and go. Graveney had forgotten how beautiful Whitby was, even at this time of the year, and only when he'd travelled with DS Cooke to interview Sandra Stewart's mother he remembered.

Louisa seemed in a much better frame of mind, and although losing your mother was something some people struggle to come to terms with, she'd shown a maturity way beyond her years. Graveney was secretly very proud of her.

Graveney offered to take Louisa to her mother's funeral – pencilled in for later in the week – but she declined. He hadn't let on he knew the reason why and didn't want to push the issue. Louisa said she knew he was extremely busy with the investigation and her family would look after her. The revelation of the photo album had come as a shock to Graveney, but in all honesty, it didn't matter if Louisa was his daughter or not. He loved her like one, and he couldn't imagine his life without her in it.

He took out his phone and flicked through his photos stopping at a selfie taken of himself and her in Whitby, he smiled and put the phone back in his pocket as Mac entered the shop. Graveney got up and walked over to the counter.

'Becks,' Graveney said. 'I'd like you to meet a good friend of mine. DI Jim Mackay. Mac, to his mates.'

'Another policeman.' Holding out her hand, Mac gently kissed the back of it.

'Nice to meet you, Becky,' he said.

'You're smooth,' she said. 'Where's Peter been hiding you, then?'

'I've just moved from Scotland. A new start and all that.'

'Well if you want good coffee, Mac, this is the place to come.'

'I'll bear that in mind, my dear.' He followed Graveney over to the table, Graveney winking at Becky as he turned away.

Andrea nudged Becky in the ribs. 'You can't help yourself, can you?'

'The clocks ticking. I can't afford to hang about any longer. I need a man in my life. I need a nice warm bum to cuddle up to. I need ...'

'I know what you need, Becks. You've told me often enough. What about Tim?'

'I've given up on Tim. He's a washout. I've only just found out he's still living with his mother. Not only that, but he admitted to me he was a virgin before we ... you know ... did it. It's like buying a horse and having to break it in yourself.'

'What's wrong with that? At least he won't come with any emotional baggage. Surely that's got to count for something?'

Becky huffed. 'I'm not about to teach a forty-something the ropes. I want a man who knows what he's doing in the bedroom. I want a man who's going to shag my brains out not stop every couple of minutes to ask me if he's doing it right.'

Andrea laughed. 'Shag your brains out? Wouldn't take him long.'

'I knew you'd say that you're so predictable.' Pretending to be offended.

'I thought you had the hots for Peter?'

'Peters gorgeous but if I'm honest though, it will spoil our friendship if we ever got down and dirty. Don't get me wrong, I'd bloody enjoy it. But Peter's not the relationship type, I can tell.'

'And his mate, Mac?'

'He seems nice. Moved down from Scotland. A story there,' Becky said.

Andrea wrinkled her nose. 'Not keen on the goatee, though.'

'That's not a problem. Men haven't a clue about looks. What Mac needs is a woman's touch.'

'A woman's touch, Becks. Not a touched woman.'

Becky rolled her eyes. 'God, Andrea, you're on fire today,' she said, leaning over the counter. 'I'll quiz Peter later. See if his mate's up for grabs.'

Graveney turned towards Mac. 'They're talking about you.'

'Really?'

'Definitely. Becky has you in her sights.'

'She's attractive. You haven't ... you know ... have you?'

'No. Becky's a friend, that's all. You could do a lot worse, sex and as much coffee as you can drink.'

Mac smiled. 'I'm not bothered about the coffee if I'm honest.'

'Let's put your love life on hold for the minute and talk about the investigation.'

'Did you speak to Bev Wilson about the post-mortem on Stephen Stewart?' Mac asked.

'Supposed to have finished it the back end of last week, but she was pulled away on to another job. I said I'd ring her this morning. Hopefully, she'll have it completed by then.'

'We've hit a brick wall, Peter. The boys and girls at the station have been interviewing anybody who stayed at Winterton, but so far nothing.'

Graveney sighed. 'Isn't there anyone able to give us information on what went on in there?'

'They all seem reluctant to. Some even seem scared. The trouble is, we can't force anyone to speak out.'

'What about the boy. The one who spoke up against Stevens?'

'Matthew Jacobs. Unfortunately, he's dead. He committed suicide in 2003. Nothing suspicious, though.'

'Christ, Mac. This case is doing my head in. Anyone connected to it is either missing or dead. It's like every time we get a strand of information it unravels and then snaps. There's got to be someone out there who knows something?'

'We'll have to hope and pray for a break.'

Graveney rubbed his chin. 'Whenever did police work rely on serendipity?' He and Mac got up and headed towards the exit.

'Off to catch some criminals, boys?' Becky said.

Mac smiled. 'Hopefully.' Stopping next to her. 'Nice to meet you, Becky. Hope to see you again.'

'I hope so too. Here's a little something for you, Mac. To keep your strength up. On the house.' Handing him a small cake, she smiled.

'Thanks,' he said

Graveney chuckled in amusement at the two of them and winked knowingly at Becky. Andrea rolled her eyes and headed into the storeroom.

Graveney went straight to his office with Mac, closing the door behind them. He spoke to the switchboard and asked them to call Bev Wilson. The two of them waited for the phone to ring. A female voice on the line informed Graveney she was putting him through. Graveney put the speaker phone on, allowing Mac to hear the conversation.

'Hello, Peter,' said Bev Wilson's familiar voice.

'Hi, Bev. I've got my colleague DI Jim Mackay here with me, so no bad language.'

'As if I would. Nice to meet you, Mac. Peter's told me all about you.'

'Now I'm worried,' he said.

Wilson laughed. 'I suppose you're calling about the post-mortems?'

'Yeah. Have you finished them?' Graveney said.

'Just. Shelby died of a gunshot wound to the chest. The bullet went straight through his heart, so he'd have died instantaneously. Stewart, on the other hand, had a gunshot wound to his left-hand side. The wound itself not severe, and I don't think it would have proved fatal if his body hadn't already been compromised.'

'In what way?' Graveney said.

'Without going into technicalities, he had a non-operable brain tumour. He probably had treatment for it, but that was only ever going to delay the inevitable. There were several secondary tumours, and I'm not an expert on this, probably weeks to live. Maybe a month or two.'

'How would this tumour affect him?' Mac said.

'Headaches, double vision, mood swings, hallucinations, etc. All, or maybe only some of these.'

'Nothing to lose in going after Shelby and the others?' Mac said.

'Not really. Another thing. Stewart had a past injury to the right-hand side, probably caused by a knife of some sort. He'd been stitched up by a professional by the look of it. It healed well.'

'This injury ... caused by the knife they found at Vale Farm?' Graveney said.

'Possibly.'

'Thanks, Bev. Invaluable as always,' Graveney said.

'One tries.' She ended the call.

Graveney looked at Mac. 'What do you think?'

Mac rubbed his goatee. 'Not sure. Stewart was obviously stabbed, almost certainly with the knife recovered at Vale Farm. If his wife didn't stab him, and I think we're sure she didn't, who did?'

'Who indeed?' Graveney said.

OCTOBER 2006 – Sandra, woken by the sound of her mobile ringing, rubbed her eyes. Putting on the lamp at the side of her bed, she glanced at the clock. It was 02.05 and checking the phone, saw Colin's name.

'Hi, Colin. What's up?' she asked.

'Sand. Have you seen Jimmy?'

She yawned. 'Jimmy? I dropped him off at the top of your road this afternoon ... about two-thirty. He said he was going to the newsagent and then home.'

'Well, he's never been home. I've tried ringing his mobile, but it keeps going to answer-phone. I've left several messages, but he hasn't got back to me.'

'Have you been in touch with anyone else, apart from me?'

'I've rung everyone I can think of. Sandra, I'm worried. It's not like Jimmy. Did he say anything else to you today?'

'No. We went for lunch in Hartlepool, and then I dropped him off.'

'Should I ring the police?'

'Maybe, although they probably won't do anything until he's missing much longer.'

'What if he's had an accident or something, he could be in the hospital or dead somewhere?' Colin's voice quivered.

'Colin, calm down. I'll ring around some of my friends and see if they've heard from him. If he hasn't turned up by tomorrow morning, we'll go to the police.'

'Ok. Sorry to call you so late, it's just ...'

'I know. Don't worry. We'll find him.'

Sandra rang off and put the phone on the bed. A terrible feeling swept over her, but unsure of what to do, she put her dressing-gown on and headed downstairs.

SEPTEMBER 2014 - DS Jones stood outside in the car park of the police station with his mobile phone pressed to his ear. 'Yes, Jones?' answered Chief Superintendent Oake.

Jones took a deep breath. 'I've got the folder, sir. I recovered it from Stewart's room at the Whitestone hotel like you asked. At great risk to myself.'

'I appreciate what you've done, Tony, and I'll get the money for you,' Oake said.

'The thing is, sir. I've seen inside the folder, and I think it's worth more than £20,000.'

'How much more?' Trying hard to maintain his outward calm.

'I reckon £50,000 is more appropriate, sir.'

'Ok. I'll get the money to you tonight.'

'Thanks, sir.' Ringing off he headed back into the building.

Oake banged the desk with his fist. Opening the contacts on his phone, he pressed a number. 'Bill, it's Charlie, we've got a problem.'

'What sort of problem?' Foxley said.

'Jones isn't playing. He wants £50,000. Not the £20,000 we agreed.'

'How the hell am I going to get another £30,000 in cash at such short notice?'

'You don't have to. Jones has outlived his usefulness. I'll get the folder, but I'm keeping the £20,000.'

'That's fine by me, Charlie, just as long as you get the folder.'

They both rang off, and Oake searched his mobile contacts again. He rang Stephanie Marne.

'I've got a job for you,' he said.

OCTOBER 2006 - Sandra hadn't slept after Colin's phone call. She'd half-heartedly called people who knew Jimmy, but deep down felt what had happened to him was serious. She phoned Colin and told him to report Jimmy missing, and he headed off to the Hartlepool police station to do that. Sandra got Jessica off to school and was sat in the living room at Vale Farm when her mobile rang.

Glancing at Jimmy's name on the screen, she quickly answered. 'Where the hell have you been?' she snapped. 'Colin and I have been worried sick.'

'Sandra Stewart?' An unfamiliar voice asked.

'Yes. Who's this?'

'My name isn't important, Sandra,' Flint said. 'We have a friend of yours here with us. I'd like you to do exactly as I say, do you understand?'

'Yes,' she said.

'If you want to see your friend again, we want the video and anything else on Winterton.'

Sandra put a hand to her mouth. 'Please ... You can have everything, just don't harm Jimmy.'

'I'll phone later to arrange a time and a meeting place. Please don't contact the police. Otherwise, you won't see your friend again. Are we clear on this?'

'Yes,' she said, and Flint rang off.

Sandra sat, stunned. What should she do? The man was obviously desperate. She wasn't keen on meeting him on her own. But if she went to the police and they found out, they would kill Jimmy. Sandra put her hands to her face and began to cry when her mobile rang again. She looked at the name on the screen and answered it. 'Oh, Angela. Please come quickly. I'm in trouble.'

CHAPTER FOURTEEN

SEPTEMBER 2014 - Marne parked her car away from Jones' flat but within walking distance to it. Carrying a plastic shopping bag in her hand, she reached the outside door to the apartment block and checking left and right pressed the buzzer.

'Hello?' Jones said.

'It's Steph, Tony.' Jones buzzed her in.

Marne climbed her way up a flight of stairs and reached a slightly open door. She entered, closing it, making her way into the kitchen where Jones leant up against the table.

'Have you got the money?' Jones said.

Marne grinned. 'Of course. I told you they'd pay what you asked.'

Jones rubbed his hands together. 'Forty for me, and ten for you?'

'That's what we agreed,' Marne said. 'Moving a little closer to him. 'What about a drink to celebrate our good fortune?'

'Vodka ok?'

'Vodka's fine,' Marne said.

Jones turned towards one of the cupboards, pulled out two glasses and a half-full bottle of vodka. Marne made her way over to him and put her hands around his waist, allowing her left hand to slide to his groin. Jones closed his eyes in anticipation as Marne nuzzled his neck and then, deftly, removed a hunting knife from the back pocket of her jeans. She moved the knife up his back, the tip of the blade in line with Jones' heart, and plunged the blade in as she brought her forearm across his neck. Jones emitted a gasp as the knife pierced his body. Marne held on to him briefly before his legs gave way and pulling out the weapon, allowed him to drop to the floor.

She rinsed it under the tap and dropped the knife into the carrier bag. Picking up the folder from the table, Marne flicked through the pages of information inside and pulled a small piece of paper from it. She studied Sandra's handwriting, briefly. Folding it back up and entering the bedroom, Marne placed the piece of paper on top of a wardrobe. Dropping the folder into the bag, and glancing at the inert body of Jones, she quietly left.

Once outside and far enough away, she removed her mobile from her pocket and rang Oake. 'I've got the folder, and Jones is no longer a problem, sir.'

'I knew I could rely on you, Steph. Keep it safe, and I'll see you tomorrow.'

Graveney arrived at the police station early on Tuesday morning. He made himself a cup of coffee, and sat at his desk when Ruth tapped on the door of his office.

'Come in,' he shouted. Ruth entered carrying some paperwork for him, which she placed on his desk.

'Morning, Ruth. How are you?' Noticing she didn't look her usual happy self, he studied her.

'Not too good. I've had some bad news. John Watney died.'

'Died? I only visited him last week.'

'Apparently, he took his own life, sir.'

'I'm sorry to hear that. John seemed like a good bloke.'

'He was. A bloody good copper as well.' She tearfully left his office.

Graveney picked up his phone and spoke to the switchboard. 'Can you get hold of DCI Anderson at North Yorkshire Headquarters please?' Replacing the receiver, he waited a minute or two before the switchboard rang back.

'I've got DCI Anderson on the line, sir,' a female voice said.

'Thanks.' He heard a click. 'Jeff, how are you?' Graveney said.

'Good, Peter. Yourself?' Anderson said.

'I'm in the middle of a real tester at the moment.'

'I've seen the paper. I bet Oake's all over you on this one. It's his neck of the woods where the murders took place, isn't it?'

'Tell me about it. What's the story regarding John Watney?'

'The ex-copper who topped himself?'

Graveney sat back in his chair. 'Yeah. Anything suspicious?'

'No, not really. Watney definitely killed himself.'

'Are you sure?'

'Yeah. There was a visitor on the day, though. A woman. His niece, she told the staff. She'd visited once before, apparently. She left about half-six at night, and a care assistant went in to see him about ten with some cocoa. He was still alive then. We haven't traced the woman, and Watney didn't have a niece.'

'And no one else visited?'

'No. Watney waited until after the care assistant left, and then injected himself.'

'Could he have injected himself?' Graveney said.

'Yeah. He had one of those inserts in his wrist, so even in his poor state of health, we think so. The woman who visited him might have brought the stuff in, or maybe someone else did. It's a crime, of course, assisting a suicide. But given the state he was in, I don't think we'll be pursuing it vigorously.'

'Have you a description of the woman?' Graveney said.

'Not a good one. There's a CCTV camera as you go in or out of the building, but she managed to avoid it, and in all honesty, it could be anyone from the description. Why the interest?'

'I'm working on a historical case. *The Vale Farm Murders*. He was the investigating officer on the original case. I travelled up there last week and talked with him. Seemed strange him dying so soon after. How did he kill himself, anyway?'

'A cocktail of drugs. Hold on a moment.' Anderson searched for the information. 'He took Succinylcholine, a drug that causes paralysis, a sedative of some sort and Potassium Chloride which stops the heart. It's similar to the drugs they use in America for executing prisoners. It would have been quick. He wouldn't have suffered.'

'Glad to hear that. Thanks for your help, Jeff.'

'Anytime. When you're next in the area pop in, and we'll have a pint.'

'I'll do that.' Although satisfied there hadn't been any foul play, it amazed him anyone with anything to do with this case was ending up dead. Graveney was deep in thought when someone knocked on his door.

'Come in.' Raz entered.

'Jones hasn't come in today, sir,' Raz said.

'And?'

'We've tried ringing him, but he's not answering his home phone or his mobile. We've spoken to his girlfriend, and she says he was supposed to go around to her flat last night but didn't turn up. She's worried.'

Graveney sighed. 'You and Steph drive around there. The lazy bugger's probably slept in.'

'Yes, sir.'

OCTOBER 2006 - Angela raced over to her sisters, concerned by what Sandra had told her on the phone. Sandra recounted what she knew to her when she'd arrived.

'You'll have to go to the police,' Angela said.

Sandra rubbed her face. 'But Ang. The man told me he would kill Jimmy if I went to the police.'

'For all we know, Jimmy's dead already. You can't go and meet this guy on your own. I've got an idea. I know a Detective Inspector who works in Middlesbrough. A friend of my dad's and a good copper. Go and see him.'

'What's his name?'

'Detective Inspector Trevor Phillips. I'll drop you off if you like.'

'What about Jessica? She's home soon,' Sandra said.

'I'll wait here for Jessica, and you go to the police.'

'Ok, thanks. I don't know what I'd have done without you?'

'When is Stephen back?'

'Tomorrow,' she said.

'Good. At least Stephen is here to support you.'

Sandra set off for Middlesbrough while Angela waited for Jessica to come home from school. She reached the police station and made her way to the reception. A uniformed sergeant stood at the desk when she arrived. He looked up from his paperwork and smiled at her.

'Can I help?' he said.

'I need to speak with Detective Inspector Phillips,' she said.

'Can I ask what it's in connection with, Mrs ...?'

'Stewart. I really need to speak to him. It's important.'

'If you hang on a minute, I'll see if he's available.'

The sergeant spoke to someone on the phone for a few moments before hanging up. 'If you'd like to follow me, Mrs Stewart.'

Sandra followed the officer into an interview room, sitting on one of the chairs.

'Would you like a drink?' the officer asked.

'No. I'm fine, thanks.'

'Someone will be along shortly.' Leaving the room, he closed the door behind him.

Sandra waited alone for ten minutes in the interview room. Eventually joined by two plain-clothed policemen.

'Mrs Stewart,' said the older of the two officers. 'I'm Superintendent Oake, and this is my colleague, Detective Constable Jones. I'm sorry, but DI Phillips is on another case. Maybe we can help?'

Sandra told the police officers everything she knew, leaving out nothing. The officers jotted down the information, and when they finished they reassured her they would do all they could.

'I want you to go back home.' Oake said. 'I'll have one of my men come over with some equipment to record any more calls you get from this man. Don't tell anyone else about this. We need to ensure we get your friend back safely.'

Jones showed her back out of the station. 'We'll be in touch,' he said, as she got into her car and left.

Sandra thought it a bit strange they told her to go home, but she'd told them she had to get back to Jessica, and maybe they thought it better she was at home with her. She reached Vale Farm and told her sister what happened at the police station. Angela assured Sandra the police knew what they were doing, and to let them handle it. Angela left to go on duty, while Jessica headed upstairs to shower, and Sandra slumped onto a seat in the front room. Her mobile rang with Jimmy's number. Reluctant to answer as the police hadn't arrived yet, but she felt impelled to do so.

'Hello,' she said.

'You've been a naughty girl,' Flint said. 'Didn't I explain to you about what would happen if you went to the police?'

Sandra was stunned, how did they know? Maybe they'd watched the house, she thought.

'When the police arrive,' Flint said. 'I'd like you to tell them it was all a joke. That Jimmy had only been fooling around. You do this, and you'll see your friend again. If they want they can ring Jimmy's mobile and speak to him. Deviate from any of this and Jimmy dies. Do you understand Sandra?'

'I understand,' she said.

'I'll ring tomorrow.' He rang off.

Sandra heard a car pull up outside the house and went to answer the door, almost in shock. She composed herself and opened the door. The DC from the police station and a thick-set uniformed officer stood outside.

'Can we come in, Sandra?' Jones said.

She beckoned them inside, and they followed her into the front room. 'I'm afraid you've had a wasted journey,' she said. 'Jimmy's been in touch. Apparently, a prank on his part. I've gone mad at him, but he said he didn't expect me to go to the police.'

'This is serious,' Jones said. 'I could charge you both for wasting police time.'

'I'm sorry. I'll ring Jimmy if you like, and you can speak to him.'

Sandra phoned Jimmy's mobile and handed her handset over to Jones. Jones left the room, and Sandra heard him shouting at someone on the phone. She glanced at the uniform officer, who appeared a little sinister. More like a thug than a policeman, a large sticking-plaster on his neck only adding to his menace. Jones re-entered the room.

'I'll speak to my commanding officer, Mrs Stewart, and he'll decide if there are any charges against you and your friend. I can't emphasise how stupid it is. I've given him a good dressing down, and we'll be back in touch.' He and the uniformed officer headed for the front door.

'I'm sorry,' Sandra said. And closed the door behind them. She leant against the wall and started to cry, but composed herself when Jessica appeared at the top of the stairs.

She phoned Angela and lied about what happened, sticking to the story she'd told the police. Angela, who was angry with Jimmy for pulling such a stunt, was sympathetic with Sandra. Sandra rang off and after getting Jessica to bed, sat on the settee in the front room feeling utterly helpless and wishing Stephen home.

The two policemen drove away from Vale Farm and stopping in a lay-by, Jones took out his mobile phone and called Oake.

'Yes, Jones?'

'We've seen her, and she's terrified. I don't think we'll have any more problems.'

'Let me talk to Flint,' Oake said.

Jones handed his mobile over to the uniformed officer, who was busy removing the large sticking-plaster from his neck, revealing the spider's web tattoo below.

'Yes, sir?' Flint said.

'What have you done with the journalist?'

'We're going to dump him tonight.'

'I don't want his body turning up anywhere. Bury it near the kid's bodies. And Flint, for Christ's sake. Do not let anyone see you. You understand?'

'Perfectly.'

'I'll get Shelby to ring tomorrow regarding Mrs Stewart. We may need some more leverage to make sure she complies.'

SEPTEMBER 2014 - Marne and Hussain stood outside Jones' apartment. They buzzed several times but had no answer. Hussain suggested getting in touch with the landlord to gain entry, in case anything had happened to him, Marne agreed. The owner promised he'd send someone over, and the two of them waited patiently. Eventually, a small man wearing a blue uniform, and the name *Nunthorpe Estates* emblazoned on the front of it, arrived. They showed him their badges, as Marne introduced the two of them. The man, suitably satisfied, entered a code on the keypad to gain access to the building. The two officers followed the man up to Jones' flat, stopping outside while he found the right key. He pushed open the door to the apartment, and Marne and Hussain stepped inside.

Hussain paused 'Do you mind waiting here, sir?' He followed Marne along the hallway.

'Tony,' shouted Marne as they headed into the front room. She listened. 'Raz, check the kitchen. I'll look in the bedroom.'

Hussain nodded and pushed open the kitchen door. He stopped and stared at the dead body of Jones, lying on the floor surrounded by a huge pool of blood. 'Steph!' he shouted. 'In here.'

Graveney was on the phone to Heather when someone tapped on his office door, and Mac ambled in. Graveney motioned for him to sit, which he did.

'I'll be there about six?' Graveney said.

'If you come earlier, I can do you some tea.'

'Five ok?' Graveney glanced across at Mac who frowned at him. 'Listen, Heather, I'm going to have to go. Something's come up.'

'See you at five.'

'What's up, Mac?'

'Marne and Hussain are at Jones' flat. They've found his body. He's been stabbed to death.'

Graveney stood up from his chair scarcely able to take in what Mac said. 'Stabbed?'

'Yeah. Bev Wilson and her team are on their way over there. I've informed Phillips. He's upstairs with Oake.'

Graveney rubbed his chin. 'What do you think, Mac?'

Mac shook his head. 'I don't know what to think. But there's something not right about this.'

'If I were paranoid, I'd say Jones' death is linked to the investigation,' Graveney said. 'Jones was ... a bit of a dark horse. Something about him that didn't ring true. Something beneath the surface I could never decipher.'

'Thin-slicing?'

'Yeah. A feeling Jones was hiding something. An arrogance about him. As if he knew more than you. Watching you struggle to work something out when he knew the answer already. If I'm honest, I didn't much like Jones, but no one deserves to die like that.'

'What do you want to do?' Mac said.

'Grab your coat. We'll go to Jones' flat.' Mac stood up to walk out.

Graveney stood too. 'When I went to see Watney at the care home, he said something strange.'

'What?'

'He told me not to trust anyone at the station except Phillips.'

'Why Phillips?'

'A decent copper, he said.'

Mac rubbed his beard. 'If Watney had suspicions there were ... *are* ... bent coppers here, we'd better tread carefully.'

Graveney nodded. 'Any relevant information goes no further than you and me.'

'Ok,' Mac said.

CHAPTER FIFTEEN

Graveney and Mac arrived at Jones' flat, greeted by a street full of police vehicles. They trudged up the stairs passing officers from Forensics coming in and out of the building. Graveney and Mac stopped outside the flat and put on white overalls and plastic overshoes. Bev Wilson glanced up from her notepad and noticing the two officers beckoned them in. Graveney stopped at the threshold of the kitchen, the body of Jones lying dead on the floor, while Forensics operatives took photos.

'Bev,' Graveney said. 'What have you managed to find out?'

'I'm sorry about this, Peter. It's always worse when it's one of your own. It appears he knew whoever killed him. No sign of forced entry. A single stab wound in the middle of his back that almost certainly went straight through his heart. There's no indication of any defence wound. So, I can only assume the murderer got very close or surprised him.'

'Possibly a female?' Graveney said.

'What makes you think that?'

'Jones was straight. I assume anyone able to get that near to him would be female.'

'Maybe,' she said. 'Or Jones might just have known the murderer well. He had his back to them, getting some drinks, I think. We found two glasses and a bottle of vodka on the worktop.'

Graveney nodded. 'So, Jones was getting a drink for himself and whoever killed him when he was stabbed?' Graveney turned Mac around and simulated what he thought happened.

'You could be right. Jones has a bruise on the throat as if someone grasped him with a free arm while stabbing with the other. We've dusted for prints, and we're checking for fibres, so hopefully, that'll help us catch who killed him.'

'Anything else we need to know?' Mac asked.

Wilson lowered her voice. 'We found some cocaine in a bedside drawer. It looks as if Jones was a user.' She put a hand in her pocket and took something out. 'I found this on one of the wardrobes.' Showing Mac and Graveney a piece of paper within a clear plastic bag.

Graveney read it and passed it to Mac. In capital letters, written, *POSSIBLE BURIAL SITE.* Under this, a twelve-figure number, and below this, two names. *GEORGE APPLEBY* and *GREGORY WATTS.* Mac jotted down this information.

'Has anyone else seen this?' Graveney whispered.

'No not yet,' Wilson said. 'Why?'

'Do me a favour. Keep this to yourself for the moment. I'll speak to you later about it, but I'd appreciate it if you'd do your usual checks on it. We'll get you another piece of handwriting for a possible match.'

'Whose handwriting do you think it is?' Wilson said.

'Sandra Stewart's.'

'Right. I can't hold on to it indefinitely, its evidence after all, but I can give you a couple of days.'

'Thanks. Appreciate that.' Graveney patted Wilson on the arm.

'Is there something else I should know, here?' she asked.

'When you're finished, give me a ring. I'll meet you at The Dubliner's on Baker Street.'

'Yeah, ok.' Mac and Graveney made their way out of the flat and headed off up the road. Once outside and out of earshot of anyone, Mac turned to Graveney. 'Those two names were boys who stayed at Winterton.'

'Are you sure?'

Mac stared at Graveney. 'The only reason I remember their names, is because they absconded and were never heard from again.'

'We may have found them. The numbers could be a grid reference,' Graveney said. The two of them headed back to the station.

OCTOBER 2006 - Reverend James sat in the study of the vicarage, drinking his usual morning coffee when his mobile rang. He glanced at the name of Shelby on the screen and hesitated before answering. 'Hello, David.'

'Reverend, we've got a job for you,' Shelby said.

'What sort of job?'

'We want you to collect a young girl for us and take her to a farmhouse. I'm sending Sheila Johnson to help you.'

'A young girl. Are we talking kidnapping?' the Reverend whispered.

'Her mother has some information we need. We want you to get the daughter to persuade her to play ball.'

'I'm not sure I'm comfortable doing this. I mean, we're talking about an abduction.'

Shelby interrupted him. 'Listen, Reverend. *The Man* wants you to do this, you understand? Unless you want the police or your Bishop to discover your liking for young boys. Is that what you want, Reverend?'

'Of course not, but I'm not sure I'll have the nerve.'

'That's why I'm sending Sheila. She's got more balls than both of us. Pick up the girl and do what Sheila says. Payback Reverend. If you don't want to do it let me know, and I'll make a telephone call.'

'No, No. I'll do it.'

'Phone Sheila and she'll pick you up. She knows the address to take the girl to. And Reverend, make sure you're not seen.'

'Yes, David.'

SEPTEMBER 2014 - Graveney and Mac met Bev Wilson and attempted to explain what they thought was going on. They told Wilson they suspected Jones was knee-deep in this case, and in some way connected to the deaths of Sandra and Jessica Stewart. They explained to Wilson they thought the numbers on the paper she'd recovered from Jones' flat were in fact, grid references. They believed the grid references indicated the location of the burial site of two boys who had gone missing, from Winterton Boys' Home, in the 1990s. They'd already checked the numbers and discovered the location was on the estate of Wyndbourne Hall. They wanted to dig some more before they approached DCI Phillips about obtaining a search warrant.

Phillips would treat Jones' death as a separate investigation, they hoped, to the one they were working on. But everything relied on Wilson keeping quiet regarding the paper she found. Wilson agreed, mainly because of her own reservations about the case but also out of respect and judgement for Graveney. Wilson told them she could hold onto the evidence until the following week and claim it was found on a second sweep of the flat. Graveney and Mac, relieved, knew what they were doing was highly irregular and likely to jeopardise the case if it ever came out. Given the stakes, they thought the risk worth taking.

Mac returned to the station to finish up some things, including ringing Sandra Stewart's mother to obtain a sample of Sandra's handwriting. Graveney headed across to Heather's.

OCTOBER 2006 - Jessica Stewart wandered along the country lane on her way home from school towards Vale Farm. A car pulled up ahead of her on the opposite side of the road, and a lady popped her head out.

'Jessica,' she shouted. And watched as Jessica made her way over to the car.

'Yes,' she said, politely.

'Your mum has sent us to pick you up,' the woman said. 'Mummy's been held up at work and wants us to take you to your Gran's.'

'I'm not supposed to talk to strangers.'

'That's splendid, Jessica, but we're not strangers. We're friends with your mum and dad.'

'I suppose it's all right.' She climbed into the back of the car.

'I've got you a drink, Jessica.' Handing her a bottle of Coke.

'Mummy doesn't allow me to drink Coke. She says it's full of sugar.'

'Well, we won't tell her if you don't.'

Jessica thought for a moment before opening up the bottle and taking a swig. It tasted unusual, but not unpleasant. She hadn't had Coke before, so continued to drink it as the car drove off in the opposite direction to Vale Farm.

Sandra Stewart stayed at Vale Farm all day waiting for the man to call about Jimmy. She had spoken to Stephen on the telephone when he landed at Newcastle Airport and lied that there was something wrong with the car, so he'd opted to get a taxi. Sandra didn't want to leave the house and wondered what to tell Stephen when he arrived home. She glanced at the clock and realising Jessica would be back soon, decided to begin tea. As Sandra stood, her mobile rang. With dread, she viewed Jimmy's number on the screen.

'Hello,' she said.

'Are you alone?' the male voice asked.

Sandra, reluctant to say she was but felt she had little choice, answered. 'Yes. Is Jimmy ok?'

'You can't help Jimmy anymore,' he said. 'You've got to think about yourself now.'

Sandra put her hand to her mouth, instantly understanding the implications of what he said.

'Where's your daughter? Where's Jessica?'

'Jessica?' she replied.

'Listen carefully. If you want to see Jessica again, you'll do exactly as I say. I'll phone later with an address of where to meet me. Bring along the video and anything else you have. Please don't inform the police like last time, or you won't see your daughter again. Have you got that?'

'Yes,' she said. Sandra dropped the phone in shock. Sobbing uncontrollably, she fell to her knees as she heard Stephen's key in the front door.

SEPTEMBER 2014 - Graveney arrived around five o'clock at Heather's. She had prepared a meal for him, and they ate together. He'd bought Luke a new Middlesbrough top for the match, which his nephew proudly wore.

'What time are you leaving?' Heather said.

'I thought about seven.'

'That's fine with me,' Heather said. 'Maddie's coming around later for a girlie night in. Make sure you have something warm on, Luke. It's a bit chilly out.'

'That's why I got you a bigger size,' Graveney said. 'You can wear it over your hoodie or something.'

'It's fantastic, Uncle Peter. Thanks. I'm going over to Tommy's to show it to him.'

'Make sure you're back before seven,' Graveney said. Luke turned, and raced out.

'I will.'

Heather put a hand on his. 'Thanks for taking him.'

'He's family. I love spending time with Luke.'

'I know. I've read the papers, I thought you'd be tied up.'

'To be honest, I'm glad to get my mind off the investigation.'

'Are you going to stay over tonight?'

Graveney smiled. 'If you want me to?'

'I always want you to.' She forced a smile and squeezed his hand.

'I'd love to stay then,' Graveney said.

'I better get on with the clearing up.'

'I'll give you a hand.' Gathering up the plates from the table, he followed her into the kitchen.

Maddie and Heather sat in the front room of Heather's home with a large glass of wine each.

'Where's Luke?' Maddie asked.

'He's gone to the match with Peter.'

'Peter ... And I suppose he'll be staying over tonight?'

Heather shrugged. 'Probably.'

'You're not going to take my advice and look for someone else?'

Heather rolled her eyes. 'You're not going to lecture me, are you? I thought you understood.'

'I do understand. It's just you have so much to offer someone. There are men out there who'd jump at the chance of dating you. I could fix you up with a friend of a friend if you like?'

'No thanks, Mad. I'll pass on a blind date.'

'I'd introduce you first. A group of girls from where I work are going out this week. Why don't you come along?'

Heather sighed. 'It's not for me.'

Maddie sipped her wine and then put down her glass. 'What happened to Luke's dad?' Changing the subject abruptly as Heather looked up. 'Doug wasn't it?'

Heather's eyes widened. The question taking her by surprise. 'Yes ... Doug. He moved abroad. Spain, I think.'

'Doesn't he ever get in touch? Isn't he bothered about his son?'

Heather shifted in her chair and replenished hers and Maddie's glasses. 'Doug isn't Luke's dad,' she said. Her eye's dropping eyes down.

'But I thought you said he was. If Doug isn't, then who is?' Maddie looked at Heather, who put her hands on her face. 'It's not Peter is it?'

Heather nodded at Maddie and blew out her cheeks.

'Does he know?'

'No, he doesn't,' Heather snapped. 'And I'd rather it stayed that way,'

'But surely he suspects?'

'He was drunk. I doubt he remembered anything of that evening. Doug was away for the weekend and Peter pitched up here, and well you know.' Heather shrugged. 'He assumed the baby was Doug's, but unfortunately, Doug couldn't have kids. He told me when we first met. When he found out I was pregnant, he left.'

'But if you told him, Heather, Peter might stay with you.'

Heather stood and walked across to the window and stared outside. 'I'm not a charity case. I want Peter to want me for me, not out of some misplaced loyalty.'

Maddie stood too. 'But it's not fair he doesn't know Luke is his.'

Heather spun around. 'I don't want Peter to know. If you tell him any of this.' She looked upwards. 'I'll never forgive you.'

'Of course I wouldn't tell him.' Maddie strode across and hugged the now tearful Heather.

Graveney woke early, gathering his clothes from Heather's bedroom before quietly making his way to the spare room. After returning with Luke from the match he and Heather talked for a while, enjoying a glass of wine until satisfied Luke was asleep. Only then, did Heather lead him upstairs. They'd undressed and slipped into bed together, making love quietly as Luke slept next door. Graveney smiled when he remembered the night before, a warm glow washing over him. Heather was a fantastic lover. Possibly the most generous lover Graveney had ever known. Her sole intention seemed to centre on his enjoyment. Graveney always tried hard to reciprocate, and it usually made for an wonderful experience for both of them.

Graveney's thoughts of Heather were interrupted by images of his encounters with Marne. The memories elbowing their way into his mind. As much as his love-making with Heather was tender and thoughtful, his sex with Marne was visceral. He couldn't help but compare the two and having them held up next to each only other emphasised the differences even more. He knew his and Marne's relationship was dangerous, and in some ways frightening. And although it sounded somewhat cliché to say it, Marne was like a drug. He couldn't imagine making love with Heather the same way he did with Marne, and he definitely couldn't believe sex with Marne being anything other than what it was. The two sexual orbits Graveney inhabited with Heather and Marne, never likely to cross. As he thought about it more, he found himself getting incredibly turned on. Tempted to sneak back into Heather's room but, it was the dark, dangerous, animalistic memories of Marne he tapped into as he made his way to the bathroom to relieve himself and shower.

OCTOBER 2006 - The Reverend and Sheila Johnson drove with the sleeping Jessica to a deserted farmhouse just off the road to Northallerton. They carried her into the house and up the stairs to a bedroom at the back of the building. Johnson gave her an injection to keep her sedated, and the two of them waited for Flint.

Flint arrived shortly after them. He pulled up outside the property and took out his mobile phone. 'Yes, Flint,' Shelby said.

'We've got the girl. What do you want us to do?'

'I've spoken with Oake. He wants no loose ends.'

'Killing them both is messy.'

'Be creative. This ends here. Make it look like a robbery, a random act of violence, whatever you want, but get the stuff from the woman and eliminate her.'

'Ok.'

Flint entered the farmhouse and walked into the kitchen where the Reverend and Johnson stood waiting.

'Where's the girl?' Flint asked.

'Upstairs,' Johnson said.

'What are you going to do?' the Reverend asked.

'Don't you worry about that.' He smiled. 'You two can go.'

'You're not going to ....?' The Reverend couldn't bring himself to say the words.

'Reverend,' Flint said. 'She's seen your faces. It's either her or you two. What would you rather I do?' He turned towards the door.

'But she's only a child.' The Reverend said, and took hold of Flint's arm.

Flint spun around and grabbed him by the throat, pushing him up against the wall. 'Listen, you stupid tosser. Get your things and fuck off. Otherwise, I'll do you as well.'

The Reverend slumped against the wall, cowering beneath his stare.

Johnson got up from the chair and pulled him by the arm. 'Come on, Rev,' she said. The two of them leaving quickly.

Flint climbed the stairs to the bedroom and pushed open the door. The girl lay unconscious on the bed. He tiptoed over to the sleeping Jessica and picked up a pillow next to her.

SEPTEMBER 2014 - Graveney enjoyed a lovely breakfast with Heather and Luke. Luke quickly finished his and went upstairs to get ready for school, leaving Heather and Graveney alone.

'Thanks again for taking Luke to the football.'

'I'm his uncle,' he said. 'It's covered in the job description. I enjoyed it. I'll take him to a couple of league matches if I can. I think The Boro might get promoted this season.'

'What's the new manager like?'

'He's not bad. I've a feeling we've got a good one there.'

'Do you need a lift to work?' she asked.

'No. Mac's picking me up from here.'

'Is he your new DS?'

'No. Mac's a DI. He's moved down from Scotland. He should be here shortly.' Trying to avoid talking about Marne.

There was a knock on the front door. Graveney got up and answered it, beckoning Mac inside. 'Mac, this is Heather, my sister-in-law.'

Mac held out his hand and smiled at her. Heather reached for his hand and shook it, smiling back. 'Nice to meet you, Mac,' she said.

'Likewise.'

Graveney kissed Heather on her cheeks, and he and Mac headed towards the door. 'Bye, Luke!' he said, as he paused at the Threshold.

Luke appeared at the top of the stairs. 'See you, Uncle Peter.'

Graveney climbed into the car next to Mac, who started up the engine.

Mac smiled, looking across at Graveney. 'So, that's the lovely Heather?'

Graveney glanced back towards the house. 'Yeah. That's Heather.'

CHAPTER SIXTEEN

OCTOBER 2006 - Sandra and Stephen Stewart waited impatiently for the phone call. She had broken down and told her husband everything. He wanted to inform the police but changed his mind when Sandra told him about Jimmy. Sandra went upstairs to the master bedroom, and Stephen followed her. He walked into the room and found her on her hands and knees putting something into the cupboard in the corner.

'What are you doing?' he asked.

'This is my secret place,' she said. 'I always had them as a child. I used to hide things precious to me. Stupid really, I know.'

'What are you hiding there?'

'She unfastened the locket from around her neck and placed it in a small metal tin. It's my locket with Jessica's picture in it. I'm going to leave it here until we have our baby back.' She began to cry.

She put the box under the floorboards, replaced the board she had removed and then the carpet. Stephen walked over and put his arms around her.

'I want my baby back.' She sobbed.

'I know.' He kissed her. 'I'll get her back. I'll bring her home.'

They waited into the next day when the call they had expected and dreaded, arrived. Stephen answered it. 'Hello,' he said.

Silence on the line for a moment or two, before a voice answered. 'Who's that?'

'Stephen Stewart.'

'Can I talk to your wife, please?' Flint said.

'Sandra's told me everything. All we want is our daughter back. You can have the stuff, and we promise we won't inform the police. Please. We just want Jessica back.'

The phone went dead as the man hung up. Stephen stared in horror at the mobile as Sandra grabbed him by the arm.

'He's hung up,' he said

'Oh, God, Stephen. What are we going to do?'

The phone sounded again, and Stephen answered it.

'I want you to follow these instructions to the letter. Do not deviate from them. Sandra is to stay at the house and not attempt to contact anyone. We'll know if you get in touch with the police and if you do, you'll never see your daughter again. Do you understand?' Flint hissed.

'Yes,' Stewart said.

Flint gave Stewart directions of where to meet him, and Sandra jotted them down as they spoke. He told him to be there for seven o'clock that evening and hung up. Sandra and Stephen hugged each other.

SEPTEMBER 2014 - Graveney and Mac arrived at Middlesbrough police station. As they'd secretly hoped, Oake and Phillips were treating Jones' murder as a separate investigation. Phillips had scheduled a meeting for 10.00 am. Mac had managed to speak to Sandra Stewart's mother and obtain an example of her handwriting, for comparison with the piece of paper recovered from Jones' flat. He despatched a PC to collect it, explaining that they needed it as another line of enquiry was being pursued. Graveney and Mac, after talking to their team, returned to Graveney's office to discuss their plan of action.

Marne made her way up to DCI Phillips' office and tapped on the door before entering.

'Sit down, Steph,' Phillips said. 'What's your take on the Jones murder?'

'Not sure. Oake hasn't mentioned anything, so I'm not certain if he had anything to do with it.'

'Would he tell you if he had?'

'I'm sure he would. Without going into details, I've managed to get close to him.'

Phillips stared at Marne, realising what she had implied. 'Steph, you're like a daughter to me, you know that. I don't want you to get in too deep. If he found out you're working with me, you'd be in danger.'

She smiled. 'Don't worry. I can look after myself. If I had any reservations, I'd tell you.'

Phillips nodded. 'Are we any closer to finding out more about the paedophile ring? It's essential we amass evidence that'll hold up in court. We want it to stick.'

'I'm getting closer. Oake trusts me implicitly, and hopefully, we can get what we need soon.'

'Who do you think killed Jones?' he asked.

'I'm not sure. Apparently, Jones had a drug habit, and we don't know what other information the investigation will throw up. Have you decided who'll lead the investigation into his death?'

'I've put DI Robertson on it. At this moment, there is no reason to assume his death is in any way connected to the Vale Farm Murders. Oake, of course, wants us to treat them as separate enquiries.'

Marne smiled again. 'He would do, wouldn't he?'

'Be careful, Steph. Don't put yourself in any unnecessary danger, and keep me in the loop.'

'I will.'

Graveney and Mac made their way up to Phillips' office.

Phillips waved them in. 'Sit down, lads.' Pointing at the chairs opposite his desk. 'What do we know about Jones' death?'

'We spoke with Bev Wilson yesterday, and she believes Jones knew the killer. Whoever it was, got very close to him. There was no sign of any struggle. We suspect someone he was intimate with, probably female, murdered him.'

'What about his girlfriend?'

'I was speaking with DI Robertson,' Mac said. 'His girlfriend has a cast iron alibi but, apparently, Jones was a bit of a ladies' man. There's possibly someone else who we aren't aware of yet.'

'Crime of passion?' Phillips said.

Mac nodded. 'Maybe. Robertson's team are digging into Jones' life, and he does have a few skeletons in his closet.'

'Such as?'

'A drug-user, and he owed money to online gambling sites. He was often seen in his local betting office placing large wagers – sometimes in the hundreds.'

'Oake wants it treating as a separate enquiry at the moment, so I think that's what's going to happen.'

Mac and Graveney briefly glanced at each other. Graveney nodded. 'I think that's probably the right thing to do, sir. Unless something to the contrary turns up.'

Phillips sat back in his chair. 'What about your investigation? Any further forward?'

'We're currently pursuing a few lines of enquiry, sir,' Graveney said. 'Nothing concrete yet.'

'Ok, boys. I've got a meeting with the brass in ten minutes. Keep me informed? You can't imagine the amount of pressure I'm getting over this.'

'We can, sir,' Graveney said. He and Mac stood and left.

Once outside, Graveney looked across at Mac. 'So far, so good. If the handwriting matches, we'll tell Phillips.'

'We'll have to,' Mac said. 'Apparently Foxley, who owns the Wyndbourne Estate, is an acquaintance of Oakes. You can imagine what he's going to say if we ask for a warrant to start digging on it.'

Graveney smiled. 'We'd better make sure to cross all the t's, and dot all the i's then.'

OCTOBER 2006 - Flint and Dec carried Jessica's wrapped body and placed it in the boot of their car. Flint turned to Dec. 'I'm going with Jones to Vale Farm. She already knows us from our previous visit there, and won't take much convincing we've got her husband and daughter safe. Get the stuff from Stewart, and then kill him. Once you've done that, text me he's dead, and we'll finish her off.'

'Is Johnson meeting me here?' Dec said.

'Yeah. Once we've killed both, bring the girl's body over to us so it looks as if Stewart murdered them and then legged it. Bury Stewart's body with the others.'

'I'll need a gun.'

Flint shook his head. 'We've had a think about it. Do Stewart with a knife, and we'll plant it at Vale Farm. When the police find the bodies and the knife with his DNA on it, they'll assume Stewart and his wife fought, and she stabbed him before he fled.'

'Bit risky, using a knife.'

'I know, mate, but that's the way we want it done.'

The two of them turned around as a car pulled into the drive of the farmhouse, stopping nearby. As Roger Johnson got out of the vehicle, Flint made his way over to it and got into the passenger seat next to Jones.

'Park near to Vale Farm,' Flint said to Jones, as they drove off.

SEPTEMBER 2014 - Mac and Graveney were sat in Graveney's office discussing the case when the phone call from Bev finally arrived. 'Hi, Peter. It's Bev.'

'What have you got for us?' Switching his mobile onto speakerphone.

'We've got a match on the handwriting. It's definitely Sandra Stewart's.'

'So, what are you going to do now?' Graveney said

'I'm taking a couple of my team over to Jones' flat to do a second sweep. We'll discover it while I'm there. Nudge, nudge.'

'Thanks for this, Bev,' Graveney said. 'We appreciate the risk you're taking.'

'You do know what this means, don't you?' she said.

'Yes. Jones was in some way linked to Sandra Stewart's death. Otherwise, why would he have a vital piece of evidence at his flat?'

'Have you considered the possibility someone planted it?' she said.

'Mac and I have discussed it, and it does throw open lots of other questions. There's no way Jones would take evidence home with him if acting legit. Maybe he was blackmailing someone. Maybe there was other evidence the killer managed to recover but unknown to them, Jones had hidden what you found.'

'Where did he get it from?' she said.

'Stephen Stewart told me he had evidence of some sort at his room at the Whitestone Hotel, but when we got there his room had been ransacked. The thing is, when Marne and I arrived, Jones was already there. It's possible he had enough time to gain entry to the room and steal the evidence.'

'Who was he working on behalf of?'

'We don't know that, but the numbers on the piece of paper are grid references. The location they indicate is on the Wyndbourne Hall Estate, owned by William Foxley. I'd say his name's in the frame. I know you'll be discreet, Bev, but keep your diary clear for the next couple of days. When the piece of paper is brought forward, we'll be asking for a search warrant to dig on the estate.'

'I certainly will. I'll ring you when I discover the paper. If you know what I mean?' She laughed.

'One more thing,' Graveney said. 'When you find it, make sure you tell Phillips yourself?'

'Why Phillips?'

'Let's just say,' he said. 'At this moment we're not sure who's involved in this, but we're kind of confident Phillips isn't.'

'Will do.' She hung up.

'What next then?' Mac said.

'We wait for the shit to hit the fan.'

OCTOBER 2006 - Stephen Stewart pulled on his jacket and gathered up the video and Sandra's notebook. He turned to face his wife as she walked over to him and put her arms around him.

'I'm so sorry for all of this. If I ...' She stopped as Stephen put his finger to her lips.

'You did it for the right reasons. Those two boys, and maybe more, deserve to have their stories told. The animals who did that to those kids need catching. I'll bring our baby home, and then we'll put this all behind us.'

'But what happens if it's a trap?'

'If I've not been in touch within an hour, phone the police and tell them everything.' He kissed her tenderly on her head.

'I love you.' Her tears flowed freely down her cheeks.

'I love you too, and I always will.' Tearing himself away from her, he headed towards the door. Glancing back at his wife one last time as she touched her lips with her fingers, gently blowing him a kiss. Stewart reciprocated, and then he was gone.

Stewart got into his car and drove off, not noticing a parked vehicle up the lane from the house. He headed towards Swainby, eventually pulling his car into a lay-by within walking distance of the meeting place. He reached into the foot-well, picked up a large wrench he had put there earlier, and slipped it into the left-hand pocket of his jacket. Removing the keys from the ignition, he thought for a moment. What if he had to make a quick getaway? He didn't want to be fumbling with keys in the ignition. He decided to take a chance and leave them in the car in case it all went wrong. His mind raced with possible scenarios. Stewart put his head on the steering wheel and tried to compose himself again. Pushing the keys back in the ignition, he got out of the car and nervously walked along the bridle path.

Sandra Stewart heard a car pull into the drive of the farmhouse and footsteps approach the door. She tentatively walked towards it and looked through the glass. Outside she saw the uniform of a policeman and what she supposed was a plain-clothed officer with him. She opened the door to the two police officers from a couple of nights ago, not knowing what to say.

'Mrs Stewart, can we come in?' Jones said.

'Yes, of course.' They followed her into the front room.

'We've watched you closely. We know what's been going on over the last couple of days. We know about Jessica's abduction, and we're aware your husband, Stephen, has gone to meet the abductors tonight. We have police following him, and we hope to apprehend the culprits and bring Stephen and Jessica home safely.'

'I'm sorry I didn't tell you. I was scared,' she said, through tears.

'Don't worry. Go and make us all a cup of tea, and we'll wait for a call from my colleagues.'

'Yes, of course.' Sandra got up, glancing at the sinister looking uniformed officer, with a large sticking-plaster on his neck.

Stephen Stewart reached the end of the track. A car parked with its full beam on prevented him from seeing into it. The shape of a man strode towards him and stopped six feet away.

'Have you got the stuff, Stewart?' He sounded different from the voice on the phone.

'Yes.' Holding out the video and book for him to see.

The man stepped forward, snatching them from him. 'Is this everything?'

'Yes. It's everything we have. Can I please see my daughter now?' He pleaded.

The man stepped closer to Stewart, close enough for him to feel the man's breath on his face. Stewart felt his heart-rate increase as he slipped his left hand into his pocket and gripped the wrench.

'You know, Stewart, you shouldn't meddle in other people's affairs, my friend.'

As the man leant nearer, Stewart spotted the knife in his gloved hand. The man thrust the weapon forward and Stewart, expecting the attack, almost got out of the way of the blade, but winced as it sliced along the right-hand side of his body. He reacted quickly pulling the wrench from his pocket and swinging it wildly, catching the man a glancing blow on the side of his head. The man dropped to the ground, stunned. Stewart turned and fled, running as fast as his legs would carry him. He pushed any thoughts of Jessica from his head, knowing the implications of what happened. His thoughts now with Sandra and heading back towards his car, Stewart saw in the distance a figure next to it. He jumped behind a hedge and reasoned he couldn't risk going back to the vehicle. He'd have to set off on foot. If he crossed the fields, along bridle paths and through shortcuts he'd discovered on his walks in the countryside, he guessed the farmhouse was only twenty minutes away. He stumbled on, his heart pounding, his thoughts consumed with Sandra and her safety. Putting his hand in his pocket, he realised his mobile was missing, and this spurred him on more. He had to get back home.

Johnson heard footsteps along the farm track and turned around to see a bloodied Dec, emerge into the lay-by.

'The bastard got away,' Dec said.

'He's left his car keys in the ignition, and the stupid idiot's forgotten his mobile,' Johnson said.

'Good. Get it across to Vale Farm. I'll get the other car and phone Jones.'

Flint and Jones sat quietly with Sandra Stewart in the front room of Vale Farm, when Jones' mobile rang. Jones got up from the chair and marched into the hall to answer the call, closing the door behind him, out of earshot of Sandra.

'Yes, Dec?' he said.

'We've got the stuff, but Stewart got away. He's injured and on foot, so if he's headed your way, it'll take him some time to get there. Johnson's bringing Stewart's car across, and I'll bring mine. We'll be about five minutes.'

'Ok,' Jones said.

Jones re-entered the living room, feigning a conversation on his mobile. Sandra Stewart stood up expectantly, not noticing the uniformed officer pick up a tie from the back of the settee and move behind her.

'They've got them safe, Mrs Stewart. I've got to take you to the police station.'

'Thank God,' Sandra said, as Jones nodded to the uniformed officer.

Flint put the tie around Sandra's throat. Sandra desperately grabbed at the tie to loosen it, but this encouraged Flint to tighten it further. He pulled and tugged as Sandra struggled to breathe. His strength incredible. He lifted her slight frame off the floor as her legs kicked wildly, and she battled for her life. Flint squeezed more as Sandra continued to struggle, kicking and thrashing to somehow escape. Flint held firm pulling ever tighter, the struggling Sandra now on top of him as they both fell to the floor. She kicked and battled as light-headedness, through lack of oxygen, took effect. Eventually, her efforts subsided as her energy failed, her movements became more sporadic and then slowed until she stopped moving altogether. Her eyes drifted across to Jones as her last moments alive sped by. Jones impassively looked on, nonchalantly putting on a pair of latex gloves. Her movement stopped entirely and Flint, sweating from his exertions, allowed Sandra's inert body to fall away from him.

Jones quickly brought Flint up to speed regarding the events with Stephen Stewart. Flint thought for a moment as a plan formed in his head.

'Get her legs.'

'Why?' Jones asked.

'We're going to put her outside.'

Jones frowned. 'Outside?'

'It'll muddy the waters regarding DNA. Look.' He pointed to the window. 'It's starting to rain.'

They opened the French doors leading to the garden and carried Sandra Stewart's body along the path before they put her down. Flint glanced across at a broken swing hanging from the tree in the back garden. The seat still connected to one of the ropes trailing on the ground, the other rope hanging freely from a branch.

'We'll tie her up on the rope,' Flint said.

Jones, though puzzled, complied as they carried her across towards the apple tree. Flint tied the rope around her neck, allowing her to hang loosely from it.

'It won't fool the police,' Jones said. He followed Flint back towards the house. Flint ignored him and stopped outside the French doors. He took out two pairs of plastic overshoes from his pocket and handed a set to Jones. They headed towards the front door as Johnson, closely followed by Dec, arrived.

'Put the girl's body in the boot of Stewart's car,' he ordered. 'Dec, have you got the knife.'

Dec handed Flint the blood-covered knife inside a clear plastic bag.

'Make sure you wear gloves. Once you've put the body in the car, Dec, you and Johnson get away. Jones, you wait for me.'

Flint headed around the back of the property. He made his way over to Sandra's body and pressed the knife into her right hand before striding back towards the house. Flint dropped the knife inside, closing the doors and headed around to the front. Once there, he motioned for Jones to get in the car with him and they sped off.

'It won't fool the police,' Jones repeated.

'It's not meant to. It'll look like a domestic. It'll appear as though Stewart panicked and tried to make it look like suicide or something. It's what panicking people do when they've committed a crime. You should know that.'

'What about Stewart?' he asked.

'If he goes back to the house and rings the police, what's he going to say? The knife has his wife's fingerprints on them and his blood. No one's going to believe his story – especially when they find his daughter's body in the boot of his car.'

CHAPTER SEVENTEEN

Bev Wilson had organised another sweep of Jones' flat, intending to place the piece of paper somewhere out of sight. Hoping one of her people would find it, rather than having to claim she had found it herself. Therefore, adding a bit of authenticity to it. She arrived first at the flat, secreting the paper within the gap behind a wardrobe and the wall in Jones' bedroom. As the other members of her team arrived, she gave out her orders.

'Right, people. It appears a woman may have killed DS Jones – someone he was intimate with – so, I want a full sweep of the bedroom in the hope we can pick up some DNA other than his girlfriend,' she said. As they set off to work, Wilson waited nervously.

Chief Inspector Phillips sat in his office, sorting through his mountain of paperwork when his telephone rang. Putting aside a file, he answered. 'DCI Phillips.'

'Sir, I've got Dr Beverley Wilson on the line for you,' said a female voice on the other end.

'Ok, put her through.'

'Hi, Trevor. How are you?'

'Fine, Bev. Yourself?'

'Well, I'm being kept busy by your lot at the moment.'

'Yeah, I bet you are. What can I do for you today? I'm sure this isn't a social call.'

'We've done another sweep of Jones' flat, and we've come up with some possible evidence.'

'What?'

'We've found a piece of paper. I'd better bring it over.'

'Ok. I'll see you shortly.'

Phillips phoned the incident room and asked Graveney and Mac to come up and see him. They made their way upstairs, Phillip's door already open. When they arrived, he beckoned them in.

'Bev Wilson is on her way over here with some evidence they've recovered from Jones' flat.'

'What's that got to do with us?' Graveney said. 'I thought—'

'I'm not sure if it concerns Robertson's investigation into Jones' death, or if it involves your case, so we'll have to wait and see.'

The three of them waited until a young DC showed Bev Wilson into the room. After closing the door, she sat down with the others and pushed a clear plastic bag across the desk towards Phillips. He examined it before handing it to Graveney who studied it himself, passing it on to Mac.

Phillips clasped his hands together. 'DI Robertson is out of the office at the moment, that's why he's not here, but what do you two make of it?'

Mac stood. 'The two names are familiar to me, Guv. Give me a moment.' Heading out of the room, he returned minutes later. 'As I thought. The two names are boys who stayed at Winterton Boys' Home in the nineties. It was thought they absconded. They haven't been heard from since.' Graveney and Wilson suppressed a smile.

'Really,' Phillips said. 'This could be a burial site for them?'

'Maybe, sir,' Graveney said.

Phillips nodded towards Mac. 'And the numbers?'

Graveney accepted the paper from Mac and glanced at it again. 'Could be a grid reference.'

'Grid reference,' Phillips rubbed his chin. 'Who wrote it, do you think?'

'Maybe Jones?' Wilson said.

'Possibly Sandra Stewart, or her friend Jimmy Hind?' Graveney said.

Phillip glanced up. 'Why do you think that?'

'Stewart and Hind were working on abuse that took place at Winterton. Maybe they stumbled across something.'

'Bev.' Phillips looked towards her. 'Check the handwriting with samples from Jones, Stewart, and Hinds. We'll decide what to do next when we have the results. You two check the grid reference, if that's what it is, for a location?'

Graveney, Mac, and Wilson stood.

Phillips studied the three of them. 'We need this information pronto, people.'

Graveney, Mac, and Wilson glanced across at each other but never said a word as they left and made their way downstairs.

Stopping between floors, Graveney put a hand on Bev's arm. 'Thanks, Bev.' He held out his hand to her. 'I'll be in touch.'

'No problem.' She shook his and then Mac's hand, turned, and continued downstairs.

Graveney winked. 'Well, Mac. Let's check the grid reference.'

Phillips flicked through his list of contacts on his mobile and selected Steph.

'Hi, Trevor.'

'We've had a stroke of luck. It looks as though Jones *was bent*, and he's left some incriminating evidence in his flat.'

'Really?'

'I'll ring later. We're still checking it out at the moment. I'll keep you informed, but it's possible Jones was killed for what he knew. So watch your step.'

'I will,' she said.

OCTOBER 2006 - Stephen Stewart set off across the countryside, racing along bridle paths and crossing fields, to reach Vale Farm as quickly as possible. He tried desperately to push any thoughts of Jessica and what might have happened to her from his mind, his primary concern Sandra, and getting to her. His heart pumped so loudly he thought it would burst. He continued his lung-busting run back home. The lights of the farmhouse in the distance a flame to his moth, driving him forward. Relentlessly, remorselessly, Stewart stumbled on. Eventually, he emerged into the lane and sprinted as fast as he could, careering into the drive and towards the door. He stopped briefly outside and glanced at his car parked near to the garage, not quite understanding how it got there.

He burst into the hall and screamed Sandra's name. Pushing away any thoughts about his own safety, he mounted the stairs two at a time and shouted her name repeatedly. Convinced she wasn't upstairs he bounded back down, losing his footing as he stumbled at the foot of them. Regaining his stride, he entered the kitchen and continued through into the dining room. Finally stopping in the living room he shouted again, only silence met him. He slumped against the wall, his heart pounding. He bent at the waist to recover his breath, his legs like jelly. Stewart stumbled around not knowing what to do, he paused and brought his hands up to his face.

He glanced to his right out of the French doors and into the garden, his interest piqued as he made his way towards them. Stewart stopped, trying to bring his vision into focus. Wanting desperately to understand what he was seeing. Opening the door, he stepped onto the patio and crept nearer. Slowly, inexorably, his mind deciphered the scene and dropping to his knees he screamed her name. Stewart stood up straight and ran across to his wife, her body hanging limply from the apple tree. Untying the rope and taking her body in his arms, he lifted her up and carried her into the house, dropping to his knees, gently placing his wife on the floor. Stewart brushed the hair from her face, her lips tinged blue, a red ring encircling her neck. He put his arms under her body and pulled her close to him. Hugging her tightly, his teardrops falling unabated as he kissed her cheek. He sat rocking her back and forth like a baby.

'I'm so sorry,' he murmured. 'I'm so sorry.' He gazed at her lifeless eyes and watched as his life, his love, and everything he'd ever treasured, disappeared from view. He gently allowed her head to rest on the floor and sat back on the settee. Mentally shaking himself from his stupor, he felt in his pocket for his phone. Realising he didn't have his, he located Sandra's handbag and removed hers. Stewart stood, trying desperately to reach a decision. Maybe they would come back, he thought. He didn't dare phone the police. How could he explain what had happened? He raced towards the French doors and spotting the flashing lights in the distance, knew instantly what he must do. He stepped out over the threshold of the house and turned to look at his dead wife one final time, before heading into the garden. Making for a gap in the hedge at the bottom, and passing through it, he found himself in the open. Occasionally stopping, as the lights of the farmhouse slowly faded from view. He began to jog and crossing fields and countryside, put distance between himself and Vale Farm. Eventually he stopped in a small copse and sitting on the floor Stewart searched through Sandra's contacts, pausing at her sister's name. He put his hand to his side and stared at it, blood covering the palm. Stewart had forgotten about it, but now it was causing him considerable discomfort. Ignoring the pain, he rang Angela.

'Hi, Sandra,' she said.

'They've killed them ... they've killed them, Angela.' Stewart struggled to say through his tears.

'Who, Stephen? Who?' she asked.

'They've killed Sandra and Jessica.'

SEPTEMBER 2014 - Bev Wilson already knew the outcome of the handwriting comparison. So didn't even bother to check against Jones' or Hind's, before phoning DCI Phillips and informing him. Phillips scheduled a meeting with Oake, Graveney, and Mac to discuss the new evidence.

Graveney and Mac climbed the stairs to Chief Superintendent Oake's office and knocked on the door, entering and sitting next to Phillips and opposite Oake. Oake finished talking to someone on the phone, hung up and looked at the three officers.

'So, gentleman. What have you got for me?'

'We've come by some new evidence,' Phillips said. 'Bev Wilson's team picked it up from Jones' flat, sir.'

Graveney viewed Oake. Watching him closely as a fleeting emotion flashed across his face, an emotion Graveney recognised instantly. One of concern.

'What sort of evidence?' Oake said.

Phillips pushed the transparent plastic envelope across the desk towards him. Oake picked up the piece of paper and viewed it casually before putting it back in front of Phillips. 'Do we know who these two names are?'

Graveney leant in closer. 'They're the names of two boys who stayed at Winterton Boys' Home in the nineties, sir. They went missing and were never heard from again. The piece of paper indicates this might be the site where they were buried.'

'I see it could suggest that, but how did Jones come by it?'

'We're not sure, sir,' he said. 'The numbers on the paper are almost certainly a grid reference.'

'A grid reference?' Oake looked again at the evidence. 'What makes you think that?'

'The handwriting matched Sandra Stewart's,' Phillips said.

Oake frowned. 'Sandra Stewart. The Vale Farm Murders?'

'Yes, sir,' Phillips said.

'What's the connection between Sandra Stewart and these names?'

Graveney picked the paper back up. 'Sandra Stewart and a friend of hers – Jimmy Hind – were working on a story concerning Winterton. Hind went missing shortly before Sandra Stewart's murder and was never heard from again. We think they discovered the burial site of the two boys and paid with their lives.'

Oake sneered. 'Bit of a leap there, Peter. I thought Stephen Stewart was in the frame for the murder of his wife?'

Graveney looked at Mac. 'We're not entirely sure he killed his wife,' Graveney said. 'There is some doubt.'

'What about this grid reference? What location does it indicate?' He stood and stared out of his window.

'It pinpoints a location on the Wyndbourne Hall estate, sir.' Phillips said.

Oake spun around and glared at the officers. 'Do you know who owns that land?'

'Yes, sir. William Foxley. I believe he's a friend of yours?' Phillips said. Graveney and Mac suppressed a smile.

'What are you implying, Trevor?' Oake said.

'Nothing, sir. I'm stating a fact. The estate is quite extensive, and we're in no way alleging Mr Foxley knows anything about this, but we'll need a warrant to dig on his land.'

'William Foxley, gentlemen, is an influential individual. You're asking me to authorise a warrant to start digging holes on his estate. This could be a wild goose chase, and imagine what the newspapers will say.'

Phillips leant forward. 'I do feel there are sufficient grounds, sir. Maybe if you have a word with him, to smooth things over. We promise to keep the excavation discreet until we discover any evidence of wrongdoing.'

Oake sat back at his desk and thought for a moment, as Graveney continued to study him. 'Ok. We'll get the paperwork together, and we'll see what we find.' He stood again and stared out of the window.

Graveney, Mac, and Phillips got up to leave.

Oake spun around again. 'I hope for your sake, Trevor, you find something.' Phillips nodded, and the three of them left.

Once outside, Phillips stopped. 'Right, boys. Get in touch with Bev Wilson and tell her we'll require her team.'

'Yes, sir,' Graveney said. He looked towards Mac, and the pair of them descended the stairs.

Oake waited for the three officers to leave his office, closed the door, and took out his mobile phone. 'Bill? It's Charlie.'

'What's the problem?' Foxley said.

'The investigation team have discovered the location of the buried bodies.'

'How?'

'Jones was holding out on us. Forensics have found evidence. He was probably going to use it to get more money from us.'

'What can we do?'

'Not much. I've had to go along with a search warrant. You've got to hold your nerve. After all, your estate is extensive. You can't be expected to know every inch of it.'

'Do you want me to stonewall them?' Foxley said.

'No. Feign surprise. Be as helpful as possible and tell them you have no idea how the bodies got there.'

'Can they find anything else out?'

Oake sighed. 'Shelby is my only concern. The investigation hasn't come up with anything yet, but I can't believe he didn't have something incriminating. We need to locate that.'

'But where would he keep it?'

'Who knows?' Oake said. 'Maybe a safety deposit box or something. Possibly in a false name? There's only so much I can do to avoid people getting suspicious. I'll have a word with my operatives and see if they can find anything out. But if evidence comes to light, we're all finished.'

'Leave it with me. I won't let you down, Charlie,' Foxley said. The pair rang off.

Oake phoned Marne's number. 'Yes, Charlie?'

'This is not a personal call, Steph. We've a problem. It appears Jones hid some evidence in his flat before you got to him. Forensics found it, and now they want to do a search on Wyndbourne Hall Estate.'

'What do you want me to do, sir?'

'Shelby must have had damaging information. We need to find out what he had, and get to it before Graveney. Check anywhere he may have hidden it? Check for aliases. I'm certain he had something. Be discreet, Steph. I'll get Flint to do some checking as well.'

'I will. Should I come over tonight?'

'I'd enjoy that. Wear something nice. I could do with some female company.'

'Seven-thirty ok?' she asked.

'Seven-thirty's fine.'

Mac entered Graveney's office and sat opposite him. 'We've arranged the visit to Wyndbourne Hall in the morning at nine o'clock,' Mac said.

Graveney smiled. 'Good. Hopefully, it'll finally crack open this case.'

'Do you think Oake will tell Foxley we're on our way?'

'I'm sure he's informed him already,' Graveney said.

'Of course, you do realise even if we do find anything on his land it doesn't incriminate Foxley?'

'Yeah, it had crossed my mind. We need something to implicate Foxley. Something linking Stevens, or any of the others who worked at Winterton, with him. Although, even that's only circumstantial. None of them are in a position to point the finger at him, so I suspect he'll deny any knowledge of the bodies.'

'What's your view on Oake?' Mac asked.

'I've a feeling Oake knows more than he's letting on.'

'Thin-slicing, Peter?'

'Something like that,' Graveney said. He rubbed his chin, deep in thought. 'How do you fancy a drink tonight, put the investigation to bed for today.'

'Yeah, I'm game. What about The Farmers again?'

'I was thinking of going to The Marton Arms. It's a little livelier.'

Mac frowned. 'It's not full of kids, is it? I'm getting a bit long in the tooth for pubs full of kids.'

'No, it gets a mixed age-group, and Becky sometimes wanders in there on a Thursday.'

'Becky? It sounds like my sort of pub. What time?'

'I'll pick you up from your hotel about half-seven. I'll leave my car in the car park and collect it in the morning.'

'Sounds good to me.' He got up. 'Are you off home now?'

'Yeah. I want to see Louisa before she leaves. She's staying at her sister's tonight. It's her mam's funeral tomorrow.'

'You're not going?'

'She doesn't want me to. Long story.'

'You'll have to tell me tonight.'

Graveney let himself into his flat and went straight to the kitchen where Louisa sat waiting at the table. 'Hi.' She got up and gave him a hug.

'You ok, darling?' Brushing the hair from her face, he looked at her.

'Yeah,' she said. 'Just waiting for my sister.'

'Are you sure you're all right? I could come with you?'

'I'm ok. My family will look after me.'

'You do know you're special to me, Louisa?' Astonished at his own candidness.

She hugged him again. 'I know, and you're special to me I ...' Graveney interrupted her, putting his finger to her mouth.

'I know. You look after yourself and give me a ring if you need anything.' He squeezed her hand. A car horn sounded outside. Louisa kissed Graveney on the cheek and then left. He watched her depart before heading to the bathroom for a shower.

Marne drove to Chief Superintendent Oake's house in Stokesley. She'd dressed provocatively to extract as much information out of Oake as possible. Things were moving along well. Marne secretly hoped Oake would allow his guard to drop again and tell her even more. She was managing to keep Phillips suitably in the dark but felt guilty about that. He'd helped her and risked so much, but she still needed to find all the people responsible for Sandra and Jessica's murders and couldn't allow anything to distract her from that goal.

The only other thing she needed to concern herself with was the safety deposit key. Sooner or later she needed to bring it into play. She knew the risks to everyone involved, especially Graveney, were necessary and nothing would stop her. Nothing would stand in her way. Absolutely nothing would prevent her from pursuing this to its bitter conclusion and bringing those responsible to justice. She got out of her car and pushed the hatred she felt for Oake back below the surface. She smiled to herself, slipping effortlessly from Angela to Stephanie, as she headed towards his door.

CHAPTER EIGHTEEN

Graveney and Mac headed into the Marton Arms at quarter to eight. The pub already over half-full as they made their way towards the bar. Graveney squeezed into a gap between two people and catching the eye of one of the barmaids, pulled a ten-pound note from his pocket. An attractive-looking woman in her mid-thirties, with blonde hair tied back in a ponytail, moved towards him.

'Hey, stranger,' she said. 'Don't usually see you in here, Peter.'

'I'm here with a friend of mine.' Pointing to Mac, who was oblivious to the conversation. 'Thought he needed cheering up a bit.'

'Usual?' She smiled at him.

'Two pints, Jen.'

She pulled two pints of Speckled Hen ale and placed them on the counter in front of Graveney. '£6.80 please.' Holding out her hand, as Graveney gave her £10.

'Keep the change, darling.' He turned and gave one of the pints to Mac, and turned back to face the barmaid.

'Thanks, handsome,' she said

'Becky not in tonight?' Graveney asked.

'She's coming in later. Anyway, what's Becky got that I haven't?'

Graveney laughed. 'She hasn't got a husband for starters.'

'Yeah, I suppose you're right. The silly bugger would only kick up a fuss. Craig's funny about that sort of thing.' Winking at Graveney, she moved along the bar towards another customer.

Graveney and Mac made their way over to a high table, vacated by a young couple, and the two of them positioned themselves on stools.

Graveney gulped his drink. 'Becky's coming in later.'

'How do you know?'

'Her cousin, Jenny, served me. She said she is.'

'It isn't the only reason I came here,' Mac said.

'No. Of course it isn't.' Graveney winked.

'What's the plan of action in the morning?' Mac said.

'We'll have to be there before Bev and her team to serve the warrant. I'll probably meet you there. If that's all right?'

'Yeah, that's fine by me.' He took a large swig from his glass.

'So, what's the story with Louisa then?' Quickly changing subjects.

'You know Louisa's mam died the other day?' Graveney said. Mac nodded as Graveney took a drink from his glass. 'When Louisa came home to the flat, understandingly upset, I tried to comfort her and sat with her until she eventually fell asleep. I decided to wash the dirty clothes she'd brought home in her overnight bag. When I went through the bag, I found a photo album. One of the photos from this album had either fallen out or had been removed. The photo was of Louisa's mam, *and me* took in 1996.'

'I didn't know you knew her mother?'

'I didn't either,' Graveney said. 'I was on a course in York. I'd just joined the force, and I met her there. I'd no idea Louisa's mam was this woman. It was a long time ago, and as you can imagine, there have been a few women since.'

Mac grinned. 'I can believe that. Does Louisa know about it?'

'I'm sure she does. When I met Louisa two years ago, she was living rough, and I thought her just another runaway. There was something in her eyes, though, something that struck a chord with me.'

'Peter, are you saying what I think you're saying? She's your daughter?'

'I'm not sure. Louisa's mother and I did have a fling, but she told me she was on the pill. I took her at face value.'

'So, it looks like Louisa thinks you're her dad?'

'Well, I can't imagine she'd come looking for someone from an old photo of her mother's unless she'd a reason too. Her mam must have told her something about us.'

'Are you bothered?'

'Not really. I'll be honest, I couldn't care more for Louisa than I do now.'

'You haven't discussed it with her then?'

'No. I got the feeling Louisa was going to say something the other day, but she had to go. I've told you how special she is to me, so I'm not bothered either way. I'll see if Louisa broaches the subject. But you understand why she doesn't want me at the funeral. Her family would probably start asking awkward questions, and Louisa is obviously not ready to tell them about me yet.'

Mac rubbed his goatee. 'The thing is, only her mam knew for sure if you're her father and well ...'

Graveney nodded. 'Yeah, I know. But I'm sure she'll tell me what she knows when she's ready.'

Mac laughed. 'You haven't got any more kids kicking about, have you?'

'I don't think so. I've usually taken care in that respect.'

Mac frowned. 'I miss not seeing my kids as much as I used to. I worry we'll drift apart, but life looks nothing like the brochure. We end up making it up as we go along.'

Graveney patted Mac's arm. 'You can have them visit when you get settled.'

'Yeah. I need to get myself a nice flat or house. Marie told me she wouldn't have any problem with them coming down here. It doesn't stop you worrying about them, though, when you don't see them every day.'

'They're still your kids,' Graveney said. 'You're still their dad. They won't forget that. You've just got to see them as much as possible.'

'You're lucky to have Louisa here with you.'

Graveney blew out hard. 'Sometimes, in this job, you become hardened to the pain and suffering of other people. Louisa keeps me grounded. It reminds me how vital our job is. God, listen to us two getting all deep.' He took another large swig from his glass.

Mac nodded. 'I know what you mean, though. The day I forget how important the families and friends of the victims are, that's the day I'll leave the force. I want to keep my humanity. I don't want to end up like some of the coppers I've known. Viewing another victim with a shrug.'

Mac stood up to get some more drinks in, and as he headed for the bar, Graveney realised how lucky he was to have both Louisa and Mac in his life.

Mac and Graveney sat deep in conversation as Becky and Kate – a friend of hers – came wandering over to their table.

'Hi, you two,' Becky said.

Mac stared at Becky. He already knew she was attractive from their meeting at the coffee shop, but tonight she looked absolutely stunning. Her hair hung in curls around her shoulders, her dark red dress clung beautifully to the contours of her curves, and she had the right amount of make-up on. Mac hated women who felt it necessary to apply too much make-up and momentarily, he was lost for words. Graveney stood and kissed Becky on her cheeks.

Becky motioned towards her friend. 'Peter. You know Kate, don't you?'

Graveney smiled. 'Of course.' Kissing Kate on her cheeks, he got up and offered his stool to her. Mac, who's jaw finally moved back into its rightful place, offered Becky his.

'Can I get you, ladies, a drink?' Mac said.

Becky nodded. 'Yes, please. I'll have a vodka and lemonade.'

'A double?' Mac said.

She smiled. 'Why, Mr Policeman. You're not trying to get me drunk, are you?'

'No ... no ... Of course not,' Mac spluttered.

Becky gently placed a hand on his and smiled. 'I'm only kidding, don't look so worried.'

'Kate, can I get you one?' he asked.

'A Coke please, I'm driving.' Mac turned and headed to the bar.

'How's your husband, Kate?' Graveney said.

'Lucas?' Kate smiled. 'He's ok. We're off on holiday to Bermuda tomorrow. That's why I'm not drinking. I don't want a thick head in the morning.'

'Bermuda. Sounds fantastic.'

Kate tossed a glance Becky's way. 'Your friend seems nice.'

'He is.' Graveney looked across at Mac. 'Any woman who manages to snare him will be fortunate.' Glancing across at Becky who smiled at him.

Mac and Becky talked all night incessantly, like a couple of love-struck teenagers. Graveney couldn't help but glance across from time to time at the pair of them. Thin-slicing their looks at each other. Reading their body language. Besotted with each other already, surprising Graveney by the speed of their attraction. Graveney talked with Kate, while Mac and Becky got to know each other. He liked Kate. She was intelligent, a quality Graveney admired in a woman. She also possessed a wacky sense of humour and self-deprecation Graveney loved. Devoted to her husband – he knew this by the signals she gave off anytime his name came up in conversation – and this put Graveney at ease. He loved women, of course, loved the flirting and the thrill of the chase, but he also loved women for who they were. It was good to talk with a woman and not feel as if it was some worn out pick-up routine he was going through. He thought, given a chance, he would enjoy a fulfilling, platonic relationship with Kate. In his already complicated life, there was always room for someone like her.

Graveney stood and headed towards the bar to get some more drinks. He stopped, spotting Heather's friend Maddie, nearby.

'Hi, Maddie.' He moved nearer to her. 'Heather not out with you?'

'Heather's at home,' she said. Brusquely, Graveney thought. But let it pass.

'I thought I'd pop round and see her.'

'What's up, Peter?' Turning to face him. 'At a bit of a loose end. Not able to pull tonight?'

Graveney, taken aback by the abruptness in her tone, backed away slightly. 'I'm sorry, Maddie. I don't know what you mean?'

'Yes you do, Peter.' Anger flashed across her face. She turned and stomped away from Graveney. He followed her outside.

'What do you mean?' Taking hold of her arm. Maddie shrugged him off and turned around once more to face him.

'You're sat inside there with a woman, and then asking me about Heather.'

'I don't know what you're on about. Becky and Kate are friends. In any case, I don't know what it has to do with Heather.'

'Come off it, Peter,' she said. 'Heather loves you – *no strike that* – she adores you. Don't ask me why, but she does. And you treat her like shit.'

'Heather's special to me. I'd never do anything to hurt her.' His irritation at what Maddie was saying now rising.

Maddie sneered. 'You drop in when you're at a loose end for a quick shag, and then piss-off again without a thought of what it does to her. Heather's beautiful. She's vibrant and sexy, but she's letting her life pass her by, waiting for someone who obviously doesn't give a flying fuck for her!' She almost spat the words

Graveney scowled. 'That's unfair. Heather and I go back a long way. You've hardly known her five minutes. How the hell can you understand what sort of relationship we have?' Finding himself getting emotional, his voice now quivering.

'Heather's my best friend, and I know when someone treats her like shit. And when they do, I think I'm within my rights to speak up. What about your responsibilities to her and Luke?'

'What responsibilities?' Graveney frowned, slightly puzzled by her remark, as various emotions flashed across Maddie's face.

Maddie thought for a moment. She'd said too much. She was drunk, but her reason kicked back in, just in time before she blurted out what she knew. 'Just go away, Peter. Piss off.' She stormed off.

Graveney, although furious, felt a sense of guilt. Some of what Maddie said to him, struck home. He headed into the bar and getting the drinks for the four of them, downed two double Jack Daniels before going back to the table. Fortunately, Mac and Becky were still besotted with each other and Kate appeared not to notice his change of mood. Graveney pushed any thoughts aside and turned to talk with Kate again.

Kate glanced at her watch soon after, and realising how late it was, turned to face her friend. 'Becks, I'm going. We've got an early start in the morning.'

Becky kissed her on the cheek. 'I'm having another. I'll see you in a couple of weeks. Have a good time.'

After Kate left, Graveney returned to the bar leaving Mac and Becky together. They came over to him a little later to say goodbye as the two of them disappeared. Graveney's mood lifted briefly as he realised how happy they seemed, before he dived once more into a bottle of Jack Daniels.

Heather, woken by the sound of the front doorbell, glanced across at the clock on the bedside table, which read 02.10. She put on her dressing gown, worrying whoever was ringing the bell would wake up Luke and her neighbours. Heather peered through the spyglass and viewed Graveney outside. She opened the door to the intoxicated Graveney as he stumbled over the threshold and inside.

'Do you know what time it is?' Leading him into the front room and closing the door.

'I'm sorry, Heather.' Looking suitably chastened. 'I ran into Maddie tonight.'

Heather closed her eyes in horror, wondering what Maddie had said to him.

'She had a right go at me, about the way I treat you,' he slurred.

'I wouldn't worry,' she said. 'Maddie was probably drunk. Sit down, I'll get you a drink.'

Graveney lowered his eyes. 'It's just that ... she's right. I do treat you terribly.' Bringing a hand up to rest on her cheek. He stroked it gently, smiling at her. 'I love you, Heather. You know that, don't you? I wouldn't hurt you for the world.' His eyes glistened with tears. 'When I look at you, I see her. It all comes flooding back. I ...' Graveney stopped, lowering his eyes as tears dripped down his face.

'Oh, Peter.' Putting her hands on his cheeks. She rubbed away the tears.

'I'm sorry,' he said. 'Sorry for hurting you. I wish things were different.' Heather put her fingers to his lips to stop him talking. 'Sit down. I'll get you a coffee.'

Graveney slumped onto the settee while Heather went into the kitchen. When she returned, he was fast asleep. She went and got a duvet from the airing cupboard and covered him with it, looking down at his face. A face she knew so well. Every crease, every fold. She brushed the hair from his brow and gently kissed him on his head.

'Peter,' she whispered. Standing, she switched off the lights and headed back to bed.

Graveney woke early, glancing around the room, allowing his senses to focus, before realising he was at Heather's. He studied his watch which read 06.03. Getting to his feet, the dizziness momentarily causing him to reach out to the wall for support. Unsure how much he'd drunk the night before, but the experience of past hangovers led him to believe it was a lot. His head thumped with the sort of a headache three-quarters of a bottle of spirit or more induced. His mouth had never felt so dry. He tiptoed into the kitchen and downed half a bottle of orange juice and two paracetamols from the cupboard. He thought for a moment, not wanting to run into Heather this morning as shame and embarrassment filled him. He wasn't altogether sure what happened the previous night but remembered enough to make him want to leave quickly. He opened the front door quietly, and closed it gently, before heading up the street away from Heather's.

Heather heard Graveney moving about below. She had thought of going down to see him and desperately wanted to, but she knew how embarrassed he would feel and wanted to save him from that. She hugged her pillow as if it was him and caught a slight smell of his aftershave left over from his previous visit. Closing her eyes, she drifted once more.

Graveney strolled the thirty-minutes-walk from Heather's to his flat. He showered and changed before forcing some breakfast into him. A combination of the stroll, the food, and the tablets he'd taken, made the hangover lift somewhat, and after reading the morning paper, he rang Marne.

'Hi, Peter,' she purred down the line.

'Can you pick me up later? I had a few drinks last night. I think I'm still over the limit.'

'Do you want me to come around now?' Graveney knew instantly what she was implying.

'If you want,' he said. Putting the ball firmly in her court.

'Ten minutes.'

Graveney should have said no. Hungover, and not feeling in the mood for company, but Marne had this way of quickly breaking down any defences he put up. He both loved and detested her for it.

Marne arrived shortly after, carrying a bag. Her hair hung loosely, the way he liked it, as Graveney beckoned her into his flat. She headed straight for the bedroom and Graveney meekly followed her, closing the door behind them.

Marne got out of bed on hearing Graveney enter the shower and crept across to his wardrobe. She located the jacket Graveney wore on the day he met Stephen Stewart at the solicitor's office. Opening her bag, she fished out the safety deposit key and dropped it into the top pocket of the jacket. She returned to the bed, but as thoughts of her and Graveney, and what they had done, filled her head, Marne got back up.

Wandering into the bathroom, she eyed him briefly before joining him in the shower.

Graveney and Marne headed over to Middlesbrough police station to collect the paperwork for the search of Wyndbourne Hall. They then headed out there to meet Mac, Bev Wilson, and her team. Marne and Graveney exchanging furtive glances with each other as she drove him there.

Marne felt pleased with herself for being able to secrete the key in Graveney's jacket. She would need to plant a seed in his head when the time was right, to set the wheels in motion. Graveney couldn't help but feel slightly perturbed by the conflicting emotions he viewed on Marne's face. He felt like a fly taking a step ever closer to the centre of the spider's web.

'Everything ok, sir?' she said.

'Fine, Steph. What makes you ask?'

'You looked deep in thought, there. Like someone who doesn't know the answer to a difficult question.'

'That about sums it up.' His eyes lingered on her. Marne smiled at him. As a, '*I know something you don't know*', look slowly spread across her face.

CHAPTER NINETEEN

OCTOBER 2006 - Angela raced across to where Stephen said he'd be. She pulled up out of sight, off the road, and grabbed the first aid kit from the boot of her car. 'Stephen!' she shouted.

He crept out from behind a hedge and towards her. Even though there was only the moonlight, she could see that his side and jeans were covered in blood. She helped him towards her car and onto the back seat, which she'd covered with a large tarpaulin. She removed some large pads from the first aid kit, lifted his blood-soaked shirt, and applied them to a large gash on his side. Thinking the injury required stitches, she gently pressed the pads against his wound while he recounted what had happened. Stephen tried to explain how the night had unfolded as Angela listened intently. He told her everything. She was shocked to discover that the kidnappers knew Sandra had informed the police and she wasn't sure if it was because someone followed her or, and she couldn't bring herself to believe it, someone at the station was corrupt. Angela thought for a moment and then taking out her mobile, rang DI Trevor Phillips.

'Hi, Steph,' he said.

'Trevor, I need your help.'

'Of course. What's up?'

'Are you at work?'

'No. I'm off, why?'

'Can you meet me somewhere?' she said. 'Somewhere safe.'

'You've got me worried.'

'Please, Trevor. I can't explain right now. I need to meet you somewhere away from Middlesbrough.'

'Ok. Do you know my holiday cottage at Robin Hoods Bay?'

'Yes.'

'Drive there and under the plant pot outside the front door, you'll find a key. I'll meet you later.'

'Thanks.' Hanging up, she turned her attention back to Stephen. 'Stephen,' she said. 'Lay down on the back seat, and I'll drive us to Robin Hoods Bay. Keep your head down.'

'Can we trust him?' he asked.

'He's my late dad's friend. He's like an uncle to me. He'll help us, I'm sure.' She sped off towards Robin Hoods Bay, hoping he would. If there was someone in Middlesbrough Police passing on information, they couldn't risk going there.

Angela and Stephen reached the cottage at Robin Hood's Bay. She helped him into the front room, making sure they weren't spotted. They waited for almost an hour before Phillips arrived. Angela took Phillips into the kitchen, relaying the story Stephen had told her, as he listened intently. He stood, strolled over to the fireplace and turned around.

'You do believe Stephen?' she asked.

'Steph. What I'm about to say goes no further. I had a meeting some time ago with the Chief Constable. Don't ask me why he confided in me, but he told me in the strictest confidence. There's an investigation in place to uncover corruption within Cleveland Constabulary. They don't know who's involved but they, the investigation team, without wanting to go too deep into it, have discovered evidence going missing. Possible tip-offs to suspected criminals, that sort of thing. They're kind of sure some of the coppers are taking backhanders, but so far, they haven't uncovered anything. It sounds to me when your sister went to Middlesbrough police station, someone either passed on that information to the kidnappers or are themselves involved. We can't risk taking Stephen back there, because his life's in danger if we do.'

'What are we going to do? He's been stabbed in the side, and it looks like he needs hospital treatment?'

'I'll make a call,' he said. 'Go and check Stephen is all right.'

Angela made her way back into the front room as Phillips phoned someone on his mobile. Stephen lay on the settee, staring blankly into space as she sat beside him. Angela hadn't even thought about what happened to Sandra and Jessica because of the need to help Stephen, but now she felt overcome with emotion. She put her arms around him and as they hugged tightly, they both began to sob.

Phillips stopped at the door and hearing the two of them, returned to the kitchen to make some tea. Gathering the tea things on a tray, he carried them into the front room, by which time the crying had subsided.

'I've made a call to a friend of mine. A retired doctor. He's on his way out here now. He owes me a favour, and he'll sort Stephen out.'

'Can we trust him?' she asked.

'Implicitly,' Phillips said.

Phillips left the room to make some more calls. It was vital he got Stephen away somewhere safe. He thought of ringing the Chief Constable, but paranoia kicked in, and he was unsure of who to trust anymore.

'Angela, why did he call you Steph?' Stephen said.

'Angela is my birth name. My adoptive parents called me Stephanie. When I met Sandra, she knew me by Angela. I didn't think to correct her. It seemed natural for her to call me it.'

'Should I call you, Steph, too?'

'Whatever you like.' Putting her hand to his cheek, she smiled.

There was a light tap on the back door of the property sometime later, and Phillips opened it to a familiar face. A slight, elderly man in his sixties stood outside with a bag in his hand, his grey hair thinning on top, his face full of world-worn character.

Phillips nodded. 'Doc.' And beckoned him in.

'Where's the patient?' he said.

Phillips led the man into the front room. 'I've looked at the wound, and I don't think the knife passed through his body, but it looks as if it needs stitching.'

He stitched and dressed Stephen's wound, giving him a couple of injections. After he'd finished, he returned to the kitchen where Steph and Phillips waited.

'It's only a flesh wound, Trevor, as you thought. I've stitched him up, so he should be ok. I'd better get going.'

Phillips held out his hand. 'Thanks for your help. We're even now.'

'Even.' Repeated the man, as he shook his and Steph's hand.

'I can rely on your discretion, Doc?' Phillips said.

'Never here. I'm currently tucked up in bed.' He smiled and left.

'What do we do now?' Steph said.

'Stephen stays here for the time being. They'll be looking for him. With his injury, we'll have to play it safe at the moment. I'm going to pull in some favours and get him a new passport. We need to get him out of the country. The thing is, I don't know what's going on at Middlesbrough Police Station. Until we find out more, it's best to keep Stephen out of sight.'

'What happens if you can't prove any of what Stephen says?'

'I don't know, Steph. I just don't know.'

Stephen Stewart stayed at Phillips' cottage for over a month. Eventually, his face disappeared from the newspaper headlines and only then did Phillips and Steph think it safe to move him. He'd grown a beard in the meantime to disguise his features and also dyed his hair. Phillips obtained a false passport for him, eventually managing to get him out of the country to Portugal where a good friend of Phillips' gave him a job in a bar. The idea was for Phillips to obtain evidence to prove Stephen's innocence, but as weeks, months and finally years passed, getting the necessary evidence to help Stephen proved increasingly less likely.

Steph visited on a regular basis to bring him up to date on how it was progressing, but eventually, it dawned on the pair of them that proving his innocence was unlikely ever to happen. Steph had advanced into the plain-clothes police force at Durham Constabulary, and in 2014, she visited Stephen at his apartment in the Algarve.

AUGUST 2014 - Stephen picked Steph up from Faro airport and travelled towards the Algarve, indulging in the usual small talk along the journey before pulling up outside his apartment.

'How are you, Stephen? Still feeling unwell?' Remembering he'd said on her previous visit he was having headaches.

'Not great. I've had some tests done, and it's not promising.'

'Is this regarding the headaches you're having?'

'There's no easy way of saying this. I'm dying. I've got a non-operable brain tumour.'

'What about treatment?' She put her hand on his arm.

'It'll only delay the inevitable.'

Stunned by this turn of events. Life was so unfair, she thought. He'd suffered so much heartache in his life and the people who killed his wife and daughter, were never brought to justice. She gazed at his face and into his eyes. She'd grown attracted to him over the years, and slowly but surely fallen in love with him. She'd never told him this. She knew he'd never recovered from the loss of Sandra and now, hearing she'd lose Stephen was almost unbearable.

'I'm so sorry. Life's so unfair.' Tears filled her eyes.

Stephen carried Steph's bag inside and placed it in the spare room. Steph composed herself, trying to be resolute for Stephen.

He stopped and turned. 'How about a glass of wine?' Smiling at her.

'Just what the doctor ordered.' She made her way outside to the terrace. Stephen brought a bottle and two glasses and sat beside her. He filled the glasses and handed her one.

Standing, he stared across the terrace. 'I see them, you know.'

'Who?' she asked.

'Sandra and Jessica. They haunt me. The doctor says it's not unusual for this type of tumour, and where it is, to cause hallucinations. They look so real, though. As if they've stepped into the room.'

'I'm sorry.' Hugging him close.

'I don't mind,' he said. 'It comforts me. The worst thing, the thing that upsets me the most, is the people who murdered them never got caught.'

'I spoke to Trevor last week, and he doesn't think they'll ever find them. He's tried his hardest, but he's all but given up on it.'

He briefly closed his eyes and wandered to the edge of the terrace. 'I need to do something.'

'What?'

'They've given me three to six months. Maybe a year with some treatment. I need to find those responsible.'

Steph joined him, taking a large swig of her wine, she turned to face Stephen. 'I've given this a lot of thought myself. Every time I think of what they did to Sandra and Jessica, I get so angry. I volunteered my services to Trevor to assist in trying to find those involved, but I knew he wouldn't go along with my plan. He says it's too dangerous. He won't let me take the risk. Trevor told me once that, according to the logbook at Middlesbrough police station, Sandra visited a couple of nights before she was murdered. She met with two officers called Oake and Jones. He believes one of these, or maybe both of them, told the kidnappers she'd gone to the police.'

'What can we do?' Stephen said.

'I've offered to get to know these two officers to find out what happened to Sandra and Jessica, but he's dead against it.'

'What are you suggesting?' Stephen said.

'We need to know what Sandra knew. We need to know the names of the people involved.'

'Sandra told me she and Jimmy were investigating abuse and murders at a boys' home. She said she had names in her notebook of people she thought were involved. Unfortunately, I handed it over to them on the night she was murdered.'

'Is there anywhere else she might have put the names?' Steph said.

Stephen thought for a moment. 'Vale Farm.'

'Vale Farm?'

'Sandra wasn't stupid. I can't believe she didn't leave some clues for us to find. Sandra desperately wanted these people to pay for their crimes. She hid something under the floorboards at Vale Farm the day before she died. A locket with a picture of Jessica inside and maybe, perhaps, left something else. There's also the possibility she left something at her mam's house. Maybe she left a clue there?'

'Vale Farm's still empty, I think,' Steph said. 'What happened there has put off would-be buyers. By rights, it's still yours. If we went there, we could recover her locket and whatever else she left.'

'If it's for sale I could pose as a buyer.'

Steph nodded. 'That's a good idea.'

'One more thing.' He paused, wondering what her reaction would be. 'If we find out the names of the people involved, I intend to kill them.'

Steph pondered for a moment before answering. 'We'd have to keep Trevor in the dark. He's as straight as they come. Maybe If I make up a story along the lines of you disappearing from here and carrying out this on your own. He'll be forced to include me in the investigation. You could hunt them down, and I'd gather any information I could from the inside.'

'Do you think it would work?'

'I don't know,' she said.

'I've nothing more to lose. I've been without Sandra and Jessica for so long. It's just ... if we could find these people.'

'I know, Stephen,' she said, hugging him. 'I know.'

'I've got another admission to make,' she said.

'What?'

'The policemen Trevor mentioned? I've got to know the two of them. For months I've cultivated relationships, and I've managed to gain the trust of them both. I thought it could come to this.'

His eyes widened. 'You've slept with them?'

'I want these bastards caught as much as you do. Trevor's hit a brick wall regarding the investigation and unbeknown to him, I took it upon myself to get in touch with them. No offence, but it was easy for me to gain their trust. It's marvellous how much a little alcohol and some womanly wiles loosens a man's tongue.'

'Isn't that incredibly dangerous, though?'

'I think, if we're going to see this through, we'll have to take risks.'

'Have they told you what happened?' he asked.

'Not totally. Hinted at, actually. There are some big players involved, along with some local people. The person who killed Jessica is someone called Flint. Along with another guy, Dec, they killed Jimmy Hind and buried his body somewhere. I've never met these two, but I suspect they were the ones who attacked you and killed Sandra. Oake uses them from time to time when he needs information getting, or people removed. We need to blow this open and nail all of them.'

'How do you explain this to Trevor?' he said.

'Oake trusts me so much, he wants me to get a transfer to Cleveland Constabulary. He doesn't entirely trust Jones. He sees Jones as a bit of a loose cannon and wants me to keep an eye on him. If I explain to Trevor what I'm doing, he may go along with it. If you're prepared to help on the outside, we can put the cat amongst the pigeons and flush them all out.'

'How far are you prepared to go?' Stephen said.

'As far as I need to. We've waited eight years to see justice, and I think it's about time we gave this investigation a nudge.'

'I don't know what I'd have done without you all these years.' Taking hold of her hand, he gazed at her. She looked back at Stephen, her emotions almost getting the better of her. She'd fallen for him, hoping maybe over time the hurt and pain he felt over the deaths of Sandra and Jessica would subside, but his illness put paid to that. She filled their glasses up once more and raised hers high.

'Here's to justice for Sandra, Jessica, Jimmy, and anyone else those evil bastards murdered.' Stephen raised his glass to touch hers.

Stephen and Steph flew back separately to the United Kingdom. He moved into The Whitestone Hotel in Great Broughton and arranged a viewing of Vale Farm. Steph met up with Phillips and informed him Stephen had disappeared from Portugal. She confabulated a story that on her last meeting with Stephen, he'd hinted he intended to kill the people responsible for Sandra and Jessica's deaths. Steph also told Phillips about Stephen's brain tumour, and that he had nothing to lose by coming back.

She confessed she'd secretly started relationships with Jones and Oake, in an attempt to push the investigation along, claiming she was trying to stop Stephen from doing anything stupid. Phillips was furious with her, but once his anger subsided, he had seen sense in her getting involved. She'd told him Oake wanted her to transfer to Cleveland Constabulary, so he'd have someone to watch Jones. And someone with eyes and ears within any investigations the force may be involved in. Steph assured Phillips she had no knowledge of what Stephen would do, or who he intended to kill, and that they would have to wait and see how it unfolded. Phillips, although unhappy with the situation, felt he had no choice. As far as she was concerned, he would have to play along and she would let him know just enough.

After meeting with Phillips, Steph drove out to meet Stephen between Stokesley and Great Broughton. She hugged him. 'Hi.'

'I've arranged a viewing at Vale Farm,' he said. 'I phoned the agent this morning.'

'Take these.' Handing him a mobile phone, a gun, and a box of bullets. 'After today we'll only communicate by phone unless it's absolutely essential. I've got one the same, and I've programmed my number under *Ang,* in it.'

'Why, Ang?'

'If anyone gets hold of the phone, there's nothing to link me. Just an accomplice called Ang helping you. When you text me, call me Ang.'

'I'll ring you after I've been to Vale Farm and tell you what I've found.'

She embraced him and kissed his cheek. 'Be careful, Stephen.'

He hugged her back. 'I will.'

SEPTEMBER 2014 – Marne headed back towards Teesside on the Hartlepool Road when her mobile sounded in the glove-box. She pulled over into a lay-by and answered.

'Steph,' Stephen said. 'I've been to Vale Farm, and I've got the locket. I found a couple of other things there as well. A key and a piece of paper. The paper has four names on it, numbered one to four. Then, next to number five, a question mark. I think the question mark could be the name of the person within Middlesbrough police.'

'Is that all it has on the paper?'

'Yes.' As he read out the names, she jotted them down.

'What about the key?' she asked.

'I'm not sure. I've never seen it before, but I know Sandra kept things up at her mam's house. Maybe it opens something there.'

'We'd have to break in if we wanted to gain access,' she said.

'There might be no need. I've still got a key to the house. Sandra's mam had one cut for each of us when she was going away, so we could check on the house for her. It was on the same key ring as Vale Farm. I also know the number of the alarm. 1940, the year her dad was born – if she hasn't changed it, that is.'

'Do you want me to come with you?' she asked.

'If you don't mind. Maybe you could take something of Sandra's to remember her by. A keepsake.'

'Yes, I'd like that.'

'What about her mother? How are we going to get her out of the house?'

'She always visited her sister in Sandsend on Saturday afternoon. If her sister's still alive, and she hasn't altered her plans, we may be lucky.'

'And if not?' she said.

'I don't know. Wait until she goes out, I suppose. Saturday?'

'Saturday,' she repeated, as she jotted down the time and the address of Sandra's mother's house.

They met not far from Sandra's mother's house and waited for her to leave. Luckily it appeared her plans hadn't altered any in the intervening years and once she had been gone for five minutes, they made their way around the side of the property. The key opened the door, and fortunately, the alarm code hadn't been changed allowing them to gain access to the house. They searched through Sandra's room, the two of them becoming emotional. Her mam having kept her room as she'd left it when she moved out. It was strange to see all her childhood toys and pictures still there after all these years. They located a box in the bottom of the wardrobe and finding it locked, Stephen tried the key. To their relief, it opened, and inside, they found paper cuttings concerning The Winterton Boys' Home abuse case and pages from Sandra's notebook.

She must have put them in there suspecting something might happen to her, they reasoned. One of the pages had written on the top – *POSSIBLE BURIAL SITE.* Below that, a twelve-figure number and two names. Gathering up all the items from the box, they made sure the room appeared the same as when they'd arrived, then re-set the alarm and left the house. Checking they hadn't been spotted, they headed back to their cars.

'Well this is it,' Stephen said.

Good luck,' she said, as they hugged each other.

'You too,' he said. 'I've become fond of you. I wouldn't want anything to happen ... In another life, Steph ...' She put her fingers to his lips to stop him talking. Tears filled both their eyes as they hugged again.

'I know,' she said. They parted and headed off separately back to Teesside, Marne clutching a bracelet of Sandra's she'd taken from the house.

After Stephen murdered the Reverend and the Johnsons, he'd only kept in contact with Steph via their mobiles. Finally transferred across to Cleveland Constabulary, Steph met Oake who had arranged for her to become DI Graveney's new DS. He wanted her to stay close to Jones and Graveney, as his eyes and ears inside the investigation. Both Oake and Jones were unaware she was secretly in a relationship with the other, giving her a unique advantage.

She picked up Graveney from the coffee shop, before heading towards Yarm where Stephen confronted Shelby. Marne instantly felt an attraction to Graveney she couldn't explain. Something within him, something behind those eyes of his, Marne found captivating. She knew she needed to get close if she was going to manipulate and bend him to her will. Maybe she'd enjoy that, unlike her unedifying relationships with Oake and Jones. Graveney offered her something different. Something dark, something she'd kept subdued, pushed deep beneath her psyche. Something now she was only too willing to allow to rise to the surface.

Graveney had got out of the car and headed towards the officers when Stephen Stewart phoned, informing her he'd found what looked like a Safety deposit key. Thinking on her feet, she'd told him to somehow get it out of the office and suggested secreting it on Graveney. It was a gamble that he wouldn't discover it before she retrieved it from him. Marne took a massive risk and offered herself to Graveney outside her flat. She knew about his womanising and hoped he'd take the bait, which he had much to her delight. Now, as Marne heard the door close and Graveney leave, she stared at the key in the palm of her hand she found in the top pocket of Graveney's jacket. She thought of Stephen. How smart he'd been to hide the key, but he was dead now. The man she loved, gone. Tears slowly rolled down her cheeks. She couldn't weaken, she thought. Quickly shoring up the last remaining remnants of her life, she pushed Angela aside and once again donned the mask of Steph.

Graveney was the key to this case. He was the man to find out who murdered Sandra and Jessica. Nothing else mattered now, just her relentless pursuit of those responsible. Yet he puzzled her. She had enjoyed immensely what happened between them. Wanting it to go much further. He had faltered though, shocked by her behaviour, but this excited her more. There would be more to come, she was sure of that. More liaisons with Detective Inspector Peter Graveney she mused, as she headed for a shower.

CHAPTER TWENTY

Graveney and Marne arrived after nine on Friday morning to find Mac, Hussain, and Bev Wilson's team already there.

Getting out of the car, Graveney wandered across to them. 'Morning, everyone.' He said to the assembled group. 'Mac, you're with me. The rest of you, wait here.'

The pair of them made their way to the front door. Stopping, Graveney rang the bell. A few moments passed before they heard someone inside. The door opened to reveal a woman in her early fifties. 'Can I help?' she said.

'DI Graveney and DI Mackay,' he said. Both presented their ID. 'Is Mr Foxley in?'

The woman beckoned them into the hallway and then pointed to a room to the side. 'If you'd like to wait in this room, I'll tell Mr Foxley you're here.' She turned and headed away from them.

Graveney and Mac found themselves in some sort of sitting room. Several leather chairs situated close to a fireplace. Numerous paintings adorned every wall, and a huge mirror spanned the width of the chimney-breast. Mac and Graveney glanced around the room, suitably impressed by the grandeur of it all.

'Sorry I was late this morning, Mac. A few too many last night. I didn't want to drive myself.'

'That's ok. I nearly slept in too.'

Graveney glanced across at Mac. Even though he instantly concealed his emotion, Graveney recognised joy on his friend's face.

'Well, well, well,' he said. 'What happened to you last night?'

Mac smiled. 'What?'

'I bet someone had his coffee at the coffee shop this morning, served by a particular lady we both know?'

'She's some woman, that Becky.'

Graveney laughed. 'Really? That's all it takes? One night with Becky and she's captured your heart?'

'I wouldn't say that. However, we've arranged a date.'

'You're a lucky man. Becky is a smashing lass. Although she could do a lot worse than you.'

Both of them turned as the door to the room opened.

Foxley entered. 'Good morning. Inspectors Graveney and Mackay, isn't it?' Holding out his hand as the officers shook it in turn. 'What can I do for you two?'

'We've reason to believe, Mr Foxley, that ...,' Graveney paused for a moment, searching for the right words. 'There's a possibility that bodies are buried on your estate.' Not entirely satisfied by how he'd put it.

'Bodies. How awful. What makes you think that?'

'We've obtained some information from a third party. I'm not at liberty to disclose any names, of course. I'm sure you'll understand. But we feel this information is both credible and accurate. I've a warrant to search an area on the outskirts of your estate. We will of course be discreet, Mr Foxley, and we'll keep you informed of developments.'

Foxley smiled. 'Certainly, Inspector. I'll assist you in any way I can. Where about on the estate do you want to search?'

Graveney passed Foxley a map of his property with a small red ring indicating where they intended to dig.

'I'll get my gardener to take you over there. It's on the outskirts, near to a small wood. No one ever goes to that area. It's a little unkempt up there, I believe.' Accepting the warrant from Graveney, he smiled.

'We've a specialist team with us, Mr Foxley, and it could take a while. Possibly several days to carry out the dig. We'll try to be as unobtrusive as possible.'

'No, that's fine. If you require any help from me, let me know.' Foxley showed the officers out of the room and into the hall. 'If you'd like to wait outside, I'll send my gardener along.' He offered his hand once more. Graveney noticing how sweaty it had become.

'Thank you, Mr Foxley.' They headed for the door. Once outside Graveney made his way over to Bev Wilson. He pulled her and Mac aside, moving out of earshot of the others, as Marne looked on.

'What did he say?' Wilson asked.

'Oh, he's ok with it. He's sending his gardener around to take us across to the site,' Graveney said.

Mac glanced back at the house. 'What do you think?'

'He knows about it all right. He tried to be convincing, showing surprise in all the right places, but behind his mask lies a troubled man.'

'Do you think he's involved then?' Wilson said.

Graveney smiled. 'Right up to the collar of his Saville Row suit.'

'Well, let's hope we find something,' Wilson said.

Graveney nodded. 'We will, Bev. We will. I'd stake my life on those kids being buried there.'

The gardener finally arrived and escorted the team of officers and forensics over to the site. Graveney couldn't help but notice what an ideal place to bury a body or two it was. Out of sight of both the Hall and the road. A small track led to the spot and stopped abruptly near some trees. If anyone had a body, it'd be easy to drive down and then carry it the short distance to the burial site. Nobody was likely to venture down here, and even if they did, they'd be visible from the end of the track allowing valuable time to get away. Bev Wilson's team marked out the area indicated by the grid reference and Graveney, deciding it'd take some time, left them to it.

'Ring when you find something,' he said.

'If we find something,' Wilson said.

'Like I said. Believe me, you will. When you do, there's a drink or two in it for you.' Graveney turned and marched away.

Bev smiled and shook her head. She resisted the urge to give Graveney her middle finger. In any case, she'd just about forgiven him for standing her up.

Graveney and Mac returned to Middlesbrough police station awaiting news from Bev Wilson. They had brought Phillips up to date on their meeting with Foxley, and he had headed to Oake's office to inform him. They didn't wait long before they received the expected call from Bev.

'Peter, we've had a result. The ground penetrating radar has located something underground, probably bodies,' she told him.

'How many?' he asked.

'At least two, possibly three.'

'The two boys, and someone else,' he said. 'Jimmy Hind, perhaps?'

'Maybe. We're currently excavating the site. We've covered a large area, and I'm satisfied that's all there is.'

'Thanks. Let me know when you've got them out. I'll tell Phillips.'

Graveney sat back in his chair and looked across at Mac. 'We need to obtain some DNA from the families of the two boys, to check for familial matches. The third body could be Jimmy Hind, so we need to get in touch with his family too.'

Mac stood and walked towards the door, pausing he turned back to face Graveney. 'I'll get some of the guys on it now. What about Foxley, though? They were found on his estate.'

'I know, but he's going to deny all knowledge of it. We'll speak with Phillips to see how he wants to proceed. Imagine what Oake's going to say, though.'

Graveney picked up his phone and rang Phillips. 'Graveney, sir. I've had Bev Wilson on the phone, and they've found some buried bodies on the Wyndbourne Estate. She's currently having them excavated, and Mac's sorting out getting DNA for the two missing boys. It's possible there's a third body, which we believe is Jimmy Hind.'

'Right. I suppose we'd better ask Mr Foxley some questions but keep it low key at the moment. We'll also need to know who worked for him since the boys went missing and interview them.'

'We'll sort that information out, sir.' Graveney said.

Marne made her way out of the police station, telling Hussain she was nipping into town to get some dinner. In reality, she expected her phone to start ringing at any moment and having stepped into the car park, it did just that.

'Hi, Trevor,' she replied, pleasantly.

'You've heard the news?' Phillips said.

'That they've found bodies at Foxley's place?'

'What's your view?' he asked.

'He'll deny all knowledge of it. According to Oake, he didn't even know where the bodies were buried. Stevens buried the boys.'

'There's possibly a third body.'

'I didn't know that,' Marne said.

'Graveney seems to think it's Jimmy Hind.'

'Possibly. Or someone who happened to get in the way. I'll try to find out what I can on that from Oake, later,' she said.

'Steph, please be careful. For God's sake, make sure Oake doesn't find out.'

'I'll be ok. I'll ring you later,' Marne said. She was about to put her phone away when it rang again. 'Hi, Charlie,'

'Steph. I need to speak,' Oake said. 'Can you come over later?'

'Of course. What time?'

'Seven-thirty. See what you can find out from Graveney. See if he's keeping anything under his hat.'

Bev Wilson phoned up later in the day, to inform the investigation team they'd recovered three skeletons from the Wyndbourne estate. Two children, approximately 8 to 12 years of age, and one adult male, late twenties to early forties. She intended to carry out checks on them the following day, and she'd be able to tell them more then. Graveney promised her DNA from the families of the boys and dental records for Jimmy Hind. He and Mac arranged to visit her the next day.

Graveney and Mac left the station together and headed for a swift pint in the bar over the road. Mac found a seat and sat while Graveney got the drinks in.

'What you up to tonight, Mac? Fancy meeting me at my local?' he asked.

'Sorry. I've got something on.'

Graveney winked. 'This wouldn't involve an attractive, curvaceous coffee-shop owner, would it?'

'It would. We're going for a meal and then on to the pictures.'

'I hope it works out for you two. But look after the woman, will you? I've a soft spot for Becks.'

'I will. I promise.' Sarcastically crossing his heart.

Mac downed his pint quickly and waved goodbye to Graveney, who was on the phone to Louisa.

Graveney waved at Mac as he left. 'What are you doing tonight, Louisa?' he asked.

'I'm going to the pictures with Beth. I'm staying over. Why?'

'I'm at a bit of a loose end, that's all.'

'I could put her off if you like. She won't mind.'

'No. I wouldn't hear of it, Lou. You go and enjoy yourself, and I'll see you later.'

'Ok,' she said. 'Love you.' And rang off.

'Love you, too.' He put his mobile away.

'Thought I'd find you in here,' Marne said.

Graveney looked up at her. Her tied-back hair exposing her beautiful face, the top two buttons of her white blouse undone giving him a glimpse of her bra below. She sat in the seat opposite and leant towards him.

'What you up to?' she asked.

'A quick pint with Mac. He had to take off. He's on a date.'

'Fancy another?' Her right hand deliberately brushed his thigh.

'I take it you mean a pint?'

'What were *you* thinking of?'

'I'd love another, but I'm driving.' Changing the subject quickly.

She smiled and pushed closer. 'Get a taxi. I'll sub you a fiver.'

Graveney couldn't work Marne out. Witty, charming and warm when she wanted to be, but then she'd flick a switch and change into this vamp. As if she was two people. He could feel an erection rising in his trousers, just by being so close to her.

'Yeah, go on then.' he said.

Marne got up from her seat, and Graveney watched her as she made her way towards the bar. He didn't take his eyes off her while she was getting served, or even when she made her way back, placing a pint in front of him.

'I didn't know if you wanted a short or not?' she asked.

'It's a little early for spirits, Steph. I think I'll stick to pints.'

They amused themselves with small talk for an hour or so. As Graveney became merry, Marne sipped her drinks slowly, trying to remain sober.

'What do you think of today's events?' she asked.

'The bodies at Wyndbourne?'

'Yeah. Do you think Foxley had anything to do with it?'

'I'm sure of it.'

'How do you know that?' she said.

'From his face. He looked guilty. He tried to hide it from me, but I know he knew why we were there.'

'Do you think you can get him to talk?'

'Maybe. Foxley's not as self-assured as he thinks. If I get him into the interview room, who knows. The problem is he's a mate of The Chief Super, and I'm sure Oake wouldn't be happy if we took a hard-line with him.'

'I wasn't aware he knew Oake,' she said.

'They both went to the same public school, and you know how much that sort of thing counts for some people.'

'Yeah.'

'What we need is something other than circumstantial evidence to link him to the bodies.' Graveney took a large swig from his glass.

'And if you can't find anything?'

'We've hit a brick wall again.'

'I still think Shelby's our best bet,' Marne said.

'Shelby? What makes you think that?'

'I remember you telling me Stewart said Shelby had information.'

'He did, but our searches came up with nothing.'

'What about Stewart? Are we sure he didn't find anything at Shelby's?'

'If he did, it would have been on him when he died – or inside Shelby's office – and we've been through it with a fine-tooth comb.'

She sipped her drink. 'What about his accomplice, Ang?'

'We've never found her. She disappeared.'

Marne licked her lips. 'Why do that? I mean, if she was helping Stewart to locate and kill these people, why has she disappeared? Is it possible he gave her something?'

'I don't know the answer to that. In any case, how could he get anything out of the office, with the place surrounded?'

'Yeah. I never thought about that. If Stewart did have anything, he couldn't have got it out.' She rubbed her chin as if deep in thought. 'And there's nobody else who could've got it out for him? Oh, well.' Draining her glass, she stood.

'Leaving?' he asked.

'Sorry I have to be somewhere else.'

'Shame. I'm at a bit of a loose end.' He stared up at Marne.

'I can maybe spare you ten minutes,' she purred, as he drained his glass and followed her. Past the bar, through a corridor and into the toilet area. She checked no one was about, before dragging him inside the disabled toilet and locking the door.

'What now?' Graveney said.

Marne undid the zip on the side of her skirt and allowed it to drop to the floor. She slipped off her black briefs and turned around, facing away from him, bending over. 'Come on, Peter. Do your worst,' she whispered, licking her lips.

Graveney opened the door to the toilet and glanced along the corridor. Satisfied there was no one there, he stepped outside. He waited a minute or two before Marne exited the bathroom and followed him out of the pub. 'I can see the headlines now.' He blew out hard. 'Police officers caught having sex in a pub toilet.'

Marne laughed. 'Ah, but we weren't caught, and that's what makes it exciting. The thought we *could* be caught.'

'Can I drop you off anywhere?' Graveney asked.

'No, I'm fine.' Graveney watched her disappear from sight, before heading to a taxi rank.

Marne jumped into her car and drove to her apartment. She needed to shower and change before heading over to Oake's house, smiling to herself as she thought of Graveney.

She knocked on the door and Oake beckoned her into the living room, handing her a drink.

'What did Graveney say?' he asked.

'He thinks Foxley is involved in the murders. He's convinced that given enough time to apply pressure on him, he'll crack,' she said.

Oake poured himself another brandy and then sat in one of the armchairs. 'He has a point, there. Foxley's not made of stern stuff. We'll have to do something about him. I've spoken with the London people, and they're concerned too.'

'Would you like me to pay him a visit?'

'No. This needs Flint and Dec,' he said. 'We'll make it look like he took his own life. Poor Bill Foxley, couldn't cope with the fact he'd murdered those kids.'

'And the other body? Won't they link it to Sandra Stewart's murder?'

'Hind found out what Foxley had done and confronted him. Foxley panicked and killed him too. The Stewart woman is a blind alley. They'll never reach the bottom of that particular story.'

'Sounds like you've got it all worked out, Charlie?'

'I'm thinking of taking early retirement and moving somewhere warm. I've got plenty put away, and I could use some company.' Standing, he put his arms around Marne.

'Mmm, I like the sound of that.' Kissing him passionately, her hand drifted towards his groin and unzipping his fly, she dropped to her knees as Oake closed his eyes in anticipation.

Graveney showered and was about to do himself something to eat when his mobile rang. 'Bit late for you isn't it, Bev?' he asked.

'Thought you might be in the mood for a drink. I'm not too far from you. I'm in The Marton Arms, fancy it?'

'What you doing there?'

'One of the guys is leaving for a new job. All the lightweights have left already, but I've still got my drinking head on.'

'I've just stepped out of the shower. I can't be bothered getting ready to go out,' he said. Graveney heard a long sigh at the other end of the phone. 'Pop around if you like. I've only got Jack Daniels in though, but I've probably got some Coke.' Feeling a little sorry for her.

'Have you eaten?' she asked.

'Not yet. Do you want me to order something in?'

'Yeah. Margarita pizza for me.'

'No problem. See you shortly,' Graveney said.

Bev arrived five minutes later. Ten minutes after that, the pizzas turned up. They sat drinking Jack Daniels and Coke while eating their food, the two of them getting increasingly inebriated. Graveney watched Bev get to her feet unsteadily, as she made her way to the toilet. She looked attractive, shorn of the usual light-blue overalls she wore on the job. Graveney was becoming increasingly interested in her. Her blonde hair curled around the edges of her face, and the small amount of makeup she had on, only added to her beauty. He stood and ambled along the corridor, stopping outside the toilet. The door opened, and she unsteadily came out. They exchanged glances as Graveney went to relieve himself, but as he came back out Bev was still there. Without saying a word, she wrapped her arms around him and planted her lips on his. She smelt wonderful. Her perfume filled his nostrils, as he passionately kissed her back.

'Are you sure you want to do this?' he asked.

She giggled. 'I'm a big girl. You're hardly my first, you know.'

'I mean, we've both had a lot to drink. I'll only break your heart.'

'I'll take the risk.' They kissed again.

Moving in unison towards the front room, Graveney was happy Louisa was staying at Beth's house for the night. The thought of her bursting in on them almost caused him to come to his senses. But when he turned his full attention back to Bev, they were virtually fully undressed. Bev pushed him onto the sofa and got on top. Any doubts Graveney had quickly evaporated as Bev got to work on him, like a woman who had waited a long, long time for this to happen. By the time they had finished, they both sat, semi-naked on the sofa, fighting to regain their breath. Graveney surprised at how passionate and vocal Bev had been. As if trying to prove something to him, pulling out all the stops. If this was her intention, she'd succeeded. He glanced across, her eyes beginning to droop with tiredness.

He nudged her. 'Do you want to stay the night?'

'If you don't mind.'

'You've got a busy day tomorrow.' He reminded her.

'That's tomorrow,' she said. He led her to the bedroom. They undressed fully and got into bed. Graveney spooned Bev, and she allowed her hand to reach back and stroke him, as he hardened again.

'Are you looking for seconds?' she asked.

'Why not?' he whispered in her ear.

'Why not, indeed.' And rolled on to her back.

Marne sat at the dressing table brushing her hair as Oake, still in bed, looked across. She stood and turned around, Oake viewing her beautiful form as he licked his lips. 'I don't suppose you want to come back to bed, do you?' he asked.

'I've got to get home for a change and shower. Otherwise, I would. I'll have to give you a rain-check.' Pulling on a pair of briefs and bra before slipping into her dress.

'You're really beautiful,' he said. 'Although I'm not sure your late dad would approve of me.'

'Graveney did say something else last night.'

'Oh yes?' he said.

'He thinks Shelby's the answer to this case. He hinted Stephen Stewart told him something.'

Oake's eyes widened. 'What?'

'He wouldn't tell me outright, but I got the impression he was holding something back.'

'Like what?' Oake jumped out of bed.

'No idea. But Graveney's a smart individual.'

'He couldn't have evidence.' Oake paced around the room. 'I mean. He wouldn't be that stupid, would he? Any undisclosed evidence wouldn't stand up in court.'

She turned away and smirked. 'Maybe he doesn't know what he has.'

Oake snorted. 'I always thought Shelby had incriminating evidence, but he'd have kept it somewhere safe.'

She turned to face him again. 'Like where?'

'A safety deposit box. But Jones checked it out and found nothing. If Graveney has the key, he may be able to locate where he kept the evidence.' Oake now sounded concerned.

'I'm sure, if he had a key to something like a safety deposit box, he'd have been there already.' Marne said. 'Unless he doesn't know what the key is for?'

'This is supposition,' he said. 'If Graveney has anything, we'd know by now.'

'You're right. I think we're worrying unnecessarily. Graveney would have checked out Shelby himself. Unless … Shelby used a pseudonym. And if he did, maybe no one would be able to find it,' she said. And strode out of the bedroom.

Oake thought for a moment. What Steph said had rattled him. Maybe Shelby had used a false name. Possibly the safety deposit box was in another name, something familiar to him. He needed to find out if he did, and also get from Graveney anything he had. Oake felt for a moment as if the walls were closing in but composing himself, he picked up his mobile.

'Yes, sir?' Flint said.

'I need something doing,' he said.

'Oh yeah?'

Graveney, woke early and quickly shaking off the thick head he had when he first woke up, decided to prepare some breakfast. As the bacon and sausages cooked, he went to wake Bev. She lay on her stomach, the sheet barely covering her modesty. He sat on the bed and gently nudged her. Bev, quickly realising where she was, as memories of the previous night flooding back, pulled the sheet around herself.

'It's ok. I saw it all last night,' he said, as Bev visibly blushed. 'I'm doing a spot of breakfast if you're interested?'

'Just toast, and coffee for me. And maybe some paracetamol,' Bev said. 'Can I have a shower?'

Graveney stood. 'Of course. I'll get you a towel.'

He prepared his breakfast and toast while she showered. She eventually emerged from the bathroom, bleary-eyed, looking slightly better. She forced the toast and coffee down, along with two tablets.

'About last night.' Staring at Graveney, who smiled at her. 'I don't normally do that sort of thing.'

'Really? You seem good at it.'

'You're enjoying this, aren't you? I mean, jump into bed so quickly.'

'Bev, we're both adults. We had a lot to drink. It happened. There's no point beating yourself up over it. I won't breathe a word.'

'Thanks,' she said.

'As long as you don't go blabbing to every Tom, Dick, and Harry. I wouldn't want people thinking I'm an easy lay.' Smiling, he got up from his seat with his dirty plate, while Bev resisted the strong urge to middle finger him.

CHAPTER TWENTY-ONE

Bev Wilson finished her examinations of the skeletons, recovered from Wyndbourne Hall, not helped by the hangover she was suffering. Her thoughts, from the night before with Graveney, causing her great embarrassment. Made worse by the fact he was due to turn up at any minute, with Mac. At least her headache had subsided a little, and she made herself a solemn promise never to drink Jack Daniels again. She sipped some water from a bottle, she'd bought to assist with her re-hydration, when one of her assistants entered, closely followed by Graveney and Mac.

'Morning, Bev,' Graveney said, cheerily. 'How are you today?'

'Fine,' she lied. 'I suppose you'd like to know what I've discovered.'

Graveney smiled. 'Well, we haven't come over just to look at your beautiful face.'

Bev ignored Graveney's apparent attempt to get her rattled and picked up a folder from one of the tables. 'The DNA matches with the ones you supplied for the two boys. It's definitely them. The length of time they were buried coincides with the time they went missing. I can't determine a cause of death because there aren't any clues on the skeleton.'

'And the other one?' Mac asked.

'Jimmy Hind. His dental records match. Almost certainly tortured before he died.'

Graveney frowned. 'Tortured?'

'He had five missing toes. When we unearthed him, I thought maybe they'd come away in our excavation, but when we got him back here and cleaned up, it became evident they'd been cut off with some sharp implement. Something designed primarily for cutting. They were clean cuts. Possibly inflicted by shears, or something similar.'

'And these were definitely before death?' Graveney said.

'Definitely is always hard to determine. I'm confident it was. I mean, why would someone cut toes off after death?'

Graveney looked at Mac. 'Ray Hetherington?' he said.

'Who's Ray Hetherington?' Bev asked.

Graveney turned back to her. 'He shared a cell with Arthur Stevens in Durham. Found murdered in his burnt-out flat in Middlesbrough. Missing some toes. He owed some gangsters from Newcastle money. Everybody assumed they'd killed him, although nothing was proven. It appears the people who murdered him also killed Jimmy.'

Bev put a hand up to her mouth. 'Will you excuse me a moment?' Racing for the toilets to throw up again.

'What's up with Bev? You'd have thought she'd be used to all this by now,' Mac said.

Bev composed herself and re-entered the Lab. 'I'm sorry about that. Something I've eaten.'

'Or drank?' Winked Graveney, as Bev glared at him. 'Thanks, Bev. Great job.' He and Mac turned and left.

Mac nudged Graveney. 'What did you mean by that?'

'She was at a colleagues leaving party last night. I think Bev had one too many.'

Graveney and Marne made their way out to Wyndbourne Hall to interview William Foxley. They were shown into the same room that he and Mac had waited in on their visit the previous day. Foxley joined them shortly afterwards. They were offered and accepted tea during the interview, which was quite informal. Graveney not wanting to antagonise Phillips or Oake. Foxley insisted he knew nothing about the bodies and could offer no explanation as to how they'd come to be buried on his land. Graveney viewed Foxley suspiciously as he tried to determine if he actually knew anything. Foxley appeared to get more nervous as the interview progressed, and his agitation increased, even more, when Graveney asked him if he knew Arthur Stevens. He assured Graveney he'd only heard of him via the media when the abuse at Winterton came to light.

After what Graveney thought was a gentle interview with Foxley, the housekeeper showed them out. But not before Graveney asked Foxley about his whereabouts around the time the boys from Winterton disappeared. He claimed he couldn't remember and that his diaries for that period had been destroyed. In any other circumstances Graveney wouldn't think this unusual, but Foxley had exhibited what Graveney could only describe as acute concern and anxiety. Most people miss this. Graveney picked up on it instantly, as emotion after emotion swept across Foxley's face.

One of Foxley's staff provided Graveney with a list of the people who worked at the hall since 1996. Fortunately for Graveney and Marne, the turnover of staff was relatively small since then, and they were able to interview most of the people on it. A couple of the staff had retired, and one of them had died since leaving, so Graveney asked Marne to arrange interviews with the ones not still employed. Once outside and back in the car he looked across at Marne, waiting for her to speak. She didn't disappoint.

'What do you think, sir?'

'He's as guilty as sin. He knows everything. Who's involved, who killed the boys and Jimmy Hind. Everything.'

'How do you know?'

'It's hard to explain, but his face betrays him. He tried desperately to keep his emotions in check, and I imagine, even though it was a somewhat informal interview, Foxley is feeling stressed at this moment.'

'You couldn't prove any of this, though?'

'No, I couldn't. Get Foxley into an interview room at the station, and apply more pressure, I think he'll crack. People handle guilt differently. Some are able to block it out entirely and push it from their minds as if it never happened. Others though, find it weighs heavy on their shoulders. These types of people need to tell someone and unburden themselves, and Mr Foxley is such a man. I'll speak to Phillips and Oake, see if we can give him an opportunity to do that.'

Marne and Graveney arrived back at the station thirty minutes later. Graveney headed straight up to the incident room, while Marne seized the opportunity to go outside and make a call.

'Hi, Steph,' Oake said, glumly.

Marne climbed into her car. 'We've just got back from Foxley's. I think you're right about him. Graveney is sure he knows everything and intends to interview him at the station.'

'What was Bill like, in your opinion?'

'Very nervous. If I were you, I certainly wouldn't want to rely on him.'

'I've already primed Flint. If I'm honest, I was hoping it wouldn't come to this, but if what you say is true, we've got no choice.'

'It's your call, Charlie. Your neck on the block.'

'Ok, thanks. Leave it to me.'

They both hung up, and a smile spread across Marne's face. She knew she had signed Foxley's death warrant, and it pleased her greatly. The only disappointment, she wouldn't be there to see his demise. To witness the low-life bastard get his comeuppance. She'd enjoyed killing Jones. Enjoyed slowly but surely undermining him with Oake, and then convincing Jones to ask for more money, allowing him to be the architect of his own downfall. When she closed her eyes, she felt the knife in her hand as she pushed it through his back, into his heart, until the life vanished from him. She gazed into the mirror at her reflection.

'Slowly, slowly, catchy monkey,' she said to herself. She applied some bright red lipstick and went inside.

Graveney quickly brought Mac up to date regarding his interview with Foxley. He told him of his suspicions regarding his guilt. The two of them had gone up to Phillips' office to persuade him to allow them to bring Foxley into the station for a more rigorous interview. Phillips agreed readily. Telling them he intended talking with Oake to convince him this was the best course of action. He asked them to delay it by a day to allow Mr Foxley to stew a little, and Graveney and Mac agreed. Graveney asked what Phillips would do if Oake stopped him from pulling Foxley in. To their surprise, he'd told them he'd go above his head if he had to, and ask The Chief Constable. Graveney and Mac left happy with themselves, feeling, at last, they were getting somewhere with this case.

Phillips had gone into Oake's office and told him they intended to interview Foxley formally at the station. To his total surprise, Oake agreed. Leaving Phillips, who'd been expecting a battle, bemused.

Oake picked up his mobile phone and rang Flint, closing his office door for privacy.

'Yes, sir,' Flint said.

'The conversation we had last night regarding our mutual friend,' Oake said. 'He's become surplus to requirements. Go ahead with what we discussed.'

'When?'

'Tonight. Do it then. And Flint, no cock-ups. You understand?'

'Perfectly, sir.'

Oake searched through his contacts and stopping at Bill Foxley he rang his number.

'Charlie, I was about to phone you,' he said.

'Well, I've saved you the bother.'

'The detective earlier. I said nothing. I'm sure I've convinced him.'

'That's why I'm phoning, Bill. You made a good impression because he believes you. I had a word with him, and he suspects someone else buried the bodies on your land. He thinks they used your property to hide them out of convenience. You shouldn't have any further trouble on that score. So how about meeting at the golf club tonight for a celebratory drink?'

'Sounds good to me. Seven-thirty?'

'Seven-thirty's fine,' he said.

Graveney headed home early, stopping off at a florist on the way to collect a bouquet. He'd changed out of his suit and into something more comfortable before picking up the flowers. He headed towards the door, meeting Louisa coming in.

'Where you off to?' she asked.

'The cemetery.'

Louisa frowned. 'The cemetery?' Before realising the date. 'I'm sorry, Peter. I forgot.'

'That's understandable. You've had a lot on your plate of late, what with your Mam and that.' He put his arms around her.

'Can I come?'

'Are you sure you want to?'

'Of course, I am.' She hugged him tightly.

Graveney and Louisa drove to the cemetery, parked up outside and strolled towards the graveyard. He stopped at the grave of his dead wife and unnamed child, placing the flowers down. A fresh bouquet already there, Graveney assumed from Heather. Louisa linked his arm, and Graveney touched her hand with his.

'Who are the other flowers from?' she asked.

'Heather, I think.'

'What was she like, your wife?'

'Wonderful. Beautiful, intelligent and charming.'

'What did she look like? There aren't any photos of her in the flat.'

'She looked like Heather.'

'She must have been beautiful. You miss her, don't you?'

'Sometimes.' He lied. He always did.

'Come on, young lady,' he said. 'Let's go for something to eat.'

Louisa spotted the tears forming in his eyes, but apparently, he didn't want to talk about Gillian, so she let it pass as they strolled back to the car. 'What about Heather?'

Graveney frowned. 'Heather?'

'I know you like Heather. You have photos of her in the flat.'

He laughed. '*My*, you're nosy.'

'Well, I'm your ... friend,' she said. Graveney noticing her pause said nothing.

'Heather's special. We go back a long way, and I've a lot of time for her. She's a good friend.'

'She's more than a friend, though, isn't she?'

'What do you mean?'

'Well, sometimes you stay over. Don't you?'

'Louisa, you don't hold back?'

'You shouldn't string her along if you're not serious.'

'I don't ... You haven't spoken to Maddie, have you?'

'Who's Maddie?'

'She's a friend of Heather's. I ran into her the other night. It's a long story.'

'Heather loves you.'

'How do you know that?' He smiled at her.

'I met her in town, yesterday. She told me how sorry she was to hear about my mam. We went for a coffee, and when we talked about you, I could tell.'

'How? I mean you're only ...'

'Only seventeen?'

'I didn't mean it like that. What did Heather say to you?'

She smiled. 'It wasn't what she said which mattered. It's what she didn't say. You should know that.'

'Louisa, you're seventeen going on forty-seven.'

'I know. I've always been older than my years. I grew up quickly.' The smile on Louisa's face fell away.

'Do you want to talk about it?' Hoping she wouldn't.

'Maybe another day,' she said.

'Well, I'll tell you all about Heather another day, too.'

'It's a deal.' She stretched up and kissed him on the cheek. It took all of Graveney's resolve to keep his emotions in check. The day, the guilt he already felt regarding Heather, almost getting the better of him.

'Where do you want to eat?' he asked.

'What about the Farmers Arms?'

'Why there?'

'They do good pub grub, and I fancy a Parmo. Well, maybe a half.'

'Ok,' he said. 'The Farmers it is.'

Foxley set off for the golf club at seven-twenty. Turning his Jaguar out of the estate, he headed along the main road on the ten-minute drive. Eventually, he reached the turn-off for the entrance to the golf club and stopped. A car with its bonnet up parked in the lane, and as the road narrowed at this point, he was unable to pass. A man appeared from under the bonnet of the car and closing it, got into the driver's seat. Foxley sighed in relief. For a moment he thought he'd have to get out and assist the man if he wanted to get past his vehicle. Foxley was about to drive off when his passenger door opened and another man got in beside him, pressing the muzzle of a gun into Foxley's side.

'Do exactly what I say,' Flint said. 'Follow that car.'

Foxley, terrified, did as he was told and followed the other car along the lane. They drove past the entrance to the golf club where they swung the vehicles around in a small parking area and headed back the way they'd come. Foxley followed the car back towards Wyndbourne Hall and turning back through the gates to his estate, he thought for a moment that they were heading back to the house. Alarmingly, they turned off the road and drove down to the area the police searched and recovered the bodies from. They pulled up near to where the digs had taken place, the site still taped off. The man motioned for Foxley to turn off the engine and get out of the car, which he did before they trudged over to the other car and got into the back.

'Please,' he stammered. 'What's this all about?'

'Bill, Bill,' Flint said, in slow, measured tones. 'I'm afraid there's no easy way to tell you this, but you've reached the end of the road.'

'But, Charlie, my friend ... He'll straighten this out. He'll explain.'

'Charlie sent us, Bill. The London people think you're a liability,' he continued in his drawl.

'But I haven't said anything. I wouldn't ... Please let me speak to Charlie.'

'Bill. Let me make this as easy as possible for you. You're going to die here tonight. It's up to you how you leave this life. Gently, like falling to sleep. Or kicking and screaming in agony. It's up to you. My friend is particularly good at inflicting pain. He enjoys it, actually.' Smiling at Dec, who smiled back.

'I can give you money.'

'Your money is no good, Bill. I'm afraid no amount of money is going to get you out of this. It would be better for all of us if you accepted that.'

Dec opened a bag he'd brought with him and removed a bottle of brandy, handing it to Flint.

'You see? We can be civilised. We've brought you a bottle of your favourite brandy. No expense spared.' He grinned.

Foxley's eyes darted between the two men. 'What do you want me to do?'

'Drink it.' Opening the bottle, he handed it to Foxley.

'What if I don't want to drink it?'

Flint edged his face close to Foxley, only inches from him. Foxley felt Flint's breath on his skin as his terror mounted. 'You weren't listening, Bill. I told you what would happen. I'll leave you to my friend, shall I?' Motioning to move as Dec pulled a pair of garden secateurs from his bag. Foxley gulped as he saw them and instantly realising what would happen if he didn't, drank from the bottle.

Flint and Dec carried the semi-conscious body of Foxley from their car and placed him in the driver's seat of his Jaguar. They dropped an empty brandy bottle in the footwell of the passenger side and then put a half-empty bottle of brandy in Foxley's hands. Foxley, unable to stay awake any longer, passed out. Dec had already connected a large hose from the exhaust through the rear window of the car, before sealing the gap with plastic and tape. Flint started the engine and closed the door as the car filled with exhaust fumes. Flint and Dec got into their vehicle and sat watching the Jaguar for thirty minutes. Satisfied Foxley was dead by now, the pair drove off into the night. They pulled off the road into a lay-by, and Flint rang Oake.

'It's done,' Flint said.

'No problems?' Oake said.

'Everything went smoothly, sir.'

CHAPTER TWENTY-TWO

Graveney got up early and prepared some breakfast for himself and Louisa. He felt in a buoyant mood this morning. Today could be the day they began to get to the bottom of this investigation. He intended to pay Foxley an early visit and hopefully catch him on the hop, taking him into custody for a more rigorous interview. He suspected Oake would inform Foxley of his intention, but wouldn't have any idea of what time they'd arrive. Even if Foxley knew they were coming, he hoped — and if he'd read the situation right — this would only add to Foxley's anxiety. He and Louisa popped into Ratano's to get a coffee-to-go, and for Louisa to speak with Becky about working part-time there. Becky had an extra sparkle in her eyes today put there by Mac, Graveney suspected. He'd briefly glanced through the morning papers while Louisa spoke with Becky before the two of them left the shop. Graveney dropping Louisa off at her friend's en route. He arrived at Middlesbrough Police Station and after exchanging pleasantries with some of the uniform boys, headed upstairs to the incident room.

'Morning, people.' Cheerfully heading into his office. Hussain followed him inside and stood opposite Graveney's desk.

'Have you a minute, sir?'

'What is it, Raz?' Maintaining his cheeriness.

'I've got some bad news, sir.' He shuffled his feet. 'I've had a call from uniform. William Foxley's dead.'

Graveney looked up from his paperwork, scarcely believing what Raz told him. 'He's what?'

'Found dead on his estate this morning, by one of his workmen. It appears he took his own life, sir. Gassed himself in his car near to where we recovered the bodies.'

'Are we sure it's suicide?'

'I think Bev Wilson's over there now, sir, but that's how it appears.'

'Is Mac here yet?'

'No, not yet, sir.'

'Send him straight in when he arrives.'

Graveney rang Bev. 'Morning, Peter. I was expecting this call.'

'What happened to Foxley?'

'He was found in his car,' she said. 'It looks as if he fixed a hose from his exhaust through the window of the car and gassed himself. That's how it appears.'

'Any sign of foul play?'

'Nothing yet. But we recovered two bottles of brandy from the car. One empty, the other half-full. First indications show carbon monoxide poisoning.'

'I'll ring later when you have the results of the post-mortem,' he said.

'Later this afternoon. I should be done by then.'

'How are you feeling today?' he asked.

She laughed. 'A lot better. I'll probably be giving Jack Daniels a wide berth from now on.'

'I would if I was you. We'll speak later.'

Mac entered Phillips' office and closed the door behind him, as Phillips stood.

'How are you, Mac?' Pointing to a chair as they both sat.

'Fine, sir.'

'And Peter? How's he?'

'He's ok, too.'

'Have you heard the news about Foxley?'

'What news is that, sir?'

'He's dead. They discovered his body this morning, close to the site where the bodies were recovered. It looks like suicide.'

'And do you think it's suicide?'

'Look, If I'm honest, I'm not sure what to think. It's a bit convenient, the one person who could give us a breakthrough in this investigation winds up dead.'

'Any signs of foul play, sir?'

'We'll have to wait for the result of the post-mortem for that.'

'And if it's suicide?'

'We're back to square one. The reason I asked you to come and see me, Mac ... I'm worried about Peter. I brought you from Scotland because you had no involvement with Cleveland Constabulary. I wanted someone to keep an eye on Peter, and the fact the two of you know each other helps significantly.'

'What do you mean? Keep an eye on Peter?'

Phillips rubbed his chin, searching for the right words. 'There's a belief within the force, some of the officers at Middlesbrough are corrupt. The fact Jones was found with evidence corroborates this, but he might not be the only one. It's possible there's someone else, someone more senior.'

'Who?'

'I can't say. But if there is, Peter may be in danger. I want you to keep a close eye on him for me, and make sure he comes to no harm.'

'Peter's not only my colleague, sir, but he's also my friend. I don't know if I'm comfortable with that.'

'Mac, I'm not asking you to betray him or anything, I'm just saying, I want him kept safe. I don't need to remind you, someone unknown, murdered Jones. It's obvious these people are ruthless and prepared to eliminate anyone they feel a threat.'

'Why not tell Peter this?'

'Peter needs to continue the investigation without having to look over his shoulder all the time. If he suspects everyone, how the hell can he run it competently? There are things I can't tell you at the moment. I'm asking you to take me on trust here. Make sure Peter is kept safe. Don't allow him to become isolated and most of all, don't trust anyone.'

'Anyone but you, sir?'

'Anyone but me, Mac.'

'I'll do what you ask, but I'm not going to betray Peter. If I feel he needs to know, I'll tell him what you've said to me.'

'That's fine. I appreciate that.' Mac nodded and left.

As Mac headed away from Philip's office, Marne, waiting nearby for the duration of their meeting, hid behind a filing cabinet until he'd passed. She walked over to Phillips' office and tapped on the door.

'Come in,' Phillips shouted, as Marne entered and sat opposite him.

Phillips glared at Marne. 'Foxley?'

'Suicide, wasn't it, Trevor?'

'Come off it, Steph. Are you seriously expecting me to believe he took his own life? Implicated in the murder of three people, suddenly he finds his conscience and tops himself.'

'I don't know anything about it, sir. Oake hasn't mentioned it.'

'I hope you're not keeping anything from me? I've gone out on a limb, allowing you free-reign on this investigation. There are other people at stake here. Other people in danger.'

'Like Graveney?'

'Yes. Like Graveney. What I'm doing, what we're doing, goes against everything we've been ...' He struggled to find the right words.

'Trevor. There's only so much I can do. Oake trusts me, but some things he keeps to himself. Or possibly, he had nothing to do with Foxley's death.'

'Are you saying there are others involved?'

'Maybe. Possibly more influential people,' she said.

'Who?' he asked.

'I don't know that. What I do know is, we have to follow this through to its conclusion.'

'For Christ's sake, Steph. This could backfire on us. We need evidence, and we need it soon.'

'I'm trying to obtain that, sir, but Oake is clever.'

'Steph, if any more officers die, I'm informing the Chief Constable, and handing it over to the internal investigation department. Do you understand?'

'Yes. I understand,' Marne said. She stood and left.

Phillips got up from his seat and paced around his office, not knowing what to make of the recent developments. He now doubted Steph. Phillips suspected she was keeping something from him, but what? Graveney, he was now convinced was in danger. Someone wanted this case buried for good and were prepared to remove anyone who posed a risk. Phillips sat back down. She was right, though. They'd crossed the Rubicon, and he'd have to hope this didn't blow up in his face.

Graveney phoned Bev Wilson late afternoon, giving her plenty of opportunity to complete the post-mortem.

'Give me the worst, Bev.'

'I can't find anything indicating foul play. A large quantity of brandy inside him, and it appears he drank it before gassing himself. No signs he was restrained, or forced to drink it, so my conclusion is, he took his own life.'

'What about a suicide note?' he said.

'We didn't find anything.'

Graveney sighed. 'Well, I'm not convinced. It all seems a little too convenient if you ask me.'

'It's possible his conscience got the better of him, and he did kill himself.'

'What about Jimmy Hind,' Graveney said. 'Are you telling me someone who tortures people would feel remorse for those kids?'

'Maybe he didn't kill Hind. Maybe someone else did.'

'But that complicates it further,' Graveney said.

'Ok. Suppose you're right, and someone did get Foxley drunk. We'll find it difficult to prove.'

'Yeah. You're right.'

'You sound down, Peter. Do you want a drink? As long as it's only a drink, mind.'

Graveney sighed. 'No thanks. I've just had a phone call. Some bad news. My aunt passed away.'

'I'm sorry to hear that. Is this aunt the one who looked after you when your mother died?'

'Yeah. A bit of a shock, actually. Just keeled over. I've got to go up to Bedale for the funeral next week.'

'Sorry, Peter.'

'Thanks. We'll catch up later. Maybe for a drink and a chat.'

Graveney gathered his things together and headed home, met by Marne on the way down the stairs.

'Off home, sir?' she said.

'Yeah. I've had enough of today, Steph.'

'What did Phillips want with Mac this morning?'

Graveney frowned. 'No idea.'

'They had what appeared to be a deep conversation when I went up to Phillips' office.'

'What were you doing there?'

'He wanted a copy of the post-mortems on the bodies we recovered from Wyndbourne.'

'Probably asking Mac how things were going with his move up here.'

'Probably.' She smiled, turned and headed for her car.

Graveney refused to look in her direction, not wanting her to know she'd piqued his interest. Mac hadn't mentioned he'd gone to see Phillips. It could be entirely innocent, of course, but Graveney was surprised he hadn't told him. He pushed the thought away and headed for the Farmers Arms.

Marne smiled as she sat in her car. Hopefully, the seed she'd planted with Graveney would grow. She needed him isolated for her plan to work, and she couldn't have Mac looking over his shoulder when the time came.

Graveney arrived at the pub just after five. Positioning himself at the end of the bar as Liz came over to serve him.

'Hello, handsome. Two days on the trot.'

'Louisa's going out with her friend. I haven't had time to go shopping, so I thought I'd have one of your excellent pub meals again. Oh, and of course, it gives me an opportunity to see you.'

'You smooth-talker.' Pulling him a pint. 'But I noticed it was the food you mentioned first.'

'That's because you're a fabulous cook.'

'How are things at work?' She pulled a pint for another customer.

'Not good.'

'What you need is a holiday. All work and all that.'

Graveney took a large drink. 'Too much on. I've got a funeral to attend next week as well.'

'Oh, I'm sorry. Who?'

'My aunt.'

'Was it the one who you lived with?'

'Yeah.'

'I'm sorry to hear that. How old?'

'Sixty-eight,' Graveney said. 'No age at all these days.'

'No, it isn't.'

Graveney shook his head. 'Heart attack. Just keeled over.'

'That's what happened to my mam. Dropped down dead in Asda. She wasn't even that old. Do you want to talk about it?' Putting a hand on his.

'Maybe later. I'm not sure if Louisa's coming home, or staying out.'

'She's special to you, isn't she?'

'More than you think, but I'll tell you later if I come back.'

Liz put her hand on his cheek and smiled at him, before moving away to serve another customer.

Graveney picked up the menu and perused its contents.

Marne made her way over to Oake's house. He greeted her at the door and took her into the sitting room.

'What's the view in the incident room, Steph?'

'Everyone at the station, including Phillips, assumes Foxley took his own life. There's no evidence to prove anything to the contrary, so I think we can put it to bed.'

Oake nodded. 'The thing we talked about the other night? About how Shelby could be our only stumbling block? I've given it some more thought, and I've decided to dig deeper and see if we can come up with something the investigation missed.'

'Such as?' she asked.

'Well, I'm certain he'd have information tucked away somewhere. Probably in a safe place. So, I've instructed my men to leave no stone unturned and find out where it is before Graveney does.'

'You think Graveney's holding something back?' Marne said.

'If he is, we'll extract it from him. But before we do that, we need to know where Shelby hid the stuff.'

'I'll keep working on Graveney, and see if I can find anything out.'

'Yes, you do that.' He poured himself another brandy. 'If we recover the information, and destroy it, the people in London have offered me a considerable payment. I intend to leave the force after this is all over, and move somewhere nice. Have you given it any further thought?'

'Clear up the loose ends, and I'll gladly come with you.' She put down her glass and sashayed towards him.

'You're so beautiful, Steph.' He kissed her.

'Shall we go upstairs? I'm feeling particularly horny tonight.'

Oake licked his lips in anticipation, as he followed Marne upstairs. Marne smiled to herself. Everything was coming together perfectly, she thought. She undid the zip on her dress, allowing it to fall to the floor. Oake stood, gazing at her beautiful form clad in bright red lingerie.

Graveney ate his pub meal and after going home, showering and changing, spoke with Louisa who confirmed she was staying at her friend's. He decided to return to the pub and Liz. The two of them tidied up the bar a little and headed off upstairs to enjoy their usual bottle of wine, before going to bed to make love. Liz lay in Graveney's arms, afterwards.

'What were you saying about Louisa?' she asked.

Graveney told her about the photo album, and how he suspected Louisa may be his, or at least, Louisa thought that. Liz wasn't surprised. She claimed she could see a resemblance between the two of them, but Graveney wasn't convinced. People often say that when they find out people are related.

'How do you feel about it?' she asked.

'I love her already. If she's my daughter, I wouldn't love her anymore. I'm not going to ask her though. If she wants to bring up the subject, we'll discuss it then.'

'Is she working at the moment?'

'She's doing a few hours in Becky's coffee shop. Why?'

'I'm looking for someone to wait on tables and clear up a bit. One of the girls has left and got another job, and I'd rather give it to someone I know.'

'That'll suit her because she's on about going back to college. She's intelligent. I think what happened to her at home affected her education.'

'I'll have a word next time she's in. What about your aunt's funeral?'

'It's in Bedale on Monday,' he said. 'I haven't been up there in a while. I spoke with her on the phone, mainly.'

'Were you close?'

'Like a mother to me. After my mam died, Andrew, my brother, would have had to go into care, until she stepped in. She never married, and she told us we were company for her. I lived up there until I went to Uni.'

Liz hugged Graveney, sensing the sadness in his voice. The two of them closed their eyes and fell asleep.

The rest of the week went by without incident. The investigation, despite the best efforts of Graveney and his team, appeared to have stalled. Mac and some of their team continued to look at other avenues, without success, and Graveney began to feel they'd never get to the bottom of it. He rang Heather, after putting it off for long enough and took Luke and Louisa to the Middlesbrough match on Saturday. Heather told him of her intention of going to his aunt's funeral on Monday, and the two of them decided to travel up together.

Graveney met up with Mac on Sunday afternoon for a drink, and as he hadn't mentioned the conversation with Phillips, Graveney decided not to say anything about it either. He assumed Marne had been mistaken, or maybe it was of no importance. Mac and Becky's relationship was proceeding at an astonishing rate, and Mac was even talking about moving in with her. Graveney ribbed Mac on his clean-shaven appearance, concluding Becky had encouraged him to shave it off. Mac admitted as much, but took the ribbing in good heart, claiming he'd been considering it anyway. Graveney went to bed at 10.00 pm on Sunday evening. With the plan of getting up to Bedale early, the funeral being held at 10.30 am. He checked his wardrobe, making sure his best black suit was clean, and satisfied it was, put it out ready for the next morning. Finally getting into bed, he quickly fell asleep.

CHAPTER TWENTY-THREE

Graveney collected Heather from her house early. Having decided to travel the more scenic route to Bedale, through Northallerton and some picturesque villages on their way, rather than the quicker journey up the A1. They'd stopped in Northallerton en route for coffees before travelling on through Ainderby Steeple, Morton on Swale and Leeming Bar, finally reaching Bedale. It hadn't changed much since his last visit. The high street consisting of two rows of shops either side, a mixture of the new and traditional. The pubs, he recognised from his youth and visits up to his aunt's, appeared as if they'd never had a coat of paint for years. Graveney smiled, pleased to see his favourite family butcher still there. He spotted a parking space on the high street outside a small Co-op supermarket and quickly pulled into it.

'We can walk from here,' he said. 'The church is about 200 metres over there.' Pointing away from the direction they'd come.

'It's a while since I've been here,' Heather said.

'I'm going to get a pork-and-apple pie.' He headed towards the butchers.

'There'll be food on after the service,' she shouted after him.

'Not like these.' Entering the shop, he came back out moments later carrying a white paper bag. He reached inside, removed a pie, and bit into it, instantly transporting him to his youth.

'Taste this, Heather.' Holding out the pastry towards her. Heather tentatively took a bite, pleasantly surprised by its taste. They finished the snack, Graveney pulled out a second and the two of them shared this too. He deposited the empty bag into a dustbin before brushing himself down. Heather, who'd already brushed herself clear of crumbs, pulled out a handkerchief and gently wiped the last vestige of pie from Graveney's face.

'You'll do,' she said, putting her hanky away.

Graveney turned. 'Right, follow me.' The two of them strolled up the high street. Graveney checked his watch as they approached the church and saw it was already 10.15. Once inside, they made their way along the aisle and sat on the front row. He glanced around the church at the relatively small number of people present. He guessed about twenty-five, but then a last-minute rush doubled the numbers. A middle-aged man made his way along the aisle towards Graveney and stopped, bending down.

'Are you Peter?' he asked.

'Yes,' Graveney said.

'Will you be able to act as one of the coffin-bearers?' he said. 'The people from the funeral directors will do it, but your Aunt Margaret would've wanted you to be one of them I'm sure.'

Graveney got up from his seat. 'Of course.'

'Sorry. I'm David Jenkins,' he said. 'I used to work with your aunt. We remained good friends.' Offering his hand to Graveney who shook it.

The two men walked outside the church and to the roadside, stopping at the parked hearse. Four other men stood near to the coffin, along with the people from the funeral directors. Graveney instantly recognised three of them. His cousin Jeff, Aunt Margaret's brother – Tom and Graveney's brother, Andrew. He knew Andrew would be here, but hadn't expected to run into him like this. He nodded at the other men, including Andrew, who acknowledged him before they all lined up at the back of the hearse. The funeral directors assisted them with getting the coffin onto their shoulders. The six of them marched slowly back into the church, matching strides until they reached the end of the aisle and placed the coffin down. Graveney headed back to Heather, who spotted Andrew and smiled at him, Andrew smiled back.

The service passed quickly, which pleased Graveney. Churches brought back memories which he preferred to remain buried. The congregation made their way outside, and friends and family chatted with each other. Graveney reacquainted himself with people he hadn't seen for years, talking briefly as people made their way back up the high street towards The George Hotel. He stared across at Heather, deep in conversation with Andrew and a woman he assumed was Andrew's wife. He waited patiently for Heather, who spotted him looking across. She excused herself and walked over to him.

'Who's the woman?' Graveney said.

'That's Andrew's wife, Alice. She seems nice.'

'Shall we go to the hotel?' he asked.

'If you like,' she said. 'You should speak to Andrew, you know.'

Graveney sighed. 'Heather. I don't want to.'

'Why not? You should forgive.'

'Please. Not now.'

'For God's sake, you can't bring her back. It was an accident. Isn't it time you made up. He's your brother.' She spoke so firmly it surprised Graveney. Heather hardly ever lost her temper with him. 'I'm sorry, but Gillian was my sister. If I forgive him, so should you.' She turned and marched away from him.

Graveney quickened his step and caught her up, grabbing hold of her arm. 'I'm sorry. It's so hard.' His eyes shining with tears as he spoke.

'I know, Peter. I know.' She put a hand to his cheek and smiled. 'Won't you do it for me? Your Aunt Peggy would've wanted you to. Please?'

'I'll do it for you,' he said. He hated people using emotional blackmail on him, but Heather was different. He owed her a lot, and she'd rarely asked him to do anything for her.

'Thanks.' She kissed him tenderly on the cheek and touched his arm.

Graveney walked over to Andrew and his wife, shook their hands, and offered to get some drinks in from the bar. As he stood, Andrew followed him.

'How are you, Andrew?' Graveney said.

'Not bad.'

'Yours was a lager and Coke, wasn't it?'

'Yeah. Coke for me and lager for Alice.'

Graveney smiled, thinking Andrew was joking but realising he wasn't. 'Coke. Are you driving?'

'No. I don't drink anymore. Not since ...' Andrew's voice trailed off.

Graveney turned to the barmaid and placed the order, before turning back to Andrew.

Andrew smiled. 'Alice likes a drink, though.'

'I never blamed you, Andrew. I couldn't look at you after, you know ... it brought it all back.'

'You did blame me, Peter. You're only talking to me because Heather asked you to. It was my fault. I should never have driven. It was idiotic and irresponsible of me.'

'You always were astute,' Graveney said. 'Well, you're right. But so was Heather. I shouldn't have allowed it to drag on so long. It was an accident. On another day you wouldn't have crashed.'

'I always looked up to you. These years we've been estranged were hard. My two kids don't even know you.'

'I didn't know you had kids.'

'A boy and girl,' he said.

'What's their names?'

'Peter, after you and Christina ...'

'After Mam,' Graveney said.

Graveney nudged his brother affectionately. 'Let's get these drinks back to the girls.'

Graveney and Andrew returned to their table, Alice and Heather both smiling at them as they did.

The four of them spoke all afternoon, pleasantly. Graveney and his brother regaling the two ladies with stories of things they got up to when they were younger. Speaking lovingly of their aunt and how she'd looked after them. Heather, pleased the two of them were getting along so well, felt proud that Graveney had decided to put their differences aside. Eventually the mourners, one by one, drifted away, and Graveney and Heather put their coats on ready to leave. Alice called Heather back over and introduced her to someone as Graveney stood near the bar.

Andrew strolled across to him and offered his hand. 'Maybe we'll meet up some time?' Shaking his brother's hand.

'Yeah, I'd like that.'

'Are you and Heather an item now?' Nodding in her direction.

'No. We're just good friends.'

'Sorry. I thought you two were … with you arriving together and that. You could do a lot worse, Peter.'

'I know I could, but ... Heather reminds me too much of Gillian. I just can't move beyond that. You're not the first to join the Heather fan club. Maddie, her friend, and Louisa. They're all trying to get us together.'

'Who's Louisa?'

'It's a long story. Better save it for another day.'

'I hope you don't mind me saying this. I always had a thing for Heather, but it was you she was mad about. No one else mattered. She confided in me once that Gillian stole you from her. She never forgave Gillian. It caused a rift between the two of them.'

'I didn't know that. Heather never let on. But it was Gillian I married. Gillian, I wanted to marry.'

'In my opinion, you married the wrong sister. Gillian was …' Andrew paused, choosing his words carefully. 'Not what she seemed.'

Graveney frowned. 'What do you mean by that?'

Andrew put his hand on his face and stroked his chin, deep in thought. Regretting having said anything. 'Look, Peter, I don't want to get into an argument over Gillian. We haven't spoken for years, and I don't want you falling out with me again.' He turned, about to head back to his seat.

Graveney grabbed hold of him. 'No, you don't get off that easy, I will fall out with you if you don't tell me what you mean.'

'Gillian played you for a fool. Heather knew. I knew. Others knew too. Only you couldn't see what she was like.'

'What the hell are you on about? Gillian and I loved each other.'

'Gillian knew you and Heather were having an affair.'

'How do you know that?'

'She told me. Listen, this is hardly the time or place.' Andrew walked towards the door and exited the hotel, closely followed by Graveney.

'Andrew, what are you talking about?' He grabbed his brother's arm.

'Gillian and I had an affair. She made a play for me, and I stupidly fell for it. I found out later Gillian did it to get back at you. I was besotted by her, but she just laughed. All one big game to her. She got so angry when she found out it was Heather you were seeing. I honestly believe if it had been anyone else but Heather, she wouldn't have minded.'

'How could you do that to me?' Graveney said. Backing away from his brother.

Andrew held out his hands. 'Because I was a stupid idiot allowing a manipulator, like Gillian, to use me to get back at you.'

'Don't you talk about my wife, like that.' He spat the words at him. 'I loved Gillian, and she loved me.' He turned to go back inside.

'I wasn't the only one. For Christ's sake, you're a detective, and you couldn't see your wife having one affair after another, behind your back.'

Graveney spun around and grabbed his brother by the lapels of his jacket. 'You fucking liar,' he shouted. 'How can you talk like that about her when she's not even here to defend herself?' Pushing his brother forcefully in the chest.

'Because it's true.' Tears formed in his eyes. 'Because it's true. You've put her high on this pedestal, and she doesn't deserve it.'

'I don't want to talk to you again. Stay out of my life.' He turned to walk away.

'For Christ's sake. The baby wasn't even yours.'

Graveney spun around and made a lunge for his brother, but Heather, Alice and a few of the other people who'd heard the commotion, got between them. Graveney brushed them off and headed back to the car. He reached it and making a fist, brought it down firmly on the roof leaving a dent in it. Heather came rushing up the high street towards him. 'Peter, what's up?'

'I'm going home. If you want a lift, you'd better get in the car now.'

'I'm not going anywhere until you've calmed down.'

Graveney jumped into the driver's seat – narrowly missing a car coming along the high street as he backed out – and sped away. He set off back towards Teesside, his mind racing, his rage intensifying as he did. Finally, he pulled into some services near Leeming Bar, allowing his anger to subside a little. He went inside and bought himself a coffee, as his temper slowly receded further. He thought of going back for Heather, feeling guilty for leaving her there, but he couldn't face his brother. What if what Andrew said was true? Had he been so blind? He would ask Andrew, but not now. He felt so depressed, so down. The funeral, the investigation, had sapped his spirits. He needed to get back home to Louisa, the one real constant in his life. He needed to hug her and tell her how much he loved her. As he drove away, teardrops fell like rain.

Graveney made his way back to his flat and parked up outside. He fished his keys from his pocket and entering, threw them onto the table near to the door. He paused, with the door still slightly open for a moment. Something didn't seem right. The sixth sense, almost primaeval, warning you when danger is imminent. He crept towards the bedroom and stopped outside, slowly pushing the door open to reveal an empty room. He smiled to himself, how stupid, he thought, allowing the quietness of the flat to unnerve him. He entered the kitchen and passed through the open door. As he did, a form moved from behind it and the metal object thudded against the top of his head. Graveney's knees crumbled, and as he fell to the floor, darkness enveloped him.

Unsure how long he'd been knocked-out for he heard the ringing of his mobile in his pocket, slowly rousing him. He reached inside his trousers and pulled it out as he attempted to sit upright, his head pounding in pain as he answered.

'Peter? It's Steph. I thought you'd fancy a drink. I'm outside.'

Graveney pushed himself against the kitchen cupboard, a pool of blood near to him on the floor where he'd lain. 'I've ... been ... I'm injured.'

He heard footsteps outside the flat and the door burst open as Steph came rushing in. 'Peter! What happened?' She put her hand gently on his face, she looked around.

'Someone was here and hit me with something.'

Helping him to his feet and onto one of the kitchen chairs. She glanced around the flat and picked up a tea towel. She ran it under the cold tap and pressed it gently to his head. 'Did you see who assaulted you?' Her voice full of concern.

'No. It happened as I walked through there.' Pointing at the kitchen door.

'Could it have been burglars?'

'I don't know.'

'I'll see if anything's missing.'

She wandered around the flat and making sure Graveney was still in the kitchen, went into his bedroom. She opened the wardrobe, found the jacket and checked the top pocket. Sighing audibly when she realised the key was still there. Returning to Graveney. 'There's no sign of any stuff being taken,' she said. 'You probably disturbed them before they'd got a chance to steal anything.'

'Louisa,' he said.

'There's no one else here.'

'She must still be out,' he said.

'We need to get that head of yours checked out. It'll need stitching.' She stood and checked the cupboards before locating some tablets. 'Take two of these. You've probably got a massive headache.'

Graveney swallowed them with the water Marne handed to him.

Marne gazed into the eyes of Graveney, touching his face tenderly with one hand while brushing the hair from his eyes with the other. 'How long were you out for?' she asked, her face full of worry.

'I don't know.' Glancing up at the kitchen clock. 'Ten, fifteen minutes, maybe,' he said. His words slightly slurred.

Marne took her phone out and called for an ambulance, worried about his head wound. She searched around, but couldn't see any objects that could've caused the injury. She checked the French doors in the second bedroom and found them forced open. Returning to the kitchen where Graveney now appeared groggy. She sat on a seat next to him and taking him by the hand, gently squeezed it. 'The ambulance won't be too long.' Her eyes met his as she smiled a worried smile. Graveney had never seen this gentler side of Marne. Her concern, genuine, writ large across her face as they sat in silence.

The ambulance transported Graveney to the hospital to be checked out. His skull wasn't fractured, but he was suffering a concussion. After having nine stitches placed in his head and refusing to be kept in overnight, the hospital reluctantly discharged him. He phoned Louisa from the hospital, but told her nothing of the incident as he didn't want her worrying and rushing home. She said she was staying at her friend's house for the night. Graveney, relieved as he didn't much like the idea of her being in the flat. Marne drove him home, and the two of them went inside. Marne, at Graveney's request, left to go to the shop to get some more paracetamol.

Graveney took the opportunity to look around the flat, primarily to establish if anything had been stolen. To his surprise, nothing had. Not only that, there was evidence his drawers and cupboards had been searched. The contents, he was sure, moved and almost returned to the correct place, but not entirely. Whoever had been in the flat wasn't there to burgle it. They were looking for something. But what? He sat on a chair, pondering the events when Marne returned with the tablets.

'How are you feeling?' she asked.

'I've got a thumping headache.'

'Take these.' She handed him two pills and a glass of water.

'What about a stronger drink?' asked a hopeful Graveney.

'I'm not sure that's a good idea,' Marne said. 'That was some whack on the head.'

'A small one won't harm.' Rising from his seat, he got a bottle and two glasses from a cupboard.

'Just one, Peter.' Taking them from him. 'I'd better stay the night with you.'

Graveney smiled. 'Now that's an offer I can't refuse.'

Marne put her hand on Graveney's cheek again, her face full of concern once more, leaving Graveney bemused. As if she had multiple personalities. The vamp, he already knew well. The professional police officer and now this almost sisterly or motherly concern for him.

'Why did you come around today?' he asked.

Her face instantly changed into a mischievous grin, her features flashed with conflicting emotions, so rapidly, Graveney had trouble deciphering them.

'Bit of a loose end and I fancied some company. A particular type.' She smiled at him, as Graveney stared into her eyes, a deep, dark, unfathomable abyss.

'I'd been to a funeral. You were lucky to find me in.'

'Bit of a coincidence. Someone should try to burgle your flat when you're at a funeral?' she said, somewhat enigmatically.

'Yeah, I thought that. I've checked around and nothing's missing, but someone's been looking through my things. I mean, what type of burglar leaves things so neat?'

'Are you saying they were looking for something specific?'

'If they were, I don't know what. Maybe whoever it was, found it.'

'Is this connected to the investigation?' Marne said.

'I don't know, Steph.'

'Maybe you should sleep on it.'

'Yeah. Maybe I should.' Graveney drained his glass.

Marne stood, and pulling Graveney's chair square to hers, straddled him.

He slid his hand beneath her skirt. 'You're not wearing any knickers.'

'What's the point,' she whispered in his ear. 'You'll only rip them off. Let's see if we can take your mind off that headache, Mr Policeman.' Graveney closed his eyes and allowed his head to fall back slightly as Marne nuzzled his neck, the pain in his head slowly ebbing away.

CHAPTER TWENTY-FOUR

Marne left at six in the morning to go home and change for work. Graveney, who'd risen later, showered and dressed. He checked his mobile and noticed four missed calls from Heather, but resisted the urge to phone. His guilt over leaving her, and the fact she'd want to know what went on with Andrew, stopped him from ringing. Some officers from the station turned up to dust for prints but Graveney, who wasn't hopeful they would find any, finally left for work at 08.30. He'd decided against going in Ratano's coffee shop for his usual coffee, knowing Becky would want to know what happened to his head. Not feeling much like talking about it, Graveney headed straight for Middlesbrough.

Marne sat in her car at Middlesbrough police station and phoned Oake. 'Yes, Steph. How did it go?'

'Those two idiots of yours nearly killed Graveney,' she said.

'Calm down,' he said. 'He was supposed to be out all day. Dec panicked, that's all.'

'What would've happened if he'd been severely injured, or worse?'

'But he wasn't, was he?'

'No. But we need Graveney. He's the key to finding what Shelby had.'

'What does he think?'

'He knows they were looking for something. If he has anything of Shelby's, it could make him show his hand.'

'We've got to keep a close eye on him. We don't want him involving his Scottish mate.'

'And Graveney?' she said. 'What happens to him?'

'Graveney doesn't matter. We'll eliminate him if we have to. A job for you, Steph. If you like?'

'Yeah. I'd enjoy that. But isn't it risky?'

Oake laughed. 'If we get the stuff Shelby had, even if we have to eliminate Graveney, the whole of Cleveland Constabulary will never fathom this case. We'll speak later, Steph.'

Marne pondered for a moment. It was vital she timed this right. So far, she had been able to manipulate Oake as she wished, but she didn't want him doing anything rash. She needed all of them there together. The full compliment. Marne opened the glove box and pulled out a photo of Stephen, Sandra, and Jessica. Gazing for some time at their faces, before she replaced it and went inside.

Graveney sat in his office as Mac entered. 'What the hell happened yesterday?' Mac asked. Placing a cup of coffee on Graveney's desk.

'Someone broke into my flat, and when I disturbed them, they whacked me on the head.'

'Let's have a look, then.'

Graveney bent forward and showed him the stitches.

'Christ! I bet that hurt?'

'It certainly did. I was out for about fifteen minutes when Steph phoned.'

'Steph? Funny you should mention her because the fingerprints came back. Apart from you and Louisa, Steph's was the only other print there.'

'She came over when I answered the phone, and did a check of the flat for me.'

Mac laughed. 'There's nothing you want to tell me is there? Because apparently, most of her prints were in your bedroom.' Graveney blanched but realised Mac was only ribbing him.

'Yeah. She probably took advantage of me when I was groggy,' Graveney said.

Mac closed Graveney's door. 'What was it about, then?'

'I don't know. Whoever was there was looking for something. Someone had checked through drawers, making sure they didn't make a mess. It's only that I'm a little bit fastidious, I noticed.'

'What were they looking for?' Mac said.

'No idea. Maybe they found it, for all I know.'

'It's got to have something to do with the case, hasn't it?'

'I'm pretty sure it has, but what and why?'

'Does anyone else know?' Mac said.

'Only Steph. The others think it a straightforward burglary.'

'Maybe we should keep it that way?'

Graveney nodded. 'I was talking with Steph the other day, and she mentioned Shelby. If you remember, when I was at his office with Stewart, he claimed Shelby told him he had information regarding the murders.' Graveney swigged his coffee and continued. 'I've thought about it. Stewart must have found something in Shelby's office, or someone believes he did. Maybe they think he gave it to me.'

'But he didn't give you anything?'

'No. I wasn't in there long before Stewart collapsed. It could still be at his office.'

'We went over it with a fine-tooth comb and found nothing.'

'Perhaps we should check again?' Graveney said.

'Maybe. It's worth a try, I suppose.'

'Let's go over Shelby's things one more time, in case we've missed something.'

Mac nodded. 'Ok, boss.'

Marne knocked before entering Phillips' office. Phillips stood looking out of the window into the car park below at Graveney, who was deep in conversation with someone outside. Phillips turned, slumping in his seat. His arms folded. 'What the hell is happening, Steph?' he said, in a calm, measured tone.

'I've no idea, sir. I haven't had time to speak to Oake yet, so I don't know if it was down to him.'

'I warned you. I told you I wouldn't risk Graveney, or anyone else, getting injured.'

'It could've been a coincidence.'

Phillips scoffed. 'Don't treat me like an idiot. What were they after? What has Graveney got that they want?'

'I've no idea. Oake hasn't mentioned anything about it. I'll see him tonight and see what he says.'

'I want to know everything you find out. Do you understand?'

'Perfectly.' Marne nodded and left the office. Phillips turned to look out the window again. Graveney ended his conversation and headed back inside.

Marne passed Mac coming up the stairs to Phillips' office but never said a word. Mac thought it strange but reasoned she may have received a dressing down for some misdemeanour. He stopped at Phillips' open door and tapped on it. Phillips, deep in thought, turned.

'Come in, Mac,' he said. 'Have a seat.'

Mac told Phillips about the conversation he had with Graveney regarding the attack. None of which allayed any of Phillips' fears. He thanked him for his co-operation and Mac left the office. Half-way down the stairs, he met Graveney coming up.

'What you doing up here?' he asked.

'Phillips was asking how I was settling in,' he said. Graveney didn't believe him, guilt writ large across his face.

Mac motioned towards Phillips' office. 'Has he summoned you then?'

'Yeah. Phillips wants to ask me about the attack. I'll see you later, Mac.' Graveney pondered for a moment as Mac disappeared out of sight. Mac had been to see Phillips the other day as well, according to Marne. He had looked guilty. Was there something Mac was holding back from him? Surely not, he thought, and tried desperately to push the apprehension he felt aside. The more he considered it, however, the more the doubt grew.

After his meeting with Phillips, Graveney headed into town to meet up with Heather. He phoned her to apologise for leaving her stranded at the funeral, and for his behaviour there. She was her usual forgiving self, which made Graveney feel worse. If only she'd balled and shouted at him a little. He deserved it, after all. He offered to buy her lunch after he indicated there were some things he needed to discuss with her. They met and enjoyed a pleasant meal. She confirmed most of what Andrew told him regarding Gillian, but was as shocked as Graveney that Gillian's baby was not his. They parted, but not before Graveney got Andrew's mobile number from her. At first reluctant to give it to him, she finally agreed when he promised not to do anything stupid.

Once she left, he phoned his brother to arrange a meeting with him in Darlington, where Andrew lived. Graveney called Louisa and told her about the attack but played it down a bit, not wanting to unnerve her. He arranged to meet her later at The Farmers Arms around five. He phoned Mac, telling him he had a bit of urgent personal business to deal with, and for him to cover for him which Mac agreed to. Graveney then headed off up to Darlington.

He marched through the doors of the pub and spotted Andrew sitting in the corner, nervously nursing a coke. Graveney got himself a lemonade and sat with his brother.

Andrew lowered his eyes. 'I'm sorry about yesterday, Peter. I didn't want you to find out like that.'

Graveney could see the remorse and more importantly, the genuineness in his brother's eyes. 'I was out of order myself. It came as such a shock.'

'It's true what I said. I wouldn't lie to you. I know you loved Gillian, but you were deceived. She would have left you eventually. She wasn't a nice person sometimes. I saw that side of her.'

'And the baby, whose was it?'

'Mine.'

Graveney put his hand to his chin and stroked it thoughtfully. 'How can you be sure?'

'She told me she was on the pill. She laughed when she said you were trying for a baby. She had no intention of spoiling her life, *bringing up your brat*. Her words, Peter. You were away on a course, I don't know if she did it on purpose or by accident. It was when we spent a few days together. She claimed she'd forgotten her pills, and we took a chance. A month later, she told me she was pregnant, and I was the father. She said she was going to get rid of it, but when you came home, to my surprise, she told you. You assumed it was yours, and she swore me to secrecy. Gillian said if I told you, she'd say I forced myself on her.'

'The day she died?' Graveney said.

'She suspected you were with Heather, and she called me up ranting and raving. I went over to try and calm her down, but she'd have none of it. Said she was going to find out where you were, and go there. She got herself so worked up she went into early labour. I managed to get her into my car. On the way there she went mad, screaming about you and Heather. As we drove along I tried to placate her, but she grabbed the steering wheel and forced us off the road.'

'But why didn't you tell the police this?'

'I couldn't let you know your pregnant wife tried to kill herself. I said I'd lost control. The rest, as they say, is history.' His eyes filled with tears and Graveney put his arm around him.

'I'm sorry, Andrew. I'm so sorry,' Graveney said.

'Like I said. You married the wrong sister.'

'I can't change the past.'

'But you can make the future. Heather loves you. She worships you. She's never wanted anyone else. And what about Luke?' he said.

'Luke? What's he got to do with anything?'

'Come on. Haven't you noticed the resemblance?' Pointing at Graveney.

'Did Heather tell you this?'

'No. Heather doesn't have to. She showed me a picture of Luke. It's like stepping back thirty years, and looking at you.'

Graveney sat back in his chair, hardly able to comprehend what his brother was telling him. A week ago, he had no children. Now, it appeared, Graveney had two. He laughed at the absurdity of it all. Reaching into his pocket, he pulled out his mobile, showing Andrew the picture of himself and Louisa.

'Is she yours?' Looking first at Graveney and then the photo.

'What do you think?' Graveney said.

Andrew smiled. He saw the likeness. It was in the eyes.

Graveney laughed. 'You wait for a bus, and then two come along together.'

Graveney went on to explain how he met Louisa, about her mother and the photo album. Relieved, as if a great weight had been lifted off him. After hugging his brother, he headed back to Teesside. He thought about Heather on the way, and what Andrew said about Luke. He couldn't believe she hadn't told him about Luke. He suspected it was true and he needed to speak with Heather, but not today. His life was so complicated. He was both physically and emotionally drained. Heather and Luke would keep for another time.

'Yes, Flint?' Oake said, answering his mobile.

'I've got some good news, sir,' he said. 'We've found Shelby's safety deposit box.'

'Where?'

'I've had a private detective working on it for us. This guy did some scratching about and got some information from a bloke who runs a small taxi firm. Apparently, he took our friend to Darlington one morning when his car wouldn't start – to a place called Harland Securities. He remembered it because he recognised Shelby from the newspapers after his death. He hasn't been in touch with the police and isn't likely to either. If you know what I mean?'

'I hope you were careful, Flint?'

'Tragic hit and run, sir.'

'And did Shelby have a box in his own name?' Oake said.

'No.' Flint said. 'The detective I used greased some palms and got a list of the people who hold boxes there. There isn't a Shelby, but there's a David Bryony-Nugent. Bryony-Nugent was his mother's maiden name.'

'Fantastic, Flint. The detective. Is he trustworthy?'

'Ah, sadly he met with an accident, sir. It's an awful world we live in.'

'We'll need documents in his name to gain access,' Oake said. 'I'll sort them out for you.'

'We'll need a key, sir.'

'Our friend, Graveney, must have it or at least knows where it is. We need to recover it from him.'

'Do you want me to pay him another visit?'

'No. I'll speak to Steph,' Oake said. 'She may have a better plan.'

Graveney made his way back to Teesside and after checking on his flat, showering and changing, he headed across to meet Louisa. She sat at the bar talking with Liz when he entered. Graveney walked over to her and kissed her on the cheek.

'Let's have a look at your head,' Louisa said. Graveney bent down to show her his wound.

'Oh, my God!' she said. 'They could've killed you.'

He laughed. 'It's not as bad as it looks.' He lied. 'Have you told her, Liz?' he asked.

'No. I was waiting for you,' Liz said.

Louisa frowned. 'Told me what?'

'I don't want you staying in the flat for the moment. The man who attacked me may come back. Liz has kindly offered to put you up.'

Liz nodded. 'I asked Louisa about working here, and she agreed.' Liz looked at Louisa. 'You could help me set the pub up first thing in the morning if you like?'

'If that's what you want, Peter,' Louisa said. 'But where will you stay?'

Graveney smiled. 'At the flat. Don't worry, I'll be ok.'

Louisa reluctantly agreed. Graveney tried to assuage her fears as best he could, and they sat at a table for something to eat.

Mac and Becky turned up a little later, and the four of them enjoyed a meal together. Graveney took Louisa back home, to pick up some clothes, returning her again to the pub. He checked all the doors and windows in his flat, deciding to have an early night. It had been an emotional day in more ways than one, but despite this, he quickly fell asleep.

Marne and Oake sat in the sitting room of his house. Oake told her about the discovery of Shelby's safety deposit box, and of his intention of getting hold of the key, which he was sure Graveney must know the whereabouts of. He went into his study to answer a call from someone before returning to the sitting room.

'So, where do we go from here, Steph?'

'I've given it some thought,' she said. 'Surely Graveney would've brought forward anything he has by now. I'm pretty sure about that. So, maybe he has it, but doesn't know.'

'How, though?' he asked.

'His team has already checked Shelby's again, so he apparently thinks something was missed.'

Oake sipped his drink. 'What do we do? If he finds something, he'll disclose it to Phillips and the rest of the team.'

'*Maybe.* We need to give him the incentive to find it and hand it over to us. Or even better, use him to recover the items. There's bound to be cameras at this security place. If we get him to collect it, he'll get the blame.'

'But he's hardly likely to do that, is he?'

'What we need is leverage.'

'What are you thinking, Steph?'

'The little street urchin he lives with – he seems to have a soft spot for her. If we use her as a bargaining chip. I'll muddy the waters with his team. Then afterwards we can dispose of the pair of them.'

'Steph, you're evil, you know that?'

'Then you and I can fly off somewhere warm, and forget all about this investigation,' Marne said.

'How do we go about it?'

'Leave it with me. I'll tell you when to get the girl. I think we'll need all of your team on this.'

Oake handed Marne a glass of wine. 'I'll get in touch with Dec and Flint, and wait for your call.'

CHAPTER TWENTY-FIVE

Graveney watched the television until 11.30 pm. He'd contemplated phoning Heather all night to discuss what Andrew told him about Luke. Deciding it was probably better to speak to her in person rather than on the phone, he poured himself a large Jack Daniels, to help him sleep, and sat in his armchair as thoughts whirled through his mind. Marne sat in her car outside Graveney's flat and phoned Oake. 'Charlie, are the boys in place?'

'Yes. I've spoken to Flint. They're outside the pub now.'

'Tell them to grab the girl. And Charlie, make sure all hell doesn't break loose. We don't want all of Middlesbrough Police Station descending on us.'

'Leave it with me. Where are you?'

'Outside Graveney's flat. I'll be with him when he gets the call, so I'll be able to tell you if he has anything of Shelby's.'

'Keep in touch.' Oake rang off and dialled Flint's number.

'Yes, sir?'

'Get the girl. I don't want a mess either. Just grab her, and tell the landlady what I told you to say.'

'Ok, sir,' Flint said. He watched the last customer leave The Farmers Arms, nodded at Dec, and the pair got out.

Graveney drained his glass, stood, and performed a check of the doors and windows in his flat. Satisfied they were secure, he headed for the bedroom when someone tapped on the front door. He wondered who was visiting so late. Picking up a large, brass ornament from the front-room, he went to answer it. He opened the door about six inches, making sure his weight was against the door should someone try to force their way in, and was surprised to see Marne standing outside with a bottle of Jack Daniels in her hand. He put the ornament down and beckoned her in. 'What are you doing here, Steph?' He smiled.

'I was passing and thought you might fancy a nightcap.' She followed him into the kitchen, where he collected another glass and headed for the lounge.

Graveney sat. 'I was on my way to bed.'

'I can go if you'd rather?' Holding out the already open, and slightly tilted bottle.

'Maybe a small one.' He handed Marne the glasses, which she half-filled with the spirit.

'On your own?' she said.

'Yeah. Louisa's staying with a friend of mine. I became worried after the break-in.'

'That's understandable. Any progress on that?'

'No, and I don't expect there to be.'

'What makes you say that?'

'Well ...' His phone sounded in another room, and Graveney held up a hand. 'Excuse me a minute, Steph.' He headed for the bedroom and picked up his mobile, intending to turn it off. But when he noticed Liz's name on the screen, he answered. 'Liz. What's she forgotten?' he asked, turning around to see Marne, who'd followed him into the room.

'Oh, Peter. They've taken her. They've taken Louisa.'

'Who has?' Graveney said.

'Two men. They burst into the pub and took Louisa at gunpoint. Please come.'

'I'm on my way.' Graveney frantically searched for his car and house keys. Finally locating them, he grabbed a jacket from the chair and headed towards the door.

'What the hell's going on?' Marne said.

'Someone's kidnapped, Louisa. I've got to go to The Farmers.'

'Where?' she said.

'It's a pub she's staying at. How much have you had to drink, Steph?'

'Only a sip.'

'Right. You drive.'

They raced around to the pub in minutes. Graveney and Marne burst in through the front door to find a slightly battered Liz, sat on a stool, with a dampened bar-towel pressed to her face.

'Steph, get on the phone to the station.'

'No!' Liz shouted, 'They said they'd kill her if you involved anyone else. Oh, Peter, they might have seen her.' Pointing at Marne.

'Liz, what the hell happened?' Graveney knelt next to her. 'Look at what they've done to you.' He put his hand to her cheek.

'It's nothing. I've had far worse from my old man.'

'Tell me what they said.'

'I was locking up when they burst in. At first, I thought the men were after the takings, but one of them – he had a large scar on his face – grabbed Louisa. I tried to help her, but he punched me. Then the other man pulled out a gun and pointed it at us. He said if we weren't quiet, he'd shoot us. He told me to phone you and say they would kill her if you didn't do as they said. They have eyes and ears at Middlesbrough police station, and if you involved anyone else, Louisa would die. That's what the men said. They made Louisa get her mobile, and they took her. He said he'd ring you later.'

Graveney stood and slumped on a stool looking up at Marne. She moved forward to have a look at Liz's injury. 'Have you any ice?' she asked.

'I'm all right,' Liz said. 'I've had dozens of black-eyes.'

'Liz,' Graveney said. 'Can you keep this to yourself until I talk to them.'

Liz stroked his arm. 'Of course.'

Marne looked at the two of them and realised they were a lot closer than Graveney let on.

'What're you going to do?' Marne asked.

He shrugged. 'Wait for them to call, I suppose.'

'Should we phone Phillips?' Marne said.

'You heard what they said. The men will kill Louisa if I do. By rights, you shouldn't even know. I'm asking for your help with this.'

Marne turned away from the two of them, so her face wasn't visible, as if deep in thought. A knowing smile flickered across it and then was masked before she turned. 'Ok,' she said. 'I think we should keep this between the three of us.'

Graveney and Liz nodded in agreement, Marne lifted the hatch to gain access to the bar. 'I don't know about you two, but I need a drink,' she said, placing a glass underneath an optic.

The three of them waited impatiently for over an hour, having a couple of drinks each, but in truth, none of them felt much like getting drunk. Graveney's phone rang. He stared down at it in front of him on the table, where he'd placed it in anticipation of the call. Louisa's name appeared on the screen, and Graveney nervously answered it. 'Hello.'

'Listen to me, and listen carefully,' Flint said. 'You've something we want. Something of Shelby's.'

'I've nothing of Shelby's.'

'If you try to be clever with me, I'll open your little friend's stomach with a knife and spill her guts all over the floor. Do you understand?'

'Perfectly.'

'Let's have no more pissing about. I'll phone at 10.30 in the morning and give you instructions. Do not deviate from them. Do not inform anyone at the station. Believe me, we'll know if you do. Are we clear on this?'

'Yes. I want to speak to Louisa,' he said.

There was a muffled noise before he heard her voice.

'Peter ... I'm all right.' Was all she said before Flint snatched the phone from her. '10.30, Graveney.' The phone went dead.

'What did they say?' Liz asked.

'I don't want to involve you any more than I need to. They're asking me to give them something, that's all.' Graveney desperately tried to play it down.

'What are you going to do?' Liz stroked his arm again.

'I'll get what they want, and then I'll get Louisa back.'

'But what if they ...' Her voice trailed off.

'I'll get her back, Liz. Don't you worry.'

'What do you have to get for them?' Marne asked.

'I'm not sure, yet.'

Graveney and Marne left Liz at the pub after making sure she was ok. He felt guilty for leaving her there alone, but Liz assured him she'd be fine. Liz said she'd phone if anything happened, realising he needed to get on with whatever he had to do to secure Louisa's release. They arrived back at Graveney's flat at 01.45 am.

Graveney sat. 'They said I have something of Shelby's.'

'What?'

Graveney shrugged. 'I've no idea. But if I don't find it, they'll kill Louisa.' He slumped into an armchair.

'Peter, what can we do?' Marne sat opposite.

'I don't know. Louisa's my life. I don't know what I'd do if I lost her.' His eyes filled with tears, and he turned away from Marne.

She sat next to him. 'We'll get your friend back.' Hugging him, Marne stared into his face. She momentarily felt guilty for what she was doing.

Graveney blew out. 'She's more than a friend. She's my daughter.'

'Your daughter? I didn't know.' Marne brought a hand to her mouth, shocked by this. Her guilt deepened appreciably as memories nudged at her conscience. She closed her eyes and pushed them away, trying to remain focused.

Graveney blew out hard. 'Not many people do. I've only told a few others about it.'

'What can they possibly think you have of Shelby's?' she said.

'They apparently believe I recovered something from Shelby's office, or Stewart gave me something.'

'But he didn't give you anything?'

'No. We've searched his office again and found nothing.'

'Is it possible he gave you something without you knowing it?'

Graveney rubbed his face. 'I can't see how. I wasn't in there long with Stewart. I was always ten or fifteen feet away from him.'

'And he never left the room while you were there?'

Graveney pondered. 'No. I did, though. To get Stewart a glass of water. When I returned, he'd collapsed.'

Marne nodded. 'Right.'

Graveney stood. 'Wait. It was warm in the office. I removed my jacket and put it on the back of the seat I was sitting on. Maybe he put something in there when I went for the water.'

'Have you checked the jacket?'

'No. It was my dark-brown tweed one.' Graveney Jumped up and raced for the bedroom closely followed by Marne. He rifled through his wardrobe, and locating the jacket, laid it on the bed. He checked the two side-pockets and then the inside ones but found nothing. He frowned deeply and stared at Marne. 'It's empty.'

'What about the top one?' Marne said.

Graveney pushed two fingers inside, and slowly retracted them, holding a key between his fingers. He grinned at Marne, who smiled back. 'This is it,' he said. 'Stewart must have put it in my jacket, knowing I'd find it. It's some sort of key. Looks high security. A safety deposit box, perhaps?'

'Maybe,' Marne said. 'What do we do now?'

'Wait for the call. I'm going to need your help, Steph. I'll phone in sick in the morning, and I'll need you to go to the station and cover for me. Maybe, if you can get away from there, you can make some excuse and follow me at a discreet distance.'

'Are we going to involve anyone else?' she asked. 'It could be dangerous.'

'We can't trust anyone else. There must be someone, or maybe more than one bent copper at the station. I don't even know how high up they are.'

'Are you sure you're not getting paranoid?'

'Maybe,' he said. 'I just don't know, but I'm not risking Louisa's life. Will you help me? She means everything to me.'

'Of course, I will.' Taking Graveney in her arms, her concern briefly genuine.

Graveney hadn't slept much after Marne left. The little he had managed, filled with nightmares. Graveney hoped Marne would be faithful to her word, and not tell anyone about the events of the previous night. He got dressed early and delving deep into one of his drawers, took out a revolver he had not used, or even seen, in years. He loaded it in readiness, placing it down on the coffee table along with his mobile, and waited.

Marne arrived at the station and headed straight upstairs to see Phillips, surprised to see Mac in there with him. Phillips waved her in as he hung up the phone. 'Shut the door, Steph,' he said. 'Take a seat. Right, what do you know?'

Steph glanced across at Mac.

'It's ok. Mac knows all about Oake, and that you've been working undercover for me. I told him we're trying to obtain evidence implicating him. What's the latest?'

'Graveney has something they want. A key.'

Phillips frowned. 'How did he get hold of this key?'

'It appears Stewart planted it on Graveney the day he died. Graveney didn't know of its existence, which is why he didn't bring it forward.'

'And this key was Shelby's?' Phillips said.

'Yes. It's for a safety deposit box. We can only guess at what's in this box, but Oake is confident it'll contain damning evidence, not just about him, but about powerful people from London.'

Phillips rolled his eyes. 'I thought we checked into Shelby's background for anything like this. How the hell was something like a safety deposit box missed?'

'Apparently it was well hidden, because we didn't know about the key, no one bothered to delve that deep. How can you look for something when you don't know it exists?'

Phillips rubbed at his eyes. 'And they know the whereabouts of the safety deposit box, I suppose?'

'Some of Oake's men have located it, sir.'

Mac leant forward. 'So, we've the key, and they know the location. What do we do next?'

'There's a potential problem, sir,' Marne said. 'They're going to get Graveney to recover what's inside the box and hand it over to them.'

'Peter would never do that.' Mac said.

Marne raised her eyebrows. 'They've got some leverage.'

'What kind of leverage?' Phillips said.

'Someone called Louisa.'

Phillips put his hands up to his face again, rubbing it hard. 'I knew this would happen. For God's sake.' He stood and paced. 'It's bad enough risking copper's lives, but a kid's. Christ, this is getting out of hand. We need to involve the Chief Constable.'

'I know it seems risky, sir, but Oake trusts me implicitly. I've persuaded him to allow me to meet Graveney at the bank, and then take him to a meeting place where they're holding the girl.'

'Steph, we can't risk people's lives like this.'

'They have someone within the station, sir. I don't know who. If you involve anyone, and they catch wind of it, *they will kill her.*'

Phillips blew out hard. 'The bank. Do you know where it is?'

'I'm not sure yet. One of Oake's men is going to ring with directions.'

Mac gulped. 'Can't we arrest Oake, and get the key from Peter?'

Marne looked at him. 'If we do that, we've nothing implicating Oake. We don't know where the bank is, and they *will* kill the girl. If they all go to ground, we'll never catch them.'

Phillips stared at Marne. 'What are you proposing, Steph?'

'The men holding the girl will phone Graveney this morning with directions to the bank. They've already arranged for false identification so Graveney can obtain entry. When he gets what's in the box, I'm to intercept him and take him to the place they're holding her. We'll probably be watched to make sure Graveney hasn't told anyone else. I'll phone Mac and keep in contact with him once I know more. When I get the address, I'll relay it to Mac and call for backup when I've secured Peter's and the girl's safety.'

'That's incredibly dangerous,' Phillips said. 'A lot could go wrong, and you'll be there on your own.'

'I'll have Peter. I'll take a second gun with me, for him. But it's essential, sir, that Mac keeps away from us at all times. I don't know how many people Oake has watching us. Any hint of police presence and the girl will be killed. Even if we're able to locate the bank and where the safety deposit box is later, we'd have a lot of explaining to do to our superiors if she dies.'

'What do you think, Mac?' Phillips asked.

Mac thought for a moment. 'I don't like it, sir. Why don't we tell Peter what we're doing? Surely he should know?'

'Peter suspects someone at the station's bent,' Marne said. 'He's paranoid about it. If we tell him, he might not believe or trust us. This girl means a lot to him, and getting her back is all he's interested in. We need her safe, of course, but we also need the evidence to convict Oake and his associates. I'll tell Peter when I collect him from the bank, but for the moment I feel ignorance is bliss as far as he's concerned.'

Phillips rubbed his chin. 'For the time being, we'll keep it from him, but make sure he knows at the earliest. Have you got that?'

'Yes, sir.'

'I'd prefer it if we had more than Mac, on standby, though.'

'Oake is watching for any activity. It will alert him. I don't think we dare risk it. For all we know, he has someone in the incident room on his payroll. If we tell anyone, anyone at all, and he finds out ... that would be that.'

'Ok,' Phillips said. 'Do whatever you need to do, but keep Mac informed.'

'Yes, sir,' she said. Marne got up, nodded at the two of them and left.

Mac shook his head. 'It's very dangerous, sir. But I don't think we have a lot of choice, do we?'

'I agree. I don't believe we do.'

'Can we trust Steph?' Mac asked.

Phillips glanced towards the door. 'Absolutely.' Desperate to convince not only Mac but himself.

Marne exited Middlesbrough police station and got in her car. She searched her contacts and phoned Oake.

'Steph. What's happening?'

'Nothing. Graveney's phoned in sick, and I've had a meeting with Phillips and Mackay.'

'What about?'

'Routine stuff regarding the investigation. No one suspects anything and Graveney is playing ball. I've made some excuse about checking on a lead so I can get away.'

'I want you to meet Graveney as soon as he exits the bank. I don't want him reading what's in the documents. Do you know the large industrial estate in Newton Aycliffe?'

'Yes.'

'We're all going to meet up there. Once I've the documents in my possession, Flint and Dec will get rid of Graveney and the girl.'

'And after?' she asked.

'I want you to clear up some loose ends.'

'Flint and Dec?' she said.

'Yeah, Flint and Dec. The London people think they're too much of a risk. They don't know about you, so when I get my affairs in order, we'll leave.'

'Sounds good to me.'

CHAPTER TWENTY-SIX

The call Graveney expected duly arrived at 10.30. He picked up the phone and answered.

'Drive to Darlington and park your car in the underground car park of Roseberry House,' Flint said. 'There, you'll find a black Vauxhall Vectra, registration number NE62TSA. Inside the glovebox, there are documents with your photo on them, and Shelby's alias. These will gain you access to the security bank. I want you to get the objects from the box and bring them out without viewing their contents. Once outside you'll be collected by someone in the same car, and they'll take you somewhere. If you follow this to the letter, you and the girl will be released. Do you understand?'

'Perfectly,' Graveney said. Flint rang off.

Graveney, of course, didn't believe they had any intention of releasing Louisa or indeed allowing him to walk away after giving them the contents from the box, but he felt he had no choice. Graveney had to do what he was told until an opportunity presented itself, allowing him and Louisa to escape. He refused to even harbour the thought it could go wrong.

Taking his mobile from his pocket and opening his contacts, he composed a text to Heather. He felt it the least she deserved, and if what he was doing didn't work out, he wanted her to know how special she was to him. He signed off the text and pressed send. Putting his phone away, he secreted the gun inside the sock of his left foot and secured it with tape. He took one last look around his flat and left.

Graveney headed towards Darlington. He'd phoned in sick, hopefully giving him a free day, and spoken to Marne earlier. She told him everything was quiet at the station, and to do what the man on the phone asked him to. After exiting the Darlington by-pass, he headed into the town centre and pulled into the underground car park at Roseberry House. He parked up and walked around for a minute or two before he located the vehicle. He retrieved the documents from the glove-box, along with a small map of how to get to Harland securities. Graveney, briefly surprised at how they'd obtained his photo for the fake passport and driving licence, put them in his inside pocket and headed off into the town.

Marne was parked in the car park. She saw Graveney drive in and wander about for a short time before he located the car. After a few moments he left and making sure he was out of sight, Marne made her way over to the vehicle. She jumped in the passenger seat and felt underneath it for the ignition keys. Someone, Flint or Dec, Marne supposed, had taped them there. Retrieving them, she started the engine. She waited long enough for Graveney to reach the offices of Harland securities and enter before she drove after him, parking on double-yellow lines outside. Turning off the engine, she got out of the driver's seat and climbed into the back to await his return.

Mac parked across the road from a petrol station on North Road. He took out his mobile phone and rang Marne. 'Steph. What's happening?'
'He's gone inside the building. I'm waiting for a call from Oake to tell me where we're to meet. I'll call you when we get somewhere near to it. I've got to go. He'll be ringing soon.'
'Ok. Good luck.'
Mac phoned Phillips.
'Yes, Mac?'
'Graveney's at the bank now, somewhere in Darlington town centre. Steph's waiting for a call from Oake. She's going to ring me with the address later. We'll have to sit tight for the moment, sir.'
'As soon as you know the address, ring me and get over there. I've already phoned a police friend of mine I trust, from Durham, and warned him something is about to happen. He's got an armed response unit waiting on standby for my say so.'
'It's lucky it's taking place outside our jurisdiction because I don't know what we'd have done otherwise,' Mac said.
'I was thinking the same. I'm surprised Oake choose somewhere outside Cleveland Constabulary, but then again, he probably didn't want to risk shitting in his own backyard. Keep in touch, Mac. Fingers crossed.'
'Yes, sir. I will.'
Mac's heart-rate rose a little. He puffed out his cheeks and blew hard. 'Come on, Peter,' he said, under his breath.

Graveney entered the old Victorian building and presented himself at the reception. A middle-aged woman, in her early fifties, he guessed, took his name and photocopied the documents he gave her while he took a seat. Graveney's heart rate increased as he waited, but he knew he couldn't afford to lose his nerve and arouse suspicions. He checked the clock, and although only five minutes had passed, it felt like an hour. He looked to his left as a large door swung open into the room. A smartly-dressed man in an immaculate suit entered, escorted by two burly security men.

'Mr Bryony-Nugent?' Holding out his hand. 'I'm James Langley.'

Graveney shook his hand firmly and followed Langley and one of the security men through the door.

'Have you travelled far?' he asked Graveney.

'No. Just from Middlesbrough.'

'They're doing well this year, with that new manager of theirs.'

'Yes. They might even get promoted,' Graveney said. Trying to appear calm.

'Have you got your season ticket?'

Graveney frowned. 'My season-ticket?'

'Yes. I thought when we spoke on the phone last month, you said you were thinking of getting a season ticket.'

'I did. I mean, I have ... I'd forgotten the conversation. You know how hectic life is.'

'I do indeed. It was my colleague, Mr Westerton, who dealt with you last time you were here, I believe?'

Graveney was getting unnerved. Was all this questioning small-talk, or was Langley suspicious? It was hard to tell. He gambled. 'Yes, I think it was.' Trying to appear confident.

'I'm afraid he's ill in hospital at the moment. It doesn't look good.'

'I'm sorry to hear that.' Turning down another seemingly never-ending number of corridors.

Langley stopped at a large metal, wrought-iron door. He showed his pass hanging around his neck, and it clicked open. Graveney followed Langley and the first security guard, the second one closing the iron door and remaining there. Langley reached another metal door, this one looking altogether more secure than the other. He flashed his pass once more, but this time entered a six-digit code into a keypad to the right of the door. Graveney heard a click, and Langley pushed the heavy-looking door open. The security guard waited outside as Langley and Graveney made their way into a large room full of different sized security boxes, stacked high on three walls.

'Have you your key, Mr Bryony-Nugent?'

'David,' he said, trying to appear less formal.

'David,' Langley said, and held out his hand.

Graveney fished in his pocket and pulled out the key, giving it to him.

Langley pulled its twin from his trouser pocket and strolled across to a bank of boxes on one of the walls. He pushed the keys in and turned them. The door opened and Langley pulled out a box, carrying it across to a booth on the far side of the room, he lay it down.

'I'll leave you to it. When you've finished, ask the guard outside to fetch me and I'll lock it back up.'

'Actually, I'm taking something away with me, and I've forgotten my damned briefcase,' Graveney said. 'You haven't a bag of some sort, have you?'

'Of course. You're not the first to ask.' He disappeared and returned shortly after with a heavy-duty Marks and Spencer carrier. Langley left, and Graveney opened the box. Inside, a DVD, which he put inside the bag. He pulled out a large folder, containing photos of individuals. A couple seemed familiar, but he wasn't altogether sure. Lots of documents on different letterheads and not believing he'd time to scrutinise them all, and more worried about Louisa than finding out what the stuff was, he dumped it all in the bag. He closed the lid to the box and replaced it in the hole in the wall, then told the guard he'd finished. Langley came back and locked the box, giving Graveney back his key.

'I trust everything's in order, David?'

'Yes, thanks.'

Langley, accompanied by Graveney and the two security men, made their way back through the maze of corridors, Graveney finding himself back at the reception. 'Thank you, James.' He offered his hand.

'Anytime. Any further assistance in the future, give me a call.' Shaking his hand in return. Graveney turned and left the building.

Marne sat in the back of the car as Graveney came outside. He instantly recognised the vehicle and pulled open the passenger door, expecting to see someone in the driver's seat. He looked shocked when he spotted only Marne in the back. 'What the hell are you doing here?'

'Do as I say, Peter, and get in the driving seat.' Showing Graveney the gun she held in her hand.

Graveney, though bemused, did as she said and got into the car. Marne sitting directly behind him. 'What's all this about, Steph?'

'No questions. Just do as I tell you, and you won't get hurt. I'll kill you if I have to.'

He believed her, viewing her face through the rear-view mirror.

'Give me your mobile,' she said, holding out her hand. Graveney reluctantly handed over his last contact with the rest of the world.

'Head for Newton Aycliffe,' she said.

He started the engine and did as she asked as his mind whirred. What was her involvement in this? How was she connected to the abductors? Suddenly Graveney felt incredibly isolated and vulnerable. He glanced at the revolver he'd tucked in his sock, and right now, the only thing giving him any comfort. They headed out of Darlington towards Newton Aycliffe. Any attempt at conversation by Graveney was ignored by Marne. Finally, he admitted defeat and kept quiet.

Eventually, they turned off onto a road signposted town centre, pulling onto an Industrial estate. They carried along another road for some distance before they pulled into a deserted compound, with a large, dilapidated building. Graveney glanced around at the vast, isolated expanse of ground surrounding them. He looked towards the two vehicles parked outside, and Marne instructed him to pull up next to one of them. She ordered Graveney to get out of the car, as she kept her gun pointed at him.

'Put your hands up, Peter, and turn around.'

Graveney did as he was told, wondering what he'd do without the gun if she found it. How could he save Louisa? If she was still alive? And she had to be alive. He couldn't allow himself to think otherwise. Marne frisked him and quickly located his gun. She removed it and emptying the bullets onto the floor, threw the empty revolver onto the back seat of the car. Taking out her mobile phone she texted, nudging him in the back with the gun, encouraging him towards the building.

Mac had not heard from Steph in a while and was now becoming concerned. He'd tried to call her several times but was met with her answer-phone on each occasion. Feeling all was not well, he rang Phillips. 'Mac, have you heard anything?' Phillips asked, as he answered.

'No. I hoped you had. I haven't heard from Steph for ages.'

'I'm getting worried. I know this is going to blow up in our face.'

'What can we do?'

Both their phones sounded together, alerting the pair that they had received a text.

'What does yours say?' Phillips asked.

'It's from Steph. It says Newton Aycliffe.'

'So does mine,' Phillips said. 'What does that mean?'

Mac pondered. 'It must be where they're heading. At least it's narrowed it down a bit, sir.'

'I'll alert Durham Constabulary and get their team over there. They'll only be minutes away when the time arrives.'

'I'll head over there myself, sir.' Ringing off, Mac quickly programmed his sat-nav for Newton Aycliffe city centre and sped away.

Phillips picked up his phone and called DCI Matt Wilberforce at Durham Constabulary. He told him they still didn't have an exact location yet but thought it somewhere in Newton Aycliffe. Wilberforce promised to despatch his team over there, and also get in touch with the local police. After ringing off, Phillips stood, pacing around his office like an expectant father. He briefly considered phoning the Chief Constable, but dismissed it. Reasoning there was nothing he could do. Finally, convincing himself, he'd tell him only when he had to.

Marne and Graveney entered an open door and trudged along a couple of corridors, finding themselves inside a vast warehouse. At the bottom, stood another building, constructed with grey block-work, with a red painted door, slightly ajar at one end. Marne nudged Graveney again, and Graveney tramped towards it. He entered and was met by Oake, Dec, and Flint.

'Ah, Peter. Nice of you to join us.' Oake joked. Graveney not seeing the humour at all.

Graveney glanced over to the corner of the room and spotted Louisa fastened to a chair, her mouth taped. He moved towards her, but Flint and Dec grasped hold of the struggling Graveney. He continued to wrestle with them but was punched in the stomach hard by Dec. He dropped onto one knee, the wind knocked from him.

'Let's not be foolish, Peter. Have you got the stuff?'

Graveney got back to his feet and picked up the carrier bag he'd dropped when Dec punched him, tossing it towards Oake. Flint and Dec still holding Graveney, sat him on a chair.

'You've got what you want Oake,' Graveney said. 'Now let the girl go.'

Oake smiled. 'Have you had a look. Maybe a little peek?'

'I'm not interested in your sordid little secrets, Oake.'

Flint struck Graveney across the side of his face, Graveney shrugging off the blow.

'Have you told anyone? Anyone at all?'

'I've told no one. Honest.' Trying to change tack and appear more amenable.

'Let's test that hypothesis, shall we? Flint, take the girl out back and kill her.'

'You fucking bastard!' Screamed Graveney as he got up from his seat, head-butted Dec and lunged at Flint. He managed to get a punch into Flint's side before Dec recovered sufficiently, grabbed hold of Graveney and pulled him onto the floor. Flint aimed his boot at Graveney, catching him in the ribs. Graveney heard a crack, followed by incredible pain in his chest. The two men rained down blows on him and he lay on the ground, powerless to fight on. Dec and Flint picked him up again, and pushed him back onto the seat, securing him with tape.

'Let me sort the girl out,' Marne said, attaching a silencer to her revolver. Graveney glanced across at her, pure hatred filling his features as Marne avoided his stare. She unfastened Louisa from the chair and escorted her out of the room. A brief pause before a faint gunshot sounded from outside. Graveney slumped in the chair, the pain in his chest irrelevant now compared to the ache in his heart.

Heather, more than a little worried, had received a text earlier in the day from Graveney. She hadn't fully understood it but was now concerned. Graveney apologised for his treatment of her over the years and said that he loved her. She knew he'd spoken with Andrew and wondered what had been said. The tone of the text, fatalistic. She picked up the phone and talked to Andrew. He told her their meeting had been conciliatory and they'd left on good terms. Andrew didn't mention to Heather what he'd said to Graveney regarding Luke, thinking it was between him and Heather. She ended their call none the wiser as to what was wrong with Graveney. She promised herself that, if he hadn't been in touch with her by tea time, she'd go to his flat.

Liz tried to phone Graveney on several occasions but only got his answer-phone each time. She left a couple of messages for him to ring back, desperate to hear news of Louisa. She left the pub to her staff and barked her annoyance with anyone who ventured into her flat. Her bar-staff, unsure what was going on, took the hint and gave her a wide berth. She sat, not knowing what to do, unable to think or concentrate on anything. Her day seemed to consist of checking for messages and watching the clock.

Becky, unable to contact Mac all day, tried ringing both Louisa and Graveney without success. Louisa, who was supposed to be helping her out, hadn't come in. Fortunately, quiet throughout the day, she had just about been able to manage. The shop finally emptied, and Becky tried the three of them again. For some reason she couldn't put her finger on, she had a bad feeling about it.

CHAPTER TWENTY-SEVEN

Flint lifted Graveney's head up with the tip of the large hunting knife he held. Graveney met his stare as Flint smirked back at him.

Oake grinned. 'Well, Peter, we've nearly sorted everything out. I just have to make sure you haven't told anyone where you were coming today.'

'Fuck you, Oake,' Graveney spat the words at him. Flint punched him in the face, Graveney absorbed the blow as blood trickled from his nose.

'Now, now. Let's not be like that. We can make this quick and relatively painless if you answer some questions.'

'They all know about you. Phillips, the Chief Constable, everybody. Whatever happens here today, you're a marked man. They'll catch up with you and all your paedophile mates.'

'You misunderstand. I'm doing this purely for personal reasons. Once you're out of the way, I'll hand in my notice. I've had enough of policing. Time to retire to somewhere warm, I think. I'm sorry it's ended like this, though. My friend, Flint, will ask you some questions. It would be best if you answer them honestly. He's quite persuasive.'

Marne came back into the room, avoiding any eye contact with Graveney. Graveney glared across at her, his look now beyond hatred, as she wandered across towards Graveney, Flint, and Dec.

Oake smiled. 'You're just in time, Steph. Flint was about to interrogate poor Peter. Unless you fancy it?'

Marne said nothing as she raised her gun and pointed it at Graveney. Graveney looked back defiantly at her but much to his surprise, and everyone else in the room, she turned the weapon towards Dec and shot him through the head. He fell to the floor, dead. Flint, stunned momentarily by what she'd done, dived towards his jacket and reached for his gun within it. Marne followed his movement and lowering the

215

muzzle of her weapon shot Flint through his right knee. He screamed out in agony, his knee exploding as the bullet ripped through it. Flint fell to the floor clutching his leg, hardly able to reason what was happening to him. Marne heard Oake shout something at her, but ignored him and fired a second bullet into Flint's right shoulder. He screamed again, louder, as the agonising pain in his shoulder vied for supremacy with his knee.

Marne swung around to find Oake levelling his gun at her, his face full of rage, his hand holding the gun shaking with anger. 'What are you doing!' he screamed at her.

'I'm sorry, Charlie. I thought you wanted them dead?' she said, so casually, Graveney scarcely believed it.

'Not now, you stupid bitch!' Oake said.

Marne sidled towards him, her gun hanging loosely in her hand. 'Why not? They're superfluous, aren't they?'

Oake saw the manic look in her eyes as fear swept through him. 'Move one step closer, Steph, and I'll shoot. I'm warning you.'

Marne continued to advance slowly towards him with a somewhat disconcerting grin appearing on her face. 'I'm sorry, Charlie-boy. You'll find that gun of yours, useless.' She stopped ten feet from him. Graveney glanced down momentarily, distracted from Marne and Oake by Flint's groans, but quickly switched his attention back to them.

'I'm warning you. I'll fire,' Oake said, his voice trembling.

'*Well fire, you thick bastard!*' Marne screamed at Oake. Taken aback by the ferocity of the outburst, he fired. The gun sounded as a loud bang echoed around the room, but Marne remained upright. He fired a second, and then a third, but Marne stood defiantly glaring at him. Oake allowed the gun to drop to his side, finally admitting defeat.

'It was so easy to fill your weapon with blanks. It's not like I didn't have plenty of opportunities. I was around your house a lot.' Moving closer to Oake. 'I mean, you don't actually believe I enjoyed screwing you, do you? You made my skin crawl, you odious bastard.' Her voice rising in pitch and intensity as she spoke. Oake stared back at her, a wild look filling her face. She raced towards him and caught him unaware, striking him forcefully across the side of his head with her gun, causing him to lose his footing and fall to the ground. He lay stunned, as Marne pulled a set of handcuffs from her pocket and fastened his hands behind his back. She pulled the still groggy Oake to his feet and sat him on a chair facing Graveney and the stricken Flint. Picking up the gaffer tape Dec had used to secure Graveney, Marne taped Oake to the seat. Graveney looked on bemused, not entirely understanding what had occurred, his eyes darting nervously from Marne to the still groaning Flint. Graveney's heart-rate picked up pace, his breathing becoming more difficult, the pain in his chest intensifying.

'You see, Charlie.' She positioned herself in front of Oake. 'Sandra Stewart was my sister.'

'Your sister?' he repeated, visibly nonplussed. 'You're Alex Marne's girl. She couldn't be your sister.'

Marne turned around, addressing the three men. 'The Marne's couldn't have children, you idiot. They adopted me when I was only a baby. My older sister, adopted by another family. You see, Peter, Sandra searched for me, and finally we were reunited. A beautiful sister and a gorgeous niece. Imagine that. Not knowing I had this fantastic family waiting for me.' She stared downwards as the memories came flooding back. 'And then Sandra had the misfortune of running into this lot. Jimmy and Sandra were doing good. Exposing these wretched men and their horrible crimes.' She lowered her face and spat at Oake. A globule of saliva dripped down his cheek. 'They tortured poor Jimmy, you know, Peter. He obviously didn't want to give them Sandra's name. How brave he was. How he must have suffered.' Closing her eyes, trying hard to push away the image. Marne wandered over to Flint, slowly pressing on his injured leg with her foot, causing Flint to scream out in agony. Graveney flinched, empathising vicariously with the pain he imagined Flint must be experiencing.

'This piece of work.' Pointing at Flint. 'Killed my beautiful niece. They drugged her – the Reverend and Sheila Johnson – and then he pushed a pillow over her face and suffocated her. How could someone do that to a little girl?' Aiming a kick at Flint, who groaned more.

Graveney gasped, struggling for breath, his breathing becoming increasingly difficult as the pain in his chest moved up another notch.

'And my beautiful sister. Do you know what he did, Peter? He strangled her with Stephen's tie, in her own house. He squeezed the life from her while that bastard, Jones, looked on. You remember Jones? He told me how it happened in great detail. How he idly stood by as she died. He told me how he watched as she struggled and fought for her life. I killed Jones. I stabbed him. I undermined him with Oake.' She looked back at the Chief superintendent. 'And then encouraged the stupid idiot to ask you for more money, Charlie. Knowing you'd have him killed. I had that pleasure. I stuck the knife through his back, held him, and watched as *his* life slipped away.'

She turned entirely to face Oake once more. 'Oh, I so enjoyed doing that, Charlie. Men. They're so easily manipulated. Put on a sexy dress, wiggle your arse, flash your tits, suck their cock occasionally, and you can lead them anywhere you want. It's as easy as that,' she shouted to no one in particular.

She strode over to Flint once more and putting her gun aside, picked up the knife he had dropped. 'People who live by the sword deserve to die by the sword. Don't you agree, Peter?'

Graveney didn't answer. He saw the manic look in her eyes. He had never encountered a crazy person before, but if he ever did, he imagined they would look somewhat like Marne.

She sat astride Flint pinning him to the floor and brought her right fist down hard into Flint's face, shattering his nose. Flint, stunned by the blow, vainly lifted his left arm in defence. Marne easily brushed it aside and bringing the knife down, stuck it into his good shoulder. Flint screamed again in agony, as Marne allowed her full weight to push it all the way through and out the back. Flint tried desperately to push her off, but her weight and his injuries made it impossible. Marne twisted the knife in the wound as Flint screamed even more, his cries of pain deafening. Graveney could hardly look, but like a car crash unfolding in front of him, he couldn't look away either. Marne pulled the knife from Flint's now-useless shoulder as he groaned, the blade making a sucking noise as she slowly retracted it.

'I want to see you die, Flint. I want to see the life ebb away from your eyes.' She pressed the tip of the knife against his neck. A small trickle of blood ran away from the end of it as it slowly entered. Flint tried desperately to kick, his one good leg flapping about uselessly.

'Shhh,' whispered Marne. Putting a finger from her left hand onto his lips. 'It'll soon be over.'

Pushing the knife further in, blood flowed freely from the wound and down the side of his neck. She pushed it in deeper, and as it severed the carotid artery, blood spurted outwards covering the top half of her. Marne didn't flinch. Ignoring the blood she pressed on as the knife continued its slow entry, massive blood loss causing Flint to convulse. Guttural noises replaced his cries of pain as his throat filled up with the viscous fluid. An animal sound emanating from him. Like some magnificent creature in its death-throws. Marne continued on, pushing the knife deeper still, as Flint's movements lessened until only the occasional blinking of his eyes remained. Marne put her face close to him and heard his final breath as lifeless eyes stared back. She stood and picked up Flint's jacket, wiping the blood from her face. The sight of her pristine trouser suit and her once-white blouse, covered in red, enough to satisfy the most bloodthirsty of horror fans. She pulled the knife from Flint's neck, leaving red footprints on the floor as she strolled towards Oake, now in utter shock at what he had witnessed. Graveney stared down. He'd never seen so much blood in his life. A vast pool of red fluid surrounded Flint's body, giving the scene a surreal look.

'You're insane,' Oake shouted.

Marne, wide-eyed, looked at Oake. 'Losing people you love does that to you. Watching the people who murdered them carry on with their lives as if nothing's happened, does that to you, Oake.' Putting the tip of the knife dangerously close to Oake's face.

'I had to hold Stephen in my arms, Peter. I held him while he sobbed like a baby.' She looked back at Graveney, tears flooding her eyes. 'Imagine that. Trying to console someone whose world had collapsed. Can you imagine how soul destroying it was for me? Watching him slowly die. Day after day, month after month. Cancer in his head or being shot wasn't what killed him. He died all those years ago, back at Vale Farm, when he found Sandra tied to a tree, like some forgotten rag-doll.' Marne glared at Oake, pure hatred for him filling her features.

Graveney tried to shift in the chair as he became light-headed. His brain reacting to its diminishing oxygen supply, his position in the seat making it difficult to breathe. Marne prowled behind Oake.

'Behind every puppet, there's a puppet-master, Peter. He did it all for money, nothing else. He had all those people – good people – killed for the money. Why don't you tell him, Charlie? Tell him how you covered up for your paedophile mate.' The tip of the knife now pressing against Oake's cheek.

'Tell Peter how you got Stevens to bury the kids after your cronies raped and murdered them. How you sent that thug, Flint, to frighten him in prison and how you organised his murder in there.'

'I ...' Stuttered Oake.

'Unfortunately, he won't get a chance to spend the money. I'll see to that,' she said.

'Graveney do something. She's insane,' he begged.

Graveney heard the words, but they hardly registered as he watched Marne grab hold of Oake's head, push the knife into the back of his neck, and up into his brain. Oake shook momentarily before he slumped forward, dead. Graveney groaned loudly, unable to breathe and gasping desperately. Marne looked at him, the look of joy on her face vanishing, replaced by one of concern. She rushed across to the stricken Graveney and untied him from the chair, lowering him to the floor. She manoeuvred him into the recovery position and gently brushed the hair from his face.

Graveney opened his eyes and stared up at Marne, her face full of worry and concern for him.

'I'm so sorry,' she said. 'I didn't mean for you to get hurt.' Tears dropped freely, mixing with the blood on her face.

'Louisa?' Graveney struggled to say.

'Louisa is fine, Peter. She's fine. Hang on. The cavalry is coming.' She smiled, putting her blood-covered hand to his face, stroking it gently, like a mother would a child.

Graveney gasped.

'I'm sorry. So sorry I involved you. You're a good man. I needed to flush them out. I needed to get them all. The stuff you found in Shelby's safety deposit box will lead you to the people in London. You need to bring them down.' She touched him tenderly again, in total contrast to minutes earlier. 'I see the pain in your eyes. I know the hurt. You and I aren't so different. Don't allow it to engulf and swallow you up like I did.' She got to her feet and picked up her gun from where she'd placed it earlier. Footsteps and shouting sounded from outside.

'In another life, Peter.' Blowing him a kiss, she put the muzzle of the gun in her mouth. As she did so, Graveney closed his eyes. He'd seen enough death to last him a lifetime. The door burst open and armed police disgorged into the room. He heard the gunshot, closely followed by the thud of Marne's body falling to the floor, before his consciousness failed him.

It was her voice Graveney heard. Her voice rousing him from his unconscious state. She shouted his name, and as Graveney raised his head up, he saw Louisa. Mac held onto her as she struggled to break free from him.

Mac attempted to placate her. 'He'll be fine, Louisa. He's in good hands.'

'I want to go with him,' she shouted through tears. 'He's my dad!'

Mac, briefly taken aback by her admission, allowed his grip to loosen momentarily, and Louisa bolted for the back of the ambulance, pushing past the paramedics inside. Mac ran after her, but one of the paramedics stopped him.

'She's fine. She can travel with us.' Mac backed away.

Louisa dropped to her knees in the back of the ambulance. Graveney smiled at her, an oxygen mask covering his mouth.

'Don't you die on me,' she said, through her tears, 'I can't lose anyone else. Please don't leave me on my own.'

Graveney lifted his left hand and held it out for her. She grabbed his massive hand with one of her tiny ones, as Graveney gently squeezed it. Staring at him concerned as he smiled back once more, trying desperately to reassure her. He heard a siren start up and looked on bemused before he realised it was their vehicle. Louisa held on to his hand, afraid that if she let him go, she would lose him forever. As if it was his life, his essence, she clung to. He allowed his eyes to fall down sleepily, unable to maintain his conscious state any longer.

CHAPTER TWENTY-EIGHT

Graveney slowly woke, not realising where he was. He lay on his left-hand side and could see the window of what, he supposed, was a hospital room. Slowly he manoeuvred onto his back, the pain in his chest still evident, although he was breathing more comfortably now. Louisa sat asleep on a chair next to the bed, her head supported by a pillow against the arm. She woke on hearing him move and sitting upright, smiled at Graveney.

'Hello,' she said. Her eyes full of tears.

'Hello back,' he whispered. 'How long was I out?' He held out his hand, and she took hold of it.

'Since yesterday. About sixteen hours.'

'Have you been here all that time?'

'I didn't want to leave you. I thought ...' Louisa's voice trailed off. 'Liz is here. She went to make some calls and get some drinks.'

'Has anyone told Heather?' Graveney said.

'I don't know. Mac may have.'

Liz entered with a drink for her and Louisa. 'Hello, sleepyhead.' Putting her hand to his cheek, she smiled at him. 'You got her back, Peter. Like you said you would.'

'Your face looks better?' He joked.

'It's marvellous what ice and make-up can do. It was Steph Marne who saved her.'

Graveney looked at Louisa. 'What happened when you left with Marne?'

Louisa recounted how Marne had taken her out of the room at gunpoint. She had expected to be shot, but Marne told her to be quiet and helped her hide in a cupboard under some stairs. She fired the gun into the air to convince the others she'd shot her. Marne then gave her a mobile phone and told her to wait precisely fifteen minutes before sending a text written by Marne. She had to ignore anything she heard coming from the room, and Marne promised Louisa she'd get Peter out safely. Louisa waited the fifteen minutes before going outside and sending the text. Within minutes – less than five, she thought – all hell broke loose, with police cars and ambulances arriving.

Graveney filled in the details, without explicitly describing the murders to Liz and Louisa, and explained how Marne saved him. They chatted some more before Graveney finally convinced Louisa he was fine, and she should go home with Liz for a shower and a change of clothes. As the two of them got up to leave, Heather entered. She looked across at Graveney, her concern for him visible.

Liz glanced at Heather. 'We'd better go,' Liz said.

'I'm sorry, I'm Heather,' she said, offering Liz her hand. 'Peter's sister-in-law.'

'Liz. I'm a friend of Peters.' She warmly shook Heather's hand.

Heather hugged Louisa as she and Liz headed off. Liz glanced across at Graveney and Heather on her way out, realising there was much more to their relationship than brother and sister-in-law. Heather sat on a chair close to Graveney and took hold of his hand.

'Mac phoned me earlier.' She smiled. 'I've been so worried since I got your text. I knew you were in danger.'

'I meant what I said, Heather. I love you.'

She kissed him and placed a hand on his cheek. 'Liz seems sweet.'

'She's nice. She's looking after Louisa while I'm in here.'

'Do you need anything?' she asked.

He squeezed Heather's hand. 'No, I think I have everything I need now.'

Graveney had a string of visitors throughout the day. Mac and Becky called, along with Phillips a little later. Phillips wouldn't talk about the case with Graveney, telling him they'd discuss it when he was back at work. He remained in the hospital another week before being discharged. Heather and Louisa collected him and took him home. His injuries were healing well. Only his cracked ribs still causing discomfort.

Louisa had taken Luke to the pictures leaving Graveney and Heather alone in his flat. Heather poured them both a glass of white wine.

'Why didn't you tell me about Luke?' he said.

'Who told you?'

'No one. Andrew guessed he was mine. He informed me of his suspicions when I went to Darlington to meet with him.'

'I didn't want you to look at us as a charity case. I wanted you to want me. I knew you'd do right by Luke, but I couldn't bear it if you stayed with me out of some misguided loyalty.'

'I wouldn't have done that to you. It took me time to see how special you are. I want us to be together … as a family.'

'And Louisa?' Heather said. 'She's yours, isn't she?'

'I had a fling years ago with her mother when I was on a course. When she died, I found a photo album. There was a picture of Louisa's mam and me from years ago. I put two and two together, but I wasn't entirely sure until the day I was injured, and Louisa blurted it out.'

'I knew when I met Louisa in town,' she said. 'We went for a coffee together. When she smiled, I saw you. It's the eyes. She has yours.'

'Really?' Graveney said.

'Absolutely. We can all move in together, and see how it goes?'

'I'd like that.' Putting his glass aside, he carefully embraced her.

ONE MONTH LATER - Graveney tapped on the door of Phillips' office and then entered. 'Sit down, Peter,' Phillips said. 'How are you feeling?'

'Very well, sir.'

'I'm sorry how it panned out. We should never have risked your life like we did. She played us all.'

'What have you told the Chief Constable?' Graveney asked.

Phillips frowned. 'Most of it. I'm afraid I left out some of the more incriminating facts regarding how much Steph and I knew.'

'Steph helped Stephen Stewart escape on the night of Sandra's murder, didn't she?' Graveney said.

'Yes, she did.'

'But she didn't do it alone?'

'No.'

'I've given it a lot of thought, sir, and I don't think we'll ever know who helped her get Stephen out of the country. I think that person is probably long gone. Perhaps even dead.'

'Thank you, Peter.'

Graveney forced a smile. 'I'll go and start on my report.' He got up from his seat and moved towards the door.

'I didn't know she intended murdering them, Peter. I'd have stopped her if I had.'

'I know you would,' Graveney said. 'Steph was smart. She fooled me too.'

'I've handed in my notice this morning,' Phillips said.

'Why?'

'I'm tired of all this.' Waving his hand around the room. 'Tired of all the death, and the wallowing in other people's filth. The wife and I have a cottage in Robin Hoods Bay, and we're planning to retire there.'

'Isn't Steph buried in Robin Hoods Bay?'

'She is. I'll pop around to the church from time to time with some flowers. It's a lovely spot.' Tears glistened in his eyes.

'You liked her, didn't you?' Graveney said.

'Like a daughter. I'm sure you'll understand that.'

'Perfectly, sir. Good luck in your retirement. And if I'm passing?'

'You're always welcome,' finished Phillips, as Graveney left the room.

Phillips opened his drawer and took out the envelope with his name written on it. He pulled out the letter and opened it again.

'Dear Trevor. I'm so very, very sorry …' It began.

Phillips read through the letter from Steph as tears slowly descended his cheeks. He put his fingers in the envelope and pulled out the photo of him and Steph standing together, smiling. He turned the picture over and read the words. 'Love always, Steph x.'

Phillips replaced the letter with the photo and pushed the envelope into the inside pocket of his jacket. He turned his chair around and stared out of the window at a beautiful, bright autumn day. In total contrast to how he felt.

Graveney dropped into The Farmers on the way home from work and found Liz in a good mood.

'Hi, Honey,' she said. 'What'll it be?'

'A pint, Liz. You look happy.'

'I've some good news. My old man's body was fished out of the Tyne last week, which means this place is now *all mine*. I know I shouldn't speak ill of the dead, but I always worried he'd come back.'

'He deserved it if you ask me. What are your plans for this place?'

'Not for this pub. My sister, the one who lives in Majorca, has asked me to go into partnership in a bar over there.'

'And you're going?' he said.

'I certainly am. I always fancied living somewhere warm.'

'What am I going to do without you to pull my favourite pint?'

'You'll be ok. There are always people ready to pull you a pint. Heather will look after you. You've a good one there, you know?'

'I know I have. It's just …' Graveney said.

'I know, Peter. It would never work with us. I wasn't what you were looking for. You came along and helped me when I needed it most, and I'm grateful for that.' She put her hand on his cheek and Graveney brought his hand up to hers.

'I still think a lot of you, Liz. You know that?'

'I know you do, darling,' she said, tearfully moving along the bar to serve someone else. Graveney finished his pint, blew a kiss at Liz, who blew one back to him and then left.

'If you're ever in Magaluf, look me up. Bring the family.' She waved at him and watched him leave.

THREE MONTHS LATER - Graveney sat staring at the Television. The volume turned off, but he could see the rolling headlines at the bottom of the screen. He read them before turning it off.

LONDON PAEDOPHILE RING SMASHED. POLICE HAVE ARRESTED FOUR MEMBERS OF PARLIAMENT AND SEVERAL CIVIL SERVANTS IN DAWN RAIDS TODAY, LINKED TO THE DEATHS OF TWO BOYS IN THE NORTH EAST OF ENGLAND. A SPOKESMAN STATED THAT MORE ARRESTS COULD FOLLOW AFTER SUBSTANTIAL EVIDENCE CAME TO LIGHT.

He got up from his seat and shouted. 'Come on you lot. We're going to be late.'

Graveney, Heather, Louisa and Luke, all dressed up, got into the car outside Heather's house. They drove towards Stokesley. Passing the Farmers Arms with the SOLD sign outside, as Louisa and Luke chatted happily in the back.
'I've a little detour,' Graveney said to Heather.
'We've got plenty of time,' Heather said. 'You've remembered the present?'
'Of course. It's in the boot.'
They drove past the turn-off for Stokesley and carried on up the road, eventually pulling off into the little village of Ingleby Arncliffe. Graveney opened the boot and picked up the small bouquet. He made for the churchyard and locating the grave, stopped. He knelt and gently placed the flowers on the grave of Stephen, Sandra, and Jessica Stewart, pausing in silence for a moment.
'I can't condone your, or Steph's methods, Stephen. But I fully understand them.' He stood and marched back to the car.
'Everything ok?' Heather asked, putting her hand on Graveney's.
'It is now,' he smiled. 'Right. Who's ready for an engagement party?' He started the engine.
'We are!' The three of them shouted as he drove off.
'Who'd have thought it? Graveney said. 'Mac and Becky getting engaged?'
Heather smiled. 'I think they make a lovely couple.'
'Not as lovely as us, though.' He winked at his wife.

THE AUTHOR

John Regan was born in Middlesbrough on March 20th, 1965. He currently lives in the Acklam area of Middlesbrough.

This is the first book he's written and fulfils a life-long ambition of his. At present his full-time job is an underground telephone engineer at Openreach and, worked for both BT and Openreach for the past fifteen years.

He's about to embark on his second novel and hopes to have it completed sometime next year.

June 2015.

Email: johnregan1965@yahoo.co.uk

OTHER BOOKS BY THIS AUTHOR

PERSISTENCE OF VISION – Seeing is most definitely not believing!

Amorphous: Lindsey and Beth separated by thirty years. Or so it seems. Their lives about to collide, changing them both forever. Could a higher power intervene and re-write their past and future?

Legerdemain (Sleight of hand): Ten winners of a competition held by the handsome and charismatic billionaire – Christian Gainford – invited to his remote house in the Scottish Highlands. But is he all he seems and what does he have in store for them? There really is no such thing as a free lunch, as the ten discover.

Broken: Sandi and Steve, thrown together. By accident or design? Steve, forced to fight not only for Sandi but for his own sanity. Can he trust his senses when everything he ever relied on appears suspect?

Insidious: Killers copying the crimes of the dead psychopath, Devon Wicken. Can Jack save his wife – Charlotte – from them? Or will they stay one step ahead of Jack?

A series of short stories cleverly linked together in an original narrative with one common theme – Reality. But what's real and what isn't?

Exciting action mixed with humour and mystery to keep you guessing throughout. Altering your perceptions forever.

Reality just got a little weirder! Fact or fiction... You decide!
Seeing is most definitely not believing!

THE ROMANOV RELIC – The Erimus Mysteries

Hilarious comedy thriller!

Private Detective, Bill Hockney, is murdered while searching for the fabled – Romanov Eagle, cast for The Tsar. His three nephews inherit his business, setting about, not only discovering its whereabouts but also who killed their uncle.

A side-splitting story, full of northern humour, nefarious baddies, madcap characters, plot twists, real ale, multiple showers, out of control libido, bone-shaped chews and a dog called Baggage.

Can Sam, Phillip and Albert, assisted by Sam's best friend Tommo, outwit the long list of people intent on owning the statue, while simultaneously trying to keep a grip on their love lives?

Or will they be thwarted by the menagerie of increasingly desperate villains?

Solving crime has never been this funny!